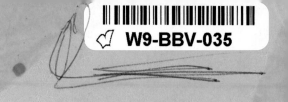

THE WATERS
UNDER THE EARTH

MARTHA OSTENSO

WILD GEESE

THE DARK DAWN

THE MAD CAREWS

THE YOUNG MAY MOON

DODD, MEAD & COMPANY

MARTHA OSTENSO

THE
WATERS
UNDER
THE EARTH

1930

NEW YORK
DODD, MEAD & COMPANY

i	Carlotta	P. 3
ii	Paget	38
iii	Tom	72
iv	Jenny	114
v	David	148
vi	Sophie	189
vii	Ruth	221
viii	Carlotta	259

THE WATERS
UNDER THE EARTH

I : CARLOTTA

§ 1

The air in the house, Carlotta thought when she stuck out her tongue, tasted of a wedding—just as it had done four years ago when her big brother David was married to Seena Nordstrom. That was a long time to remember a taste, for she had been only six then and now she was ten. She drew in a deep breath to make really sure that it was the same. It might, of course, be a smell— there was so little difference between a smell and a taste. She had discovered that fact by tasting a curl of dust under the parlor sofa, the dainty fairy mold on a jar of jelly, the rust on an old lock, the ink on a form in her father's printing office, the oil in the barrel of David's rifle, library paste—of which she was fond—and once, accidentally, a gooseberry bug.

Of course, there were smells that were disappointing when put to the test. Sophie's perfume, for example, which she kept hidden beneath her underwear in the middle drawer of her bureau, because it was a vanity of the flesh—or so their father had said—despite its fragrance of valley lilies, was rank to the taste. With roses it was different, certainly, and now there were roses in great profusion, waxy white ones, yellow ones like sun and dew petaled together, heavy red ones that seemed to be

3

fainting of their own perfume, standing in vases every-where in the parlor, the hall, the dining room. Standing as though they were waiting for something. Mrs. Well-and had grown them all and cut them all, out of her own garden. Ruth was the first of her daughters "to go," and there should be no sparing of the flowers. It was not as if it were a funeral they were to be used for, she had said. And Ruth, standing still and looking out of the window, had replied, "Not exactly." One would almost think Ruth didn't want to be married.

Carlotta moved through the house, her hands clapped to her ears to keep out the sound of the voices. She wanted to think only of the tastes and smells. From the east wing —that was where David and his family lived—there came a terrible uproar. Seena was spanking her little son, Matt, again. Seena was a harridan. Carlotta had culled the word from the vocabulary of her elders, and now never thought of Seena as anything else. Seena was a harridan.

By the grandfather's clock in the hall—Carlotta had never been able to understand how anyone knew it was a grandfather's clock because it had been bought at an auction sale along with little Matt's baby carriage—she found that there was only an hour's freedom left for her before they would hustle her upstairs and put her into her white georgette crêpe dress—her flower girl's dress. She hated georgette crêpe because it was wrinkly under the fingers. That had been Jenny's idea, to have her in white georgette crêpe. As though it was Jenny who was getting married, and not Ruth! Ruth hadn't even cared what her own wedding dress was made of. She had said to Sophie, in Carlotta's hearing, "Oh, make it sackcloth and ashes and be done with it!" Her voice had been shrill, and queer, not at all like the voice of one who was going to be married. And then, mysteriously, there had appeared at Ruth's place at the dinner table one day a box containing the loveliest ivory satin. When Ruth opened it, her father, Matt Welland, had cleared his throat and rubbed his nose and forehead with two fingers of his right hand, and almost whistled, but then he remembered, of course, he was at the table. Ruth had said, "It's beautiful, father! Thank you!" And Matt's thin little beard had looked very silvery against his sudden blush, and his bright blue eyes had gone watery and anxious. In the next instant his look was fixed upon his plate and he was mumbling, "Hrmph —hrumm—urr! It's little enough, little enough, my dear." And then he had bowed his head and said the long, careful grace.

Sophie and Mrs. Welland had sewn Ruth's dress, and Ruth had fidgeted impatiently when it had to be tried on.

Upstairs, in the boys' room, Carlotta had been overcome by the scent of mothballs, hair tonic and shoe polish. But here, in the doorway between dining room and kitchen, she breathed rapturously of chicken roasting, hot cinnamon buns, pop-overs, fresh green peas, sweet potatoes, mayonnaise in the making, green peppers, lemon pie, and chocolate layer cake.

She permitted her eyes to rove over the long table that crowded at one end right into the geraniums and wandering Jews and fuchsias and elephant's ears. The white tablecloth was the one the church had given Mr. and Mrs.

Welland on their last wedding anniversary. It had never been used before, and the pattern on it showed like islands of thin ice. The silver was not *all* silver, but Sophie and Mrs. Welland had polished each piece to within the merest membrane of its spurious vitals, and except for the unreclaimable horn-handled pieces at Carlotta's and Tom's places, they shone not unpleasingly.

Carlotta leaned as far as she dared over the back of a chair in the direction of the watermelon pickles on their imitation cutglass dish. She imagined she could capture *their* flavor, but the cucumber pickles were too far away, and the green tomato preserve too elusive. The celery she disliked, and as for the guava jelly—that was an idea of Jenny's. Who had ever heard of such rubbery, uninteresting stuff before? Carlotta actually thought of pouring a little juice from the cucumber pickles over it, just to surprise people. But she quickly dismissed the thought at the sound of a voice behind her.

"What are you doing there, Carla?" It was Jenny, her blondish hair piled high in a cascade of ringlets fresh and a bit stiff from the curling iron. Father will frown at those curls, Carla thought, wedding or no wedding. Jenny would probably stay out of his sight until the wedding march began. "As though I had polished the rung of that chair for fun! You get upstairs and get washed, and stop snooping around this table. I declare— as though there wasn't enough to do without watching you! Look at that fork, all cock-eyed! *Ma*-ma! Can't you keep this brat out of the way? After me fixing everything just right, here she comes and messes it all up!"

6

Jenny snick-snacked away in her black satin mules, on one of which there was a scarlet ostrich pom-pom; Lulu, Carla's semi-setter bitch, had eaten the ornament off the other.

"Stuck-up, embryonic tart!" said Carla after the vanishing heels. She had no idea what an embryonic tart was, but Tom had called her that, and Tom ought to know.

"Carla, dear, come away from the dining room."

Poor mamma! Her voice was so tired. When Carlotta grew up she would marry a rich man—no, she would get money some other way, because marriage meant drudgery and a lot of children—and she would buy a chalet—or was it a *château?*—for mamma in Chicago or New York, where mamma could go to the movies every night and have no end of pineapple ice cream sodas and a bicycle—no, a car—and wear black glasses in church so she could go to sleep and no one would be the wiser.

"Yes, mamma."

She moved docilely out through the hall, taking one last lingering whiff of the turbulent roses, and at the end a delicious run at the little braided rug which skated agreeably out from under her and landed her on her small rump. This time-hallowed thrill experienced, she wrinkled her nose, straightened the rug, and sedately opened the screen door upon the sky-full world of June.

On the porch Lulu lay flat on her side, her maternal, unlovely underpart arranged in a row of pinkish freckled cushions on the floor. Lying thus, Lulu was not so much setter as spaniel, although any argument on the point must necessarily have come to naught. Carla squatted beside her, and the dog raised lazy eyes of love at her caress.

"I'll never get married and leave you, Lulu," said Carla, and kissed the silky, limp ear in her hand. Lulu yawned with contentment, making a quite human sound at the back of her throat. Carla hugged her and got up.

She stood teetering, just at the edge of shadow on the top step, her hands clasped behind her back. The sky had the lightest powder of heat across its blue, so that it looked like the petal of a great prairie anemone. And there, low in the west, was a silver-ribbed cloud, like an anemone leaf. The sun would be at the half way point now, back of the house, just above the "Alhambra"—Tom's word for it—which wasn't used any more since the plumbing had been installed, and which was all charmingly grown over with wild cucumber vines. The front lawn sloped down terrace-wise, with three cement steps at the end of the short walk. The boys, after work last night, had mowed the grass and pulled every dandelion. No—there was one—hiding at the edge of the rose garden! Carla darted down from the porch and covered it quickly with a leaf which she pulled from a rose bush.

Standing up, and breathing hard, she looked toward the windows of the east wing, where Seena would just about now be dressing little Matt. It would be quite like Seena to be spying on her, and to tell. Carla stooped again, elaborately lacing her shoe. Then she pursed her lips and whistled a little as she sauntered back to the brow of the lawn, where she could look down and observe that her hop-scotch chalkings on the sidewalk had been rubbed out. Jenny's work, she decided. You would think Ruth was marrying a preacher, or a millionaire, instead of just a lout of a farmer. That was what Sophie had called him, not knowing Carla was around while she was talking to her mother. Sophie had refused to explain, but Carla had looked it up in the dictionary and, sure enough, that was exactly what Clint Proles was.

The air towered with the smell of roses; smaller scents spired up beneath—sweet pea, petunia, phlox, bachelor's button. Once, Carla, lying beneath the rambler rose hedge on the far side of the garden, absorbed in a snail's oozing out of his shell, had overheard Mrs. Linklater, next door, telling someone that it was a miracle the way roses grew for Mrs. Welland. "But still and all," she had said, "when you knew her, it wasn't surprising. Flowers would be just glad to grow where she was. And yet, somehow or other, she just didn't seem to be really happy. She had a funny, far-away look. It was queer that none of those seven Welland children were at all like her. Except, perhaps, the youngest one." And Carla, her heart swelling with pride and tenderness for her mother, had cried into the grass and got the snail in her hair, subsequently being unable to find it.

The flower garden ran southward along the eastern limits of the two acres and better of the Welland "homestead," as the family affectionately called it. The northern part of it, which ended at the terrace above the street, was a pattern of orderly beauty, but on the south it merged with the rich tumult of shrubs and underbrush and incontinent grape-vines, blackberry and elderberry bushes, and splendid, unapprehensive weeds. Beyond this democratic paradise were the plum and apple trees, and the ox-heart cherry tree which Carla's father had planted himself fourteen years ago when the family had first moved here from Iowa. Whosoever of the children found the first ripe cherry upon it each year, always brought it to Mr. Welland, even now when they were nearly all of them grown up, and he, enormously pleased, would smack his lips and eat it with great ceremony and relish. Then, past the orchard, worlds away from the house it seemed to Carla, at the southern extremity of the Welland place stood the tall poplars, a gold green spume against the sky. Across the lane, between the sunny gloom of the tree columns, one saw the small house and garden of Mrs. Gale, the widow, who was of no importance to Carla aside from the fact that she was the mother of Jared.

A path had been trodden firm and smooth in the soft earth between the Gale place and the Welland, by the feet of Jared and Carla and Carla's brother Tom. Following the path toward the Wellands', one passed first the outmoded Alhambra, then the vegetable garden and the chicken-coop and the tool-shed, and the dog-house, which no Welland dog had ever inhabited. The beauty of so spacious a world as this, Carla always thought, was that there was more sky above it than above any other place she knew, except, of course, the homes of the rich people who lived east of the church, before the deep woods began, and she never went to their places anyway and did not care. It was quite possible, however, that the sky was never so blue above the estate of Cranford Reed, the banker, and that such airy little boats of clouds never sailed within his ken.

On the west side of the Welland house, and separated from it by a lilac hedge, stood the Welland printing office, long, low and gray, with a half story façade which in profile seemed to crane a bit forward, giving the building a somewhat horned look. The structure, built before Matt Welland took it over fourteen years ago, had been a bakery shop. It had in that time never been painted. What improvements the capricious income from it would permit had been made on the rambling, indeterminate domicile which housed the Wellands.

Not that the house, for that matter, showed any signs of having been pampered. Five years ago it had been painted a sort of buff, and the gables shingled dark brown, all except the one looking out to the back yard, for which there had not been enough shingles left. The boys had done the job themselves, and luckily they had before Seena Nordstrom married David, and moved into the east wing, because she, four years older than David, was so contrary and opinionated that in all likelihood she would have insisted on having her wing of the house painted a different color from the main body of it. And all because she had brought two thousand dollars with her to tide the printing office over one of its many difficult periods.

Carla looked toward the building where her father and David were at work even now, two hours before Ruth's wedding. They would be emerging shortly to come home and dress. Their Sunday clothes were laid out, freshly pressed by Sophie, who, as the eldest of the girls, naturally assumed this responsibility. Paget would be coming home on his bicycle from the garage where he worked at the other end of town, any minute now, and Carla would be permitted to scrub the grease off the back of his neck, unless they made her dress up too soon. It was he and Tom who had used hair tonic so freely that morning that upstairs smelt to heaven of it. They both had straight, stubborn hair with cowlicks in the wrong places. Tom said that indicated mental eccentricity, and it might mean genius, but it was a darn nuisance. Aside from the cowlicks, Tom and Paget had very little in common.

Across the street, Mrs. McClintock was beating rugs on the line in her side yard. It was Saturday, of course, and she had every right to beat rugs, but Carla had overheard Jenny say that she was doing it so she could keep an eye on the goings-on at the Wellands'. Mrs. McClintock had not been invited to the wedding, because she was not a church member, and, worse still, card parties were held at her house. It was said, too, that before prohibition came into effect, she served grape wine at meals. She'll be smoking cigarettes next, Matt Welland said, and more's the pity, since she seems a decent woman at first glance, and her husband pays his bills promptly, they say. Mr. McClintock was an alderman, but one might have overlooked that, other things being equal.

Carla, standing on the edge of the terrace, sighed and looked away down the street, eastward, as she saw Diana McClintock, her own age and lovely with red hair, come out of the house to skip rope. Before the McClintocks had moved across the street a year ago from west of town, Carla had been enchanted with Diana at school. But since her father would never permit the children to bring strangers home, she had not been able to cultivate Diana's friendship. Her delight at finding that the Mc-Clintocks had become neighbors had made her bold, however, and she had promptly brought Diana over to climb trees in the Welland orchard. But before she had even determined her new friend's skill, her mother had called her indoors, telling Diana very kindly that she had a task for Carla to do. It was Carla's father who explained to her that evening, taking her on his knee and stroking her hair, that it was best for her not to play with the McClintock children, because they were different from the Wellands. Frieda Gertner, now, she was a nice little girl, and the Gertners were nice people. But Frieda was so dull, and wore glasses and didn't have short hair like little tongues of fire. Carla had crept away and cried bitterly alone, because her father always said, "Shame, shame!" when anybody cried.

She continued to gaze down the street, down along the deep elm shadows to the end, where the charred ruin of the First Methodist church stood. It was a pity, she thought, that the rebuilding of the church couldn't have been completed in time for Ruth's wedding. Carla had no interest in churches except for weddings and funerals, but on such occasions they made up for all the boredom one had to suffer in them at prayer-meetings and Sunday school, not to mention ordinary service. No, she would modify that slightly: revivals were exhilarating. One witnessed the most entrancing phenomena then, such as an enormous bead of sweat hanging and never quite dropping from the end of old Trudy Gallop's nose, and Shep Summerfelt, the town drunkard, zigzagging up the aisle to testify to the Lord and then going to sleep afterward. On the other hand, she would not have missed the burning of the church for anything. The steeple had been splendid, pluming black and mortified red to the stars like the ferocious belching of a dying dragon, rearing above his murderers. And then when they had hauled out through the window the casket of Lucas Trimm, lawyer and notary public, the glass of the coffin had burst and a fragment had nipped his partner's nose. "There's meaning in that," somebody had whispered. "The talk about Lucas's wife and Gannet wasn't all talk." And then somebody else said, "It ain't all of us gets a chance to sizzle in hell and on earth at one and the same time." But at that moment her father had found Carla hiding behind Tom and had sent her home.

§ 2

It was getting very hot, and there was a quiet communing stillness among the dense trees that avenued down to the gaping ruin of the church. The leaves of the bright copper beech on the west side of the lawn seemed jelled in the sunlight, and everything within sweep of the eyes appeared in that charmed mold of the eternity of the instant. A robin stood in the shade under the beech, head up, transfixed, like a stuffed bird uncanny with

14

paused life. Small bows of white and yellow butterflies hung over the rose trees, as though on taut, invisible wires, their wings vibrating no more palpably than the vibrating air in which they were poised. A sudden feeling of uneasiness, ennui, smote Carla. It made her nervous. She turned abruptly, without thought, and ran around the side of the house and down through the garden to the wild space which she and Tom called the "jungle."

She knew now that it was Tom she sought. He would be out here somewhere, reading or idling with Jared Gale.

There was no answer to her soft call. The locusts sang themselves dizzy, the grasshoppers snapped like twigs off other twigs, and dragonflies threaded the air with their gracile blue shine. But somewhere in the shrubbery Tom was hiding, Carlotta knew.

She found him at last, with Jared, both sprawled flat on their stomachs, under the rank growth beneath an ancient crab-apple tree. It required valiancy to approach them when they were in this attitude. If they were playing catch they tolerated her company with grudging grace, because then she could retrieve the ball for either of them if he happened to miss it.

But they appeared not to notice her now. She sat back on her haunches and regarded them wide-eyed. She pulled a feather of sweet-grass out of its sheath and nibbled its succulent end. Jared was quite close to her, and she could smell the damp, starchy smell of his freshly ironed blouse. Presently, when he turned his face a little and surveyed her with one eye, she could see that his cheek bulged with a "jaw-breaker." There was a little high-light stretched in the tan of his cheek where the candy was hidden.

"Got any more jaw-breakers?" Carla asked, in a small voice.

Tom looked up, blinking. He was sixteen, three years older than Jared, but Jared's father had been a schoolmaster, and had spurred his son on so that he was already in high school. The friendship between him and Tom, therefore, had not lessened with the years, but had become as close a relationship as any Tom had with his own brothers.

"Jaw-breakers aren't good for girls," Tom said gruffly. "Anyhow, we've eaten 'em all."

"You can have what's left of mine," Jared said, grinning. He showed a formidable gold tooth-brace when he grinned. Carla envied him his possession of the brace, which had a smart, professional air of authority about it and which gave him a charming lisp.

She longed for the jaw-breaker. Her eyes were fixed on Jared's mouth as he removed it and wiped it on his sleeve. Lately she had wondered how it would be to kiss him, and had decided that she would do it some day when he was off his guard. It was with a mingling of regret and pleasure that she was obliged to take her eyes off his face to accept the jaw-breaker, furry and white now with lint off Jared's blouse.

"Thank you, Jared," she said politely, stretching sociably out upon her back before Tom could discourage her staying.

"What is your mother going to wear to the wedding, Jared?" she inquired after a while.

Before Jared could reply Tom sat bolt upright and shouted at her. "If you want to stick around here, don't talk about that wedding!"

Carla was amazed, but thrilled, too, at his ferocity. Even Jared looked up, startled:

"Why not, Tommy?" Carla asked fearfully.

Tom looked sullenly away. "Because"—he blurted out—"Ruth doesn't want to get married. She just wants to get away from home so she can have a good time, so she took the first guy that asked her. Clint Proles, the poor fish! Ruth could have married anybody in town if father hadn't been so suspicious that he wouldn't even let her get acquainted with them. Gosh!"

Jared sat up, his eyes round with an intimation of things beyond his years. "Your father was awfully mad that night after the Old Timers' picnic when Cran Hale drove Ruth out in the country in his car. He didn't say much, but I was scared the way he looked."

"You ran home as fast as you could, didn't you, Jared?"

In reply to this, Jared favored Carla with a withering look.

"Ruth should have had more sense than to let him drive her right home," Tom said angrily. "She knows what father thinks of the swells in town who've got cars. And right after that she meets this rube Proles at the ice cream social and he falls for her and comes calling on father the next day! Gee whiz! Can you beat it?

I feel sorry for the poor guy, I do, when he finds out that she just grabbed him so she could go to dances. That's what she did, just grabbed him. Sophie knows it, too, and she despises her for it just as much as I do. Huh!"

Carla struggled to arrange things in her mind. Sophie and Ruth—they had been inseparable. And now Sophie despised Ruth because she was going to get married. It was all very difficult to arrange in the little opening places in one's mind.

"How can Sophie despise Ruth, Tommy? She gives her things all the time—"

Tom shrugged. "I don't know anything about girls," he said disdainfully. "But I can remember when Sophie used to give Ruth her best dolls and things. I don't blame Sophe, though, for despising Ruth now. She's a"—he searched heroically for the right word—"a slut!"

The word wrote itself in bizarre colors on the tablet of Carla's mind. It was, for some reason, unnecessary to ask what he meant. She looked at Jared to learn whether he was sharing her excitement, and found that his face bore a pained, tight expression. Perhaps he did not understand any more than she did what Tom was talking about, but merely wanted to look superior and knowing. She felt that she would like to pull his hair, but instead she began to stare fixedly at his face with its blue solemn eyes and its dark cheeks with red in them like fruit stains.

"What in the Peloponnesian peninsula are you staring at Jared for?" Tom demanded. It was a habit with him

18

to use big words to dumbfound her, so she was unimpressed. It was the small words now that fascinated her. She ignored Tom's rebuke, and began to watch Jared empty his pockets in search for something. Carla was lying flat with her chin on her hands, quite close to Jared, and when one of his pockets was inside out, right before her eyes, she could see the grit in the seams, and smell the dingy pungency of the contents that were spilled out on the grass. There were two jack-knives, a compass, a cotton tobacco bag with draw-strings in which coins jingled, half a stick of gum, a fish line rolled about a gaudy fly, the stub of a pencil, and a nail file. It was the file that Jared evidently wanted. He put the other things back into his pocket and began diligently to work at his nails. Carla watched him raptly.

"Don't you go talking to anybody about what I said," Tom warned her as an afterthought, "or there'll be trouble."

"I don't know what people want to get married for," Jared remarked. "Believe me, I'm not going to be. I'm going to make money and take care of Mom."

Only a short time before, Carla had vowed to Lulu that she would never marry and leave her, but now, at Jared's declaration, she felt a twinge of disappointment. She had not realized before that she would like to marry Jared. Oh, well, he was only a boy, anyway!

"Oh, Ruth is *old* enough to get married," Tom said with a large manner. "She's twenty-one, and she was never much good for anything else. But—!"

"Sophie's twenty-three, though," Carla observed. "And she's not married."

"She's different," Tom said darkly.

"I wish I had a lot of sisters and brothers like you have," Jared said with a wistfulness that made Carla's heart melt toward him. It must be awful being an only child.

"I know the ages and birthdays of every one of us," Carla said proudly. "Dave's almost as old as father. Not quite, but he might as well be. He's twenty-five. Then there's Sophie, she's twenty-three, and Ruth's twenty-one, and Paget's twenty, and Jenny's eighteen, and Tom's sixteen. Why am I so much younger, Tommy? Maybe I'm really older. Maybe they made a mistake. Wouldn't that be funny if I was really as old as Jared?"

The idea excited her so that she sat up wildly and clapped her hands. But Tom and Jared both looked bored.

"You s'pose you'll go to college when you're out of high, Tom?" Jared said, pointedly excluding Carla from the conversation.

Tom rolled over and pulled up a handful of grass. His eyes narrowed, shining goldly under their lids. "Shucks, I guess not," he said. "There won't be enough money unless I want to be a minister. Father said Paget could go if he would be one, but Paget wouldn't. Father doesn't believe in a college education unless you have the call. I dunno. Did you ever wonder if there really is a God, Jerry?"

Jared looked shocked, and Carla promptly disliked him once more. "Of course there is a God," he said stoutly. "If there isn't, who made everything? These trees"—he waved his arm eloquently above him—"the sky—the sun— Why, of course there is a God! And who made Jesus, if there isn't?"

"They might have all just come by themselves," Tom frowned. "Still, Jesus was all right. He did a lot of good, anyhow."

The concession seemed to trouble Jared, but he had no reply for it.

"I wouldn't mind being a minister myself," he said complacently. "I've talked to Mom about it, and she says if I don't want to be a minister the next best thing is to teach theology. So I've got to go to college to learn that. It takes a long time, though, and Mom hasn't got much money. I'd work my way through."

Tom was growing restive. His eyes flared, gold-hazel, with large, short-sighted pupils, and his hair stood upright like the feathers on a rumpled blackbird. Carla knew how he longed to go to college, just to learn, and then be what he felt like being. She had heard him talking to Paget. . . .

There was a call from the house. The three rose, stretched in the heat, then Jared went his way home through the orchard and Carla and Tom moved toward the house.

"I may not be on hand for this affair," Tom told her magnificently, "if anybody asks you."

Carla snickered. She knew very well he would be on

hand. Nobody in the family would dare not to be, because that would give someone in Thrace something to talk about.

As she skipped away from him she called back over her shoulder, "Oh, is that so! You know father would never stand for that."

But Tom was shuffling his feet through the grass, kicking at fallen leaves, his hands gloomily in his pockets.

§ 3

"Where *have* you been?" It was Jenny, meeting Carlotta in the doorway. "Get upstairs and take a shower this minute. You're a great help, when everybody's so busy!"

On her way to the bathroom, pulling her dress over her head, she could hear her father moving about in the big front bedroom. He was whistling softly, breathily, and she could picture how his red lips would be pursed above his short graying beard, and how his blue bright eyes would be puckered in a frown. He always frowned when he had to "dress up," because he was a "common man and had no use for gauds."

Carla emerged triumphant from her ablutions, and surveyed the really good map of Africa that she had achieved on the green calcimine with the hand spray. Jenny opened the bathroom door and, after an angry and wordless scrutiny of the place, piloted Carla into the bedroom the child would share with Sophie now that Ruth was going. Jenny had always wanted a bedroom to herself, and now she would have it, with the rearrangement.

While Jenny was seeing to it that Carla's muslin drawers and vest met securely, the sound of clumping feet came from the stairway, and the voices of Paget and Tom.

"Now I can't wash Paget's neck, can I?" Carla said regretfully.

"You certainly can not," said Jenny, beginning to brush Carla's hair.

"Ouch!"

"All right—all right! You've got to pay something for having naturally curly hair," Jenny said grudgingly. Then she relented. "But it *is* lovely, Carla. It's the loveliest hair I ever saw. It's like—marigolds."

Suddenly Jenny had an idea. "Do you know what, Carla? I'm going to paint a portrait of you. I'd like—I don't know if I dare—but I'd like to paint you in the nude."

"What's that, Jenny?"

Jenny sat back on her heels and looked the child over, her eyes dilating with pleasure. "Without any clothes on. It would have to be a secret, because father would have a fit. Oh—it's not fair for him to be so set against my painting! I don't know why it is. Mother says there's a reason. . . . Let me see, where could we do it?"

She puzzled, one sensitive finger to her lip.

"I know," Carla said excitely. "Under the grape-vine back of the woodshed. Nobody ever goes back there."

"That's a fine idea!" Jenny exclaimed. "You can stand

23

under the vine with the sun coming through. That's a fine idea! We couldn't do it in the house, because there's no telling when father is going to come snooping over from the shop to see what we are all doing. Oh, we'll have a lot of fun! We'll start to-morrow."

She threw her arms about Carla and kissed her. Carla was thrilled, not at the idea of posing, but of doing it unclad. There was nothing she loved more than being naked in the heat. Tom was generous with her in this respect—he permitted her to go swimming with him way down the creek where nobody ever went, and she splashed about naked as a fish.

The wedding slipped to a place of secondary importance in her mind now, but it was with a measure of delight that she regarded herself in the tilted mirror of the imitation bird's-eye maple dresser when Jenny had finished clothing her. What she beheld was a small, finely built girl with strained-honey gold hair, falling in slippery ringlets to her shoulders, and caught up at one side with a pink bow. Her nose was straight and short, dusted faintly with gold freckles, her eyes fusing from gray to bronze near the great pupils. There were little black flecks in the gray, too. Cat eyes, Jared said. She wished they were blue, like David's and Sophie's. Her mouth budded into a dimple at the left, and her small throat rose straight and fine to the tilt of the chin. She glanced down at the white dress that she hated to touch, and the pink sash at the waist, and her short white socks and patent leather slippers below.

"I think I'm beautiful," she said confidently, and went

up and kissed her image, leaving a dewy nebula on the mirror.

Jenny clicked her tongue. "Don't ever let father catch you doing that," she said sharply. "You mustn't be vain, even if you are pretty. See what happened to Ruth—" She checked herself, getting abruptly to her feet.

"What happened to Ruth?"

"She disobeyed father. Now run along. I have to get dressed." Then, closing a dresser drawer which stuck and had to be opened and straightened twice, she murmured, "If something only *had* happened to her, the poor fool!"

She called to Carla, in the doorway. "Remember to have Clint Proles come straight to father's room."

Carla tiptoed out, feeling very devoted to Jenny, and very grown up and full of intrigue. For Jenny, who was eighteen and through high school, to have taken her into her confidence that way, was flattering in the extreme. And to think that Jenny, who sketched adorable little water colors in her own room, was to paint her to-morrow in the—what was it?—it was too thrilling! The more so because nobody but Carlotta knew that Jenny even had a box of paints, locked securely in her cedar chest.

Matt Welland, in one of his talks at prayer-meeting, had said in his beautiful voice, his prophetic head thrown back on his short neck, his arms tight at his sides, his hands clasped before him:

"Whoso strays from the common way findeth damnation. Let us, therefore, brothers and sisters, be meek and

humble in the eyes of the Lord, and His grace shall
provide for us amply, in body and in soul, Amen."

§ 4

Into the room where Sophie and her mother were dressing Ruth, Carla minced, not so much to see the bride
as to look at herself in the full length mirror there.
While she pirouetted before it, she could see in its oily
depth, her mother, tall and smoothly brown, in her
sand-colored gown with the tatted collar and cuffs
Sophie had made after the Armistice, when there was
no longer any need to knit socks. Sophie wavered dimly
in the mirror, tall with the loveliness and look of courage of a slender tree beside a creek in spring where floods
come. She was colored like piano keys, Carla thought,
her skin so white and her hair so black; and her eyes
like blue asters painted in. Ruth's satin dress nearly
reached the floor, so that her tiny feet in their white kid
slippers dartled out only now and then. There was a
drape at the side, held with rhinestones, and a bertha
gathered at her breast with white rosebuds. In semi-
profile, even with the bertha, the pout of her full breast
could be seen, the satin high-lighting it. Ruth had rus-
set-colored hair, like October oak leaves, and it was curly
like Carlotta's, but pinned back in a flat knob at her
neck. Her color to-day was not good, mottled, with a
suggestion of an eruption on the chin.

"Mother," Ruth said angrily, "it's perfect nonsense
that I can't have a little face powder to-day at least.

Look at my skin! It's a fright—all greasy and spotty! Does father think he can keep me from using it to-morrow, too? Not much! Thank God, I'll be free and out of this house."

In the mirror Carla could see Ruth's veil trailing like a captive mist across the bed.

Mrs. Welland anxiously twisted the skirt of the wedding dress a little to the right. "You'll be your own mistress now, child," she said softly. "And I don't know whether to thank heaven or not. Dear me! I think I'll go and lie down for five minutes. People will be coming soon. Funny Clinton isn't here yet, isn't it? You look lovely, Ruthy. And don't worry about your complexion. That will clear up. It's just the excitement. He isn't marrying your complexion, anyhow."

"No," Ruth said with narrowed eyes. "He isn't marrying me at all. I'm marrying him, because there's nothing else to do."

"Sophie will help you with your veil," Mrs. Welland said faintly from the doorway. "Carla, you'd better go down to the front door soon, and help."

Carla looked at her mother, the slim brown woman with hair like satinwood, and saw her face strange and far away, the eyes wide as a person's are when there are tears in them, tears that are trying not to drop. But she was bright and smiling with her lips. Carla wanted to run and throw her arms about her, but there was something queer and incomprehensible in the room, and she couldn't move. She felt uncomfortable and embarrassed, and wanted to be away. She thought at once of the dog,

Lulu. Dear Lulu. She would run away from here and find Lulu.

But then Sophie picked up Ruth's veil, and Carla decided to stay and see it put on.

Ruth stood, stiff and expressionless, while Sophie adjusted the veil. Sophie was half a head taller than Ruth, and her eyes, as they looked across Ruth's head while she pinned the cap, closed heavily once or twice. The cap was of real lace, and had been on her mother's wedding gown, years ago.

"Ow!" Ruth squealed. "That pin went right into my scalp. Can't you be careful?"

Sophie sighed. "I guess I'm a little nervous. I'm sorry."

"You, nervous!" Ruth said petulantly. "What have you got to be nervous about, I'd like to know?"

Sophie stood back and gathered the veil out in her strong hands, fluffing it into a wide cascade down Ruth's shoulders to the floor. When Sophie bent down to pick up a pin, Carla could see her through the dripping veil, and her face looked misted and silvery, like a cocoon.

"See how pretty you are now, Ruth," Sophie said, turning her toward the mirror. "Maybe you *could* soften your hair a little at the sides—"

Ruth went close to the glass and stared at herself. Her eyes, a lighter blue than Sophie's, and inclined to be prominent because of a thyroid condition, took on a sudden glassy fright. Her red, excessive lips shook, and with a quick movement of her hand she snatched the veil off her head and stared at it while it collapsed aimlessly to the floor.

"I won't do it! I won't do it!" she cried. "He drove me into it—I was crazy—I won't go through with it—I'll run away—"

"Oh, you will!" Sophie's voice was low, but it had a steely sound. "You ungrateful little minx! You flirt with a man until he proposes to you, comes here to marry you, and then you are willing to make a fool of him because you haven't got the heart of a stuffed squirrel! You've got a good man, and you aren't worth his shoe-strings! All you wanted was a chance to play around. Well—why didn't you get out and work for your living? You'll blame that on father, too, I suppose. You'll say he sheltered you to death, so you didn't have the spine to do anything for yourself. What about me? Do you suppose I adore teaching school, and giving most of what I make to this house? Do you? Tell me that!"

"I suppose you'd jump at the chance to marry a farmer. And Clint Proles at that," Ruth said sarcastically.

Sophie's mouth tightened savagely. "I would!" she burst out. Then her eyes filled in a terrible way, and her face seemed to go entirely vacant. "I'd marry almost anybody, if it would make me forget things."

Everything was strange and impossible to understand. Ruth suddenly began to cry, and there was Sophie with her arms about her telling her to hush. But Sophie's eyes, looking across the bowed, disheveled head, were hard and distant as winter stars.

Carla, forgetful of her dress, had seated herself on the floor. She thought of a certain Bertram Seiffert who had taught in the high school at Redlands, and had come calling on Sophie, a year or so ago, when there was still a war. She thought of how beautiful Sophie had looked then, in the spring of the year. But Bertram had suddenly stopped coming, and Carla had heard Paget and Tom talking about him, and about some articles he had written in a magazine, in which he wondered about God. Because of the articles he wasn't permitted to teach at Redlands any more, they had said. But also because of the articles he wasn't allowed at the Wellands' any more. And then in the fall his name had appeared in the *Thrace Advocate* among those who had gone to the war and were *missing*. The Wellands never spoke of the war at home, even though Paget had been in it for a few months, so Carla never learned what that word *missing* really meant. How could a tall, strange-looking person like Bertram be missing very long? Surely someone would find him.

"You'd better go downstairs, Carla," Sophie said. "The doorbell just rang."

When Carla stepped out of the room, Paget and Clint Proles had just reached the landing of the upper hall on their way to the large front bedroom. Clint stopped her progress to the staircase, standing before her with his feet in their shiny new shoes spread wide apart.

"Hullo, young one!" he bawled out, and plunged a thick forefinger into the pit of her stomach. "All dolled up, eh? How about a kiss for your new brother?"

He caught her up over his broad front and tossed her above his head, so that when she came back down to a level with his face her skirts were up under her arm pits and her underclothes were hurting her. Clint kissed her with heavy good humor on the mouth. A star of rage burst before Carla's eyes. She spat with venom and precision into the middle of Clint's face.

"You little she-devil!" Clint exclaimed and dropped her abruptly to the floor. "You've got the makings, all right, all right!" He looked angrily at Paget, who was wiping a smile off his stolid face with the back of his hand.

Carla fastidiously brushed her mouth with her handkerchief, rearranged her clothes and proceeded down the stairs. Clint had smelled obnoxiously of sen-sen and perspiration and cheap toilet water. His fingers were stubby and strong, his eyes were too close together, and he had a large and prospering farm a mile from Thrace. She disliked Clint with all her might, and he should never kiss her again. She stretched a little and held her head high and looked down upon the people in the lower hall. There were her mother, Jenny, Mr. and Mrs. Holt (which of the two was the mayor of Thrace nobody knew) and their niece, Elmira Beckman. Voices of others came from the parlor.

With charm and dignity, as outlined in Jenny's *Book of Etiquette,* Carla received Deacon Loftus, the sixth wedding guest to arrive. There were to be ten in all, which, with the preacher and the bridegroom and the family, would make twenty-two. Fifteen would be seated at the large dining room table, seven at the small one near the hall door. It would be almost like a restaurant,

Carla thought, as she guided the Deacon to his place in the parlor.

§ 5

A gray, hot hush lay over that room, and the smell of wilting roses was sickening, sadly sweet. Carla looked up at the dim photographs of Grandmother and Grandfather Welland in their heavy gilt frames, and there seemed to her to be cobwebs over them. Beside the oval marble-topped table between the two front windows, the minister, Mr. Lambert Willsie, stood talking with her father in a low tone. The hair fern had been pushed back to the edge of the table, and a Bible lay upon the marble at Mr. Willsie's hand. Now and then he tapped it gently, without looking at it, as though he merely wanted to make sure that it was still there.

Mr. Willsie, a tall, thin man with a noble and poetic look, was not at ease with Mr. Welland, the printer. Frequently he would glance down at him from beneath his shaggy, somber eyebrows, as a mastiff, weary from his own height, might glance down anxiously at a sprucer, more stocky breed. Matt Welland was in high spirits. He kept smiling from the minister to the door where new guests were arriving, and back to the minister again, patting the palms of his hands softly, rubbing his nose with the tips of his fingers, and shifting his weight from one foot to the other. Just where his silky, graying hair swept up from his forehead, there was a constellation of sweat drops, and at the back of his neck his hair curled up from his collar like a darkly silver sill.

"Mr. Willsie," he said, his voice, so extraordinarily rich in a shortish man, eloquent with restrained emotion, "Mr. Willsie, this is a great moment for me, a great moment. The first of my daughters to go, Mr. Willsie. And I am not letting her go without a great searching of soul, and a great fear that I may, after all, not have properly fitted her for life. There is so much these days —so much to combat. My children have had a good home here, brother. I chose a place with large grounds, trees, flowers, so that they could have a generous space to play in and build normal bodies and healthy minds. *Mens sana in corpore sano*—that's a good motto, Mr. Willsie. A sound mind in a sound body. I have done my best, and I trust the Lord will do the rest."

"No doubt—no doubt, er-hmph!" said Mr. Willsie, gazing at the switch coiled at the back of Mrs. Linklater's head, which was so much redder than the neighboring territory. Elmira Beckman, he noted, was blond and warm-looking—warm in that it was an oppressive day, he amended to himself. What Mr. Willsie was really thinking with earnest ruefulness was that he wished he himself had some of the devout sense of obligation to the morals of the young that some of his flock had. Mr. Welland, for instance— But he, Mr. Willsie, alas, spent most of his time wistfully envying the young their access to harmless sin.

Carlotta left Deacon Loftus seated in a red plush wing chair beside the upright piano, with his back to the chenille portières through which the glitter of the dining room table could be seen. She remembered how, at ice cream socials, the Deacon's eye always roved busily over the tables, and it pleased her to place him where he could only guess at the edibles in store.

The parlor was filling with people. Jared Gale came in, escorting his mother, a small, timidly smiling woman. David Welland and his wife Seena entered, and Carla thought how weary his narrow, dark face looked, with steep hollows under his grave eyes. There was nothing weary about Seena, however. She began at once, in an energetic whisper, to tell Mrs. Gale how much hotter than this it had been on her own wedding day, four years ago. Four years, just think, and it didn't seem more than a month! Time certainly did fly, didn't it! Sophie sat at the piano, ready to play the wedding march. Carla could see the goldfish in their bowl on the other side of the piano, near the window, cleaving with curious nervousness the bar of sun that cut the water. The smell of the roses stooped into the room, from the top of the piano, from baskets hung in the windows, and from the shelf where the gilt marble clock ticked under the polite rustle of people. Carlotta was suddenly frightened. She saw her father walk from the room with his quick, short steps, his head thrown back. "The bride was given in marriage by her father, Matthew Welland. . . . The bride's little sister, Carlotta, acted as flower girl. . . ." Across the room she saw her mother motion to her to go upstairs.

Carla slipped along the wall, so close to it that she could smell the wallpaper, sharp and musty. In the hall she glanced back, but no one was watching her. Quickly she opened the screen door to the porch and tiptoed out. Lulu was lying on the grass in the shadow of the lilac hedge. Carla whistled to her softly and ran around the house and through the garden. The dog padded after her, and presently the two were lying deep under the wild cucumber vine which clambered down and made a web over an old birch tree back of the Alhambra. Here the ground was sweetly moldy and dark and cool. Lulu stretched her body gratefully upon it, and Carla laid her head on the dog's forepaw and in a short time was sound asleep.

§ 6

This, in Sophie's room, must be the darkest darkness in the world, Carla thought. It thickened down upon the bed, wet and hot. And yet she dared not stir, because Sophie, lying far over at the other edge of the bed, was not asleep. Sophie was crying, and worrying her pillow with her hands. Once Carla thought she said something, something that sounded like "little stuffed squirrel." Then she did say, "Bert, Bert," over and over again.

Sophie was feeling terribly, but she would feel worse if anyone knew. Carla lay still and tried to think of what had happened to her that afternoon. As punishment for running away she had been obliged to eat alone in the kitchen, but everybody in the family, even father, had taken pity on her so that she had had two helpings of everything and felt a little sick afterward. Especially when Mrs. Holt had bent over her with her greenish teeth and had complimented her on her recitations at

Temperance League. Mrs. Holt's voice was narrow as the voice of someone playing on a comb. She had suggested to Carla that she might put just as much expression into the plea of the drunkard's wife as she put into descriptions of snow-storms and the like. Carla had been evasive on this point, because the drunkard's wife had always bored her; why didn't the woman simply get up and walk out into the gorgeous snow-storm that was like fairies flying, and snarled witches, white and mad? But there was no use in trying to express her feelings to Mrs. Holt.

Rain was pattering along the eaves now, first lightly, experimentally, then on strong, drumming feet. Sophie got out of bed, and Carla could hear her going softly to the window. The dim white of her nightgown sank down before it.

Did being grown up mean that you had to be so miserable, always? Everything was confusing, and tight and prickly. Carla sat up in bed, swept with wretchedness for Sophie. She got out, and felt the floor clammy under her feet.

"Why aren't you asleep, Carlotta?" Sophie said, her voice polite as though she were speaking to a grown person.

"It's too hot," Carla said.

"Come back to bed and I'll tell you a funny story about when I was little," Sophie said. "Then you'll go to sleep."

Carla slipped her arm about Sophie's smooth hip, and

noticed how her silk nightgown slid like soap in a basin. The bed was cool after being empty for a few moments, and Sophie's voice was low and mysterious and full of the soft folds of sleep, and the rain felt along the eaves, here, there, and farther away, farther away.

II: PAGET

§ 1

The Wellands were seated at supper on a Wednesday evening, in early May. All but Paget, who had not yet come home—and Mrs. Welland, who, on Paget's account, was shaking the potatoes once more over the coal fire of the kitchen range. It had been Matt Welland's custom never to say grace until every member of the family was present. The eyes of Tom, Jenny, and Sophie, consequently, were fixed apprehensively upon the vinegar cruet in the exact center of the table. Carla alone was uninterested in the vinegar cruet. She sat where she could look out upon the lilac hedge that was tightly, heavily in bud, and her fingers played thoughtfully upon the pure curve of her cheek. She was thinking how exquisite it was to be fifteen on a day in early May—or rather on an evening—when the first swallows swept down from the eaves against the extravagant red gloom of the sunset, and caught your heart away.

Matt Welland looked again at his watch. "Three minutes past six," he said, and laid his watch upon the table beside his napkin.

He did not ask if anyone knew where Paget could possibly be. It was his boast that he could trust his children implicitly in their absence. He had brought them up so that they could be trusted. But punctuality at meal time was an expression of respect for the family. It implied a considerateness for others which would leave its mark upon character. It was one of those good, old-fashioned, sound principles of self-discipline which people nowadays were forgetting, and with lamentable consequences. He could not tolerate any such show of forgetfulness in his own family.

"Paget is probably over talking with Kepler about the vineyard, father," Jenny ventured, inspecting the gloss on her thumb-nail. The nail was a little too short to be genteel, and certainly much shorter than good taste, as dictated by her course in manicuring, demanded. But the hands that entered Kelly's Barber Emporium, where Jenny worked, were such that common sense told her it were best, in the interests of hygiene, to keep her own nails short. "Won't it be lovely with Paget raising grapes, though! I think that grapes are such romantic fruits, anyway. And it will be so nice for Paget to be doing what he has always wanted to do. There's money in it, too, isn't there, father?"

Matt Welland raised his large head, so incongruously majestic upon his short body, and looked calmly down the table. "No doubt, no doubt," he said absently, his blue eyes totally without expression. Lifting his napkin, he carefully covered the bread and looked again at his watch. "Four and a half minutes past six," he said, stroking his short beard between forefinger and thumb.

Mrs. Welland brought in the dewy jug of ice water.

39

The screen door opened at the front of the house, and Paget came in.

§ 2

Paget had hurried from north of town where he had been walking in the woods, full of the unease of breaking beneath his foot the brittle leaves of a dead year, and full of anxiety lest he tread upon one fragile tendril of fern, or one pale, brave jack-in-the-pulpit struggling up out of shadow.

The mood was not one that he often indulged, but he had been walking with Dorie Mayhew. He had stood with her under an elm and had seen the look of desperation and beauty in her face, and the late light falling upon her in a green, dewy pattern. Dorie Mayhew—the daughter of Sam Mayhew, a Roman Catholic, a man who had been charged with smuggling liquor across the Canadian border. Paget had left her there, in the green light under the elm, and had hurried away, running along the river bank until he was out of breath.

Even now, as he stood and looked at the family about the table, he could not resist the feeling of anxiety lest he might be treading upon some tender growing thing. Tom looked up at him from beneath his heavy black brows and saw Paget's ecstasy all over him like a betraying light upon someone hiding under a thicket.

Matt picked his watch up from the table. "Six minutes late, Paget," he said, pushing his glasses up over his eyes. "Six minutes waiting—six minutes apiece—and there are six of us here. That makes you thirty-six minutes late, Paget, my boy."

"Sorry, father," Paget said, holding his rapture in.

He saw his father lean back in his chair, his head high and rigid, his blank, hypnotic blue eyes fixed upon him. Was he going to chastise him? He had said he was sorry. Was that not enough? Anyhow, he didn't give a damn what the old man said, not a damn! He thrilled and shrank, knowing what he knew.

As Paget looked at him, the old man relaxed and waved his hand slowly toward the vacant chair at Carla's side. "Come along, my boy. And Tom—will you—will you please say grace?"

Paget took his accustomed place at the table and bowed his head as Tom began speaking the familiar words.

Jenny was the first to speak after Tom had finished asking the blessing.

"I looked in at the garage on the way home, Paget," she said with an arch look at Paget, "but you had already gone. I thought we might have walked home together."

"Come, children," Matt interrupted cheerfully, "we'll be late getting to prayer-meeting. You remember the old lines about how a kingdom was lost—because of the loss of a horseshoe nail. One thing leads to another—one thing leads to another."

Damn Jenny, and her glibness, Paget thought. Always talking, like a rattle-trap. He didn't know which he hated in her more, her chatter or her china-painting. China-painting, good God! He sat looking down at his hands, thinking back upon one hideous day five years ago when

41

Jenny had been caught by her father making a water-color sketch of Carla, behind the woodshed and under the grape-vine. Paget had been splitting kindling in the back yard. He still remembered the smell of pine split open and hot sunlight splintering into it. Matt Welland had come out of the printing office and had gone into the woodshed to look for something. A moment later there had been a scream—Jenny's scream. Matt had come slowly around from behind the woodshed, his face white and lifted against the pitiless sky, his hands clenched before him as though he were handcuffed. He was carrying something. Jenny's paints, her brushes, her ridiculous, childish easel, and a thick pad of drawing paper torn unbelievably in two. Matt had built a bon-fire of chips, precisely, painstakingly, and had placed the painting materials upon it. Then he had stood back, his face without a flicker of expression, and had watched the pile burn. Long after there was nothing left but a small heap of charred flakes and smoldering chips, Matt had stood there, his face empty, his eyes wide open and glazed, his graying, soft hair lifting a little in the spells of hot wind. Paget had not even thought to wonder about the girls, Jenny and Carlotta. They must have slipped through the garden east of the house, and in at the front door. But Jenny had never been the same after that. She was becoming more and more garrulous, and she laughed in the wrong places, and the men in Kelly's barber shop laughed at her. She had taken a correspondence course in manicuring, and Matt Welland had never been quite sure whether it was respectable or not, until he saw that in it she had quite forgotten her early folly, and was earning a decent living. She was living at home, moreover, where she was being cared for and guided in the paths of righteousness.

"We might have made a party for our baby girl, mother," Matt said, when they were all eating at last. "Just to think our little Carlotta is fifteen years old! It isn't given to many men to grow old with their families about them as my family is."

"You ought to be happy, father," Jenny observed.

"Happy—and grateful," Matt replied. "God has been very good to me."

There was a sound on the front porch. Matt looked up from his plate to see Ruth, hatless, coatless, her blouse caught crazily together with a cheap beauty pin, her curly, leaf-brown hair in a tumbled knot low on her neck. She trailed her two children after her.

"Why, Ruthy!" Matt greeted her in jubilant mood, then drew back suddenly as he saw the look in Ruth's face.

§ 3

Paget had seen that look in Ruth's face the moment she came through the door. He had meant to talk about his plans to-night—his plans to rent and later buy the old Kepler vineyard over toward the Detroit road. Perhaps he would even tell them about Dorie Mayhew. There was no cringing in Paget, no beating about the bush. He would let them have it, straight from the shoulder, full blast. But Ruth's coming had spoiled the setting. The peach glow over the old walls had faded, and Sophie got up and turned the switch on the wall behind her, lighting the chandelier.

In the flood of light, there was no mistaking Ruth's mood. Heedless of the children, who withdrew, a wide-eyed, ill-kempt pair, and stood a little apart, Ruth faced Matt Welland.

"Well," she said, in a voice that seemed whipped out of her throat, "I'm home! And here I stay, whether you like it or not, till I can get work for myself and my kids."

Her eyes flung about from one to the other of those at the table, and came at last to rest upon her mother, who sat gazing up at her and pushing her hair back over her ear. Then Ruth stiffened and her mouth worked tightly against her teeth.

Matt turned mildly about in his chair, his short hands on his knees. His eyes opened and closed slowly once or twice.

"Now, now, now, Ruthy," he said, a little humorously, a little protestingly. "Come and sit in with us. Bring chairs for the children, mother. Come, have a bite before you say anything more, my child. You're at home—you're at home, Ruthy! Tell us all about it after you've had a little something."

Ruth threw back her head and laughed piercingly. Carla turned her rapt gaze upon her, wide pupiled, from far away. The coming of Ruth was a little unreal upon her fifteenth birthday, in May, with a wash of lilac air outside the open window, all through the evening. . . .

"I can tell it all now," Ruth said. "I'm going to be free of Clint Proles. That's all there is to tell."

"Come, come, daughter," Matt Welland said, smiling almost roguishly, his eyes twinkling now, "it can't be so bad as all that. Tut, tut, Ruthy! Sit down with us and don't carry on with your dramatics. It isn't worthy of a sensible girl like you."

Ruth bent suddenly forward, her small, flushed face full of a shocking venom. "Dramatics! Do you know what it is for a man to come in drunk every night and outrage his wife—and bring children into the world that smell to heaven of alcohol? Do you—"

Matt Welland stood up. "Stop—in my house!"

Mrs. Welland had slipped forward and taken the children into the living room, closing the folding doors behind her when she had returned.

Ruth was now inflamed by the sound of her own voice. "I'll not stop! I'll not stop till you know what *you* brought upon me. You wanted me respectably married, didn't you? Well, look at me, the wife of Clint Proles! Look at me! Married five years, the mother of four children, only a merciful God—*your* God—took two of them before they could open their eyes and look on their drunken sot of a father! But I'm through with Clint Proles if I have to work my fingers to the bone—and I don't give *that* for what you or your God may think of it!"

She snapped her roughened fingers and tossed her head back with a harsh laugh. Matt had stood watching her without the twitch of a muscle in his face. Now he turned back to his place at the table, his hand fumbling over the back of his chair.

"Mother," he said quietly, "I wish you would take Ruth

upstairs and make her lie down. She ought to have a cup of hot tea. She isn't herself. She—"

He paused, frightfully shaken at last, and sat down. Then he bowed his head over his clasped hands and Paget saw a tear make its way unchecked down the bridge of his prominent nose. Ruth must have seen it, too. She stood for a moment, uncertain, incredulous, then broke into tears. Mrs. Welland was at her side, her arms about her shoulders, urging her out into the hall and upstairs.

The family ate in almost total silence, keeping their eyes averted from Matt's face and its embarrassing emotion. Mrs. Welland returned presently, leading Ruth's two children out of the living room and seating them on chairs wedged in at the table. The two youngsters huddled together, taking almost with distrust the food Mrs. Welland set before them. Norris, a boy of four, kept staring at Matt with a sort of resentful fascination. The little girl, Helen, two and a half, a tiny, wan replica of Ruth herself, suddenly drew her mouth down into a trembling inverted crescent and burst into tears.

"Ma-*ma!* Ma-*ma!*"

Mrs. Welland put her arm about the child and stroked her pale hair, but Helen merely thrust out her tiny chest, drew down her chin, and went rigid.

"Carla," Mrs. Welland said quietly, "will you make a pot of fresh tea and take it up to Ruthy?" Then she turned to quiet the child. "Hush, hush, darling. Drink a little milk now, for gran'ma. Be a big girl! That's the way, dear."

From the other side of the door that shut the east wing

of the house from the dining room, came a child's bellow of rage, followed by another's squeal of pain. Two of David's brood embattled again, Paget thought, looking over his shoulder at the locked door. He twisted his mouth in disgust. What a damned zoo! From cage to cage the jungle bedlam rose, a diabolic contagion, ripping along the senses. Matt Welland—the keeper. Well, damn it all, there was a way out of it, thank the Lord! He would never force Dorie Mayhew to become a part of the family. They could do what they liked about it, Matt Welland and the rest of them. Paget and Dorie would have their own place out along the Detroit road and they would stay there. His eyes shot down the table to where his father sat staring before him, his tea untouched. Pity and anger mingled in Paget's blood. . . . He wondered vaguely if the old man had ever walked through the woods in May, picked his way carefully among the tender buds, paused before a vision enshrined in the green light under a spreading elm. . . .

Ruth's child, Helen, was tossing the ball back to David's progeny in the east wing with a despondent wail. Carla came from the kitchen, carrying the steaming teapot. Paget, looking at her, was for the first time in his life struck with her grave, sky-clear beauty. She was outside all this. He had known it, of course, for years, but it had never come to him just like this before. She would live her life out in her own way, whatever came of it. And she was right. He would live his life, too, in his own way —and damn the consequences! He would begin to-night, by telling the old man just what he planned to do. He would tell him about his talk with Kepler. He would tell him about Dorie Mayhew. Why not? One time was as good as another.

For the matter of that, he was already outside this family. He had been no real part of it since the day he had returned from his three months in France, answered their questions about the war, and taken a job in Phelan's Garage. What did they know about the world he had been in? To the Welland consciousness, in feudal subjugation to Matt, there was something indecent, gross, in whatever went on outside the narrow limits of their own lives, whether it was a war or the birth of a bastard in Thrace.

Tom had commented upon Paget's reticence on the subject of his weeks in France. "You came back and took your place at the table as though you had just been around the corner."

Well, why tell them any more than that? They would never understand any of it if he did tell them. And as for revealing what the war had done to him and his old beliefs—God, that would be tragic! He had never forgotten, nor would he ever forget, the night he had let slip an impatient "damn" in his father's hearing. There had been prayers for him, and Matt Welland had sat late into the night writing in the leather-bound book that held the daily record of the old man's thoughts.

§ 4

The family was getting up from the table.

"Carla, will you take Helen up with you to Ruthy?"

Mrs. Welland lifted the storming child down from her chair. Carla took the small hand in her own, without so much as glancing down at the child. Helen abruptly stopped crying and threw her head back to gaze up at Carla with wide, wet-lashed eyes, her mouth open and a little askew. The boy, Norris, joined them of his own accord and the three proceeded in silence into the hall and upstairs.

Matt and Tom had gone into the living room. Mrs. Welland had retired to the kitchen. Sophie and Jenny had remained to pile up the dishes. Paget stood at the dining room window looking out into the knitting blue dusk.

"Funny how handy Carla is with kids and animals," Jenny was saying, "and without the least bit trying to be. I read the other day somewhere that criminals have the same gift."

"Criminals!" Sophie exclaimed tartly. "Do you mean to say that Carla is—"

"Well, for goodness' sake! I can't say a thing lately without you jumping on me. You must be getting old, Sophie, or something."

"I don't need you to remind me of that," said Sophie, marshaling the crumbs into a pile on the tablecloth with the edge of her hand.

"Oh, dear!"

Jenny's limp exasperation irritated Paget almost beyond endurance.

"Oh, dear—oh, *hell!*" he exploded, though he kept his voice to a harsh whisper.

Sophie paid no attention to his outburst, but Jenny dropped her hands and looked at him. "Well, I must say working in that garage is not helping you much, Paget. I don't understand how you can use such language with —with everything the way it is."

"Bah!" he replied. "You love it!"

"What do you mean?" Jenny asked.

"Just what I say. You love it—all of you love it. You couldn't live without it."

"Without what?" Jenny demanded sweetly.

"Without everything the way it is—Ruth and all the rest of it. If you didn't love it you'd get out of it, wouldn't you? That's what I'm doing."

He turned away and made for the hall. Jenny stared after him. "Well, I never!" she sighed.

Paget strode through the shabby living room—the "sitting room" of the old days—where suddenly the rag carpet which his mother had made on the loom in the attic, the comfortless, clumsy chairs, Carlotta's little red rocker which she had got for Christmas when she was five, the family pictures on the wall, all seemed unfamiliar to him. As he turned to go into the hall, his eyes fell upon his father, writing at the old oak desk. Painstakingly, in his hair-fine script done in blue ink, he was entering in the shiny, black-covered book, his "thought for the day."

Paget paused for a moment. He might sit down here and wait for the old man to complete his entry and then he might talk to him about the Kepler place and about Dorie Mayhew. But Matt Welland did not turn from his task for as much as a glance toward Paget. Damn it all, he

was an amazing old man, Paget thought. With Ruth upstairs on the verge of God only knew what, and with children squalling on every side of him at once, he could sit
there writing his stuffy avowals of faith and humility and
a thankful heart!

He turned into the hallway and trudged up the stairway in the darkness. Matt was too frugal to keep a light
burning in the hall, either upstairs or down. Paget caught
the ring of Carla's laughter as he passed the door of
Jenny's room. Then he heard the voices of Ruth's children. Carla had succeeded in bringing a measure of peace
to the house and was doing her best to preserve it. Ruth
must be in there, too. What a fine showing she had made
before the family—and how miserably she had foundered
finally, pulling all her brave sails down with her! Paget
felt a twinge of pity for Ruth, but she had brought it all
upon herself, damn it, and now she was paying for it.
But she wasn't afraid to speak out, he would say that for
her. She might have amounted to something if she had
had the nerve to speak out five years ago.

As he passed on and into the bathroom and turned on
the light, he heard again Carla's fluted laughter, an airy
sound of abandonment to something absurd, to something
delightful. The sound made him chuckle to himself,
amazed him not a little. That kid could laugh any time,
anywhere, when the spirit moved her to laugh. Nothing
touched her. He brushed his hair vigorously before the
mirror, washed his hands, and inspected an ingrown hair
on the back of his neck, with the aid of the small shaving
mirror. Then he went out, switching the light off at the

door, and tiptoed to the room where Carla and Ruth were with the children.

"No more stories now, Helen," Carla was saying. "Aunty Carly is going to brush your mamma's hair. Poor mamma has a headache, and Helen must go to sleep and let her rest."

Paget turned away and went to the room he shared with Tom. He threw himself into the wicker chair beside the heavy, old-fashioned chiffonier, in front of which Tom was changing his tie.

"Going to prayer-meeting?" Paget asked Tom.

"I was thinking I might. Father is pretty badly shaken up over Ruth and I thought I'd go along with him just to be pleasant."

"Yeah," Paget said. "Ruth sure knows how to put on a show, doesn't she? As if we didn't have enough with one lunatic in the family."

He meant Sophie, of course. Tom scowled and tucked his tie beneath his vest. For a moment Paget thought of Sophie and almost repented what he had said. It wasn't quite fair to Sophie, perhaps. She was twenty-eight now, still teaching in the Redlands country school, and bringing more than half her earnings home. Matt Welland had consistently turned his disfavor upon any of the town boys who had dared to look upon Sophie with an interested eye. But that was precisely why Paget ordinarily felt little more than contempt for her.

"You're kind of rough on Sophe," Tom retorted. "She's got more brains than the rest of the family put together."

"Why doesn't she use them, then?"

"She's not doing so bad. Sophe hasn't a chance, really, to show what she can do. Father still treats her like a kid. I just about blew up this afternoon before she got back from school. Someone called up and asked for her. The old man answered the phone and asked who was speaking. Whoever it was must have said, 'Just a friend,' or something like that. Father told him, in that voice of his that makes everybody feel like dirt, that a man who wouldn't give his name wasn't fit company for *his* daughter. It made me boil!"

Tom hitched his trousers up over his meager hips and drew his belt in more snugly.

"Sophe will never get over Bert Seiffert, I guess," Paget mused. "It'll drive her off her nut if she doesn't stop thinking about him."

"She'll probably get over it in time," Tom replied. "If she had a chance to get out once in a while with someone else it would help some."

"Some people don't get over their love affairs as easily as that," Paget observed quietly, "and Sophe is one of them, I guess."

Tom got into his coat and turned once more to the mirror as he ran the brush over his hair. "You're not coming along with us, are you?"

"Nothing doing," Paget replied. "I have work to do to-night."

"Meaning the girl-friend, eh?"

"Meaning anything you like," Paget retorted. "I'm in no mood to go trailing along with the family to make prayers for the souls of the heathen."

"Sh-h!" Tom cautioned. "He's coming upstairs."

"And I'll bet a dollar he gets Ruth to go to church for the comfort of her soul. Passing the buck to the Almighty!"

While Sophie, Jenny, Carlotta and Mrs. Welland were dressing for church, Matt was closeted with Ruth. In their room, Tom and Paget could hear Ruth's fitful sobbing, and Matt's low, earnest voice. Presently Ruth was quiet. There was a movement in the room, and the two emerged into the hall. Matt's voice, hearty, almost jubilant, exhorted the family to hurry or they would all be late for the service.

Paget looked at Tom and grinned a little sourly. "There has never," he said with mocking pompousness, fixing his head in Matt Welland's attitude, "been a divorce in the Welland family."

Tom might have replied had not Matt thrust his head in at the door just then. "Come along, boys. Paget, my boy, are you not going to be with us?"

"Sorry, father," Paget explained, "but I have to go back to the shop for an hour or so."

"Well, it can't be helped, it can't be helped, son. We'll remember you, just the same. Come along, Tom."

§ 5

Thunder moaned low in the southwest, as out of the heart of some forlorn, purple sea whose tided agony, creeping forward, creeping and spreading, struck at last with a coil of livid foam upon the last headland spur of

54

sunset. In the wake of the thunder there was undreamable stillness; and heat; and the moist smell of lilacs. Carla would remember this night in May, this night when she was fifteen.

She would remember, too, vividly as a legend remembered from childhood, the figures sculped out of the shadows on the veranda. Tom, seated on the top step; David, dark and narrow and speechless, squatting on a camp chair set back in a corner; David's wife, fanning herself politely where she sat between Jenny and Mrs. Welland on the porch swing; the Reverend Willsie, in one of the big wicker chairs, timidly scraping his throat in an effort to agree with Matt Welland without, at the same time, conceding too much to a man who, after all, was not ordained in the service of the Almighty. Ruth had gone to bed with her two children—she would return to Clint Proles after breakfast, Carla knew very well. Sophie was upstairs, supposedly reading composition papers for her classes on the morrow. But Carla had seen her in the upper hall, clad in her kimono, her hair undone, and guessed that she was at this moment enjoying one of her long, warm baths. The family had come tacitly to ignore Sophie's frequent and prolonged bathing—there was something about it secretly reprehensible, obscurely embarrassing, as there might be in a wild animal's doing something disturbingly human.

The prayer-meeting had been unwontedly brief, probably on account of the rather unseasonable heat, and the Reverend Willsie had walked home with the Wellands. Carla listened with one ear to the underbreath of the thunder, and with the other to her father's conversation with the minister. The Reverend Willsie called usually once a week and sat for an hour in strained and piteous gravity and deference while Matt Welland expounded his views on life and morals. Or if it wasn't Mr. Willsie, it was the more plastic and acquiescent Deacon Loftus, who interpreted the precept, "to thine own self be true," with an eye to gustables. Or it might be Herman Crane, editor of the *Thrace Advocate,* who would flatter his host with a lively but hypocritical argument, since business which he turned Matt's way drew a neat commission to himself.

"Reverend Willsie," Matt was saying, "it is scarcely my place to criticize a man of your calling, but—"

"We are all human, after all, Brother Welland," the minister reminded him.

Matt drew a long, significant breath. "Ah, yes. But it seems to me that the church has been steadily losing its grip, because its leaders are not using their power in the community. The church should be a tower of *strength* in the community—not only on Sunday, but throughout the *week* as well."

His emphases reverberated sonorously through the stillness, making of the violet gravity of the air something loose and voluptuous.

"You are entirely right, brother, entirely," the Reverend Willsie replied in his pleading voice. About the man there was that same pathetic helplessness you observed in a sleep-walker, something comic and yet infinitely touching. It was in some such way that the dead might grope in the beyond. "But the young people—they have so many outside interests these days. There are so many—"

"Exactly!" Matt interrupted with cheery satisfaction. "And that's just where you come in, Reverend Willsie. I am presuming a little, perhaps, but I feel that you are not getting into the *homes* of the people. *That's* where the real work is waiting for you—before these outside influences have had a chance to do their work. If we cannot do that, Reverend Willsie, the church is doomed to defeat—and civilization is going to totter into the abyss!"

He relaxed back in his chair after this delivery, and Carla, glancing up at him, saw him push his glasses up above his short, grizzled eyebrows and regard Mr. Willsie in challenging silence.

The Reverend Willsie cleared his throat with a brittle, piping sound and drew himself up straight and high. "Civilization, Brother Welland, has suffered a very severe shock in our own day," he observed. "We are struggling during these years to adjust our home life to the effects of a devastating war. We are endeavoring to recover from a hysteria—"

"The Christian home, Reverend Willsie, has no re-adjustment to make—no hysteria to recover from," Matt Welland argued. "If the church had done its part early enough there would be no groping our way back now to a sound faith."

"There are those who would urge that if the church had done its part, Brother Welland, there would have been no war in the first place."

"My family, I am proud to say, Brother Willsie," Matt

went on without offering any reply to the minister's observation, "—and with them all about me here, I am *proud* to say it—has had nothing to vex it in the matter of what you call re-adjustment—and recovery. My son, Paget, served his country with honor and returned to take up his duties quietly—and to resume his wonted place as a member of a Christian family. As a father, I am proud to say, I never had a moment's anxiety during the absence of my son—nor a moment's concern over his recovery, once he was home with us again."

"You are a very happy man, Brother Welland," remarked the Reverend Willsie.

"Happiness, brother, is the result of wisdom. I had hoped that one of my boys might have heard the call to God's service, but that was not His will, and I have contented myself. I can trust my children, because their training has been *thorough*. They have been reared in the fear of God—as I was reared myself. My father"—Matt's voice fell softly, as it always did when he spoke of that remote personage, whose chin whiskers were fading in the mists of years from the photograph on the parlor wall, "my father gave us—gave me—what he considered adequate education to meet the demands of this life. Beyond that, he always contended, lay vicious prying into what was none of our business—none of our business."

Carla heard the scrape of Dave's feet back in the dark corner. Perhaps Dave was thinking of Uncle Felix—that mysterious brother of Matt Welland's, whose name was never mentioned in the family, and who had presumably died long ago and far away. Carla knew nothing of Dave's thoughts. He lived in his part of the house, was thirty now, had three children, listened patiently and without retort to Seena's sneering reminders of the money she had brought to the almost archaic printing office with its moldering columns of religious tracts tottering in the corners, came in and went out of the house like a lean shadow, and stole away at dawn of an odd Sunday when there was no possibility of Matt's hearing of it, to fish on a little lake a few miles west of Thrace. Years ago, he had made sailboats for Carla, and sailed them in the laundry tubs on wash days.

"That's true, Brother Welland," the Reverend Willsie said with an effort at sturdiness. "Quite true. But times change, and as the poet says, 'God fulfills Himself in many ways, lest one good custom should corrupt the world.' You cannot force—"

"Tommyrot!" Matt interrupted impatiently. "That was written before the world had come to such a pass. The world to-day is losing its grip on fundamentals. And why? Because the fundamentals are not planted in the children of to-day. If I am happy in my own children, it is because they have their roots down in the rock of truth."

Matt took a deep, quivering breath, unconscious of his transferred metaphor.

"When I come to die, Reverend Willsie," he went on after a pause, "—and I'm getting to be an old man, now, I'm getting tired—I'll go gladly in the knowledge that my children are living after me, decent and respectable lives."

"Yes, yes," the minister conceded humbly. "After all, I

have no children. Ah—you are a very happy man, Brother Welland."

A crackle of thunder ran just overhead, it seemed, and for an instant the lawn and the flower garden were white under lightning.

"My, my," Mr. Willsie exclaimed, "I must be getting along. I had no idea—" He got up with the alacrity of profound relief. Jenny hurried indoors to get his hat, and when she returned he had shaken hands with each member of the family and murmured his blessing.

He sped down the steps, glancing apprehensively at the sky when he reached the walk. Matt accompanied him as far as the edge of the terrace and stood for a moment watching him as he disappeared down the street to the parsonage a block away. Then Matt returned, his shoulders drooping, his head bent, his attitude one of near exhaustion. Tom hastened down the steps and took him by the arm.

"Hurry inside, father," Tom urged. "The storm will be on us in a minute."

"Yes, yes, son. Is everyone home? Paget—I don't remember seeing Paget about. Has he not come home yet?"

"He'll be all right wherever he is," Tom assured him.

§ 6

Carlotta remained alone on the porch steps. David and his wife had gone, separately, around through the east angle of the porch to their own quarters, and now Seena could be heard slamming down the windows. Great drops of rain began to fall like leaden plummets on the walk, drumming hollowly on the leaves of the copper beech, and on the veranda roof. Carla lifted her face, pressing forward with her eyes open, staring up into the bewildered purple of the air. Over her head her bright hair foamed like a nimbus. At the sound of running feet coming along the sidewalk, she started up. That would be Paget now.

In a moment he mounted the terrace steps and was running up the walk. He halted abruptly as he saw Carla limned against the darkness of the porch by a flash of lightning.

"Come indoors, kid," he said roughly.

His voice was crushed under a clap of thunder. The lightning flared balefully over the blackened grass, so that each blade stood up poignant and illumined. The thunder struck this time near as thought; it seemed like something splintering outrageously in the caverns of your own mind. Paget laughed and opened the door for Carla. But she stood for a moment looking out, large-eyed, contemplative.

"That isn't what will kill me," she said gravely.

"What will, brat?" he asked, giving her a push into the hallway.

"Depraved old age," said Carla glibly, and took herself off to the kitchen with her curious light waltzing walk, where she would, Paget supposed, hunt herself up a cold meat sandwich. He paused a moment in the hall to take off his coat and hat, then followed her into the kitchen.

The window shades were not drawn as they were in

the other rooms of the house and the lightning flamed against them in livid spasms of white and green and a translucent magenta through which the buildings in the back yard, the bushes and the trees, stood black and alive. The rain slid in rattling sheets along the panes. The thunder had suddenly become almost incessant. It had risen like a manacled, insane universe bearing down upon the earth with a ferocious dashing together of its chains. It began with hideous, soft, preparatory knots of sound, like something desperately, cunningly mad, gathered together in an appalling instant's pause, and laid the world open with one prodigious blow.

Carlotta seated herself on the table, sandwich in hand, and hunched down, afraid with her body, though her eyes shone out with a curious detached interest in the pandemonium.

"I got out of it just in time," Paget said.

Carla shrugged her shoulders. "You were with Dorie Mayhew," she said softly.

"Yeah? What of it?"

"Nothing. That's why you're late. That's why you were late for supper."

"Listen, brat—you know too much for your age."

"I'm fifteen."

"Yeah? Well, I'm old enough to remember the night you were born."

His thoughts buckled back to that scarcely discernible, troublous memory of Carla's birth. Himself sleeping with his father, or rather not sleeping, and not daring to stir for fear of that rebuking voice in the darkness, "Stop fidgeting, Paget!" Himself lying rigid until the insides of his thighs quivered and there was a hot dew all over him, and his father thought he was sound asleep and got up and knelt beside the bed, praying hoarsely. Paget believed he could see the words, like broken, fiery scrolls in the darkness, still. . . . "Forgive me, O Lord, for my lust, forgive me, I beseech Thee, for the weakness of my flesh. Visit not my sin upon this child of my iniquity. Strengthen me, O Lord, that my accursed seed may not . . ." Paget was no longer sure as to how much was really memory and how much was his own supplementing. The first line, he knew, he had carried down through the years intact, because, with a sort of awed mimicry, he had appropriated it and embodied it, in silent parenthesis, with his own prayers. There had been something about not visiting sin upon a child, and then the next morning Carlotta had been in the family, with his mother at the point of death. It had been when Mrs. Welland was almost given up that Matt had consented to her wish that the child be baptized that frivolous and somewhat worldly name, although he worried his lip disapprovingly over it and for a long time never called her anything but "Lottie."

Carla finished the last crumb of her sandwich and hopped down from the table.

"I'm going to bed," she said, and was off into the hall and up the stairway.

Paget stood a moment in the darkness, listening to the storm without, then went directly to the living room where Matt sat before the roll-top desk looking over bills and letters Dave had folded neatly away only a day ago.

Paget knew the old man was waiting for him. Matt held uncompromisingly to the rule that the children should be at home, if not in bed, by ten o'clock. There was no logical excuse for their being out after that hour. Church benefits and ice cream socials were a different matter, as he himself was then present to insure decorum in their conduct. Not that he didn't trust them, of course, but they were young and impulsive and he understood youth so well. They might conceivably fall in with some of the less desirable youth of Thrace, who somehow managed to squeeze in at the most respectable of functions.

When one of them was out after ten, then, Matt always sat up until he returned. It was a difficult thing to face Matt's grieved look, and to hear him say, in his tired, incredulous voice, "I can't believe that you would keep your father up until this late hour, after a hard day. But the clock doesn't lie, my son, the clock doesn't lie." And then he would trudge wearily upstairs, pausing now and then to lean on the balustrade and draw a deep, hurt sigh. And the culprit below would feel desolate and futile, sensing something askew within himself.

In his anxiety about Paget he had put letters back into the wrong envelopes, and envelopes into the wrong pigeon holes. He had taken out from a drawer a dummy for a circular on mushroom culture which David was preparing for a couple of cranks who had a newfangled idea and a farm south of town. Matt couldn't quite approve of Dave's printing stuff that might be used, after all, to bamboozle the public. But he was getting too old to cope with David's protests that the shop couldn't support itself on the printing of greeting cards and religious tracts. David had done very well with the shop, he had to admit, though he couldn't bring himself to acknowledge that the machinery was rotten with age and that what David did accomplish was done under the handicap of Matt's slow, stubborn ineffectuality. Nor did he ever permit himself to doubt that David was heart and soul in the business he would one day inherit. David, indeed, had never given him an anxious moment.

Matt did not feel so comfortable when he thought of Paget. There was this scheme of his for raising grapes on a rented vineyard. The boy was young to go off on an independent tack. Besides, he would be alone out there on the Kepler place, with no home influence. And yet, Paget had apparently set his heart on it. He had been seeing a good deal of Kepler of late, it seemed. Or—*had* he been with Kepler during all his absences from home in the evening? Of course, there was his work at the garage, but Thrace was corrupt with pool-halls and bowling alleys, dim establishments above barber shops, and back rooms of ice cream parlors. Matt himself had gone prowling once and had not for days got over what he saw. No, no, it could not be that one of his boys should fall into the ways of the town. He had gone over his papers with unsteady hands, his mind upon Paget. He left them in an untidy heap at last and reached for the Bible on its shelf above the desk.

It was thus Paget found him. Matt looked up slowly and spoke in that gentle, regretful tone of his. "Ah, it's you, Paget. I have been anxious about you, my boy. Were you caught in the storm?"

"I got in just as it started, father," Paget said.

The house was suddenly shaken with a crash of thunder that seemed to break within the very walls of the place.

"It seems to be getting worse," Matt said. "I thought it had gone over."

Paget narrowed his eyes and regarded the old man shrewdly. In another moment, he knew, Matt would begin to question him about coming in late. Well, he would beat him to it.

"I've got it settled with Kepler," he burst out before the old man had a chance to speak again.

"Settled?"

"I have his proposition. I thought I'd tell you about it before I went any further in it."

"That's right, my boy. I hope he has made you a fair offer."

"He'll let me have the house free, and split fifty-fifty with me on the profits of the yield. He'll stake me to one-third of the expenses of the first year. That sounds fair enough to me. What do you think?"

"We shall have to think about it, Paget. No need of rushing into anything, eh? And now, my son, do you think it was quite necessary for you to prolong your discussion of the business till this hour?"

"No, father," Paget replied. Damn it all, why did he have to feel this way about it? "I—to tell the truth, I wasn't with Kepler at all this evening."

"Ah, of course. You mentioned something about having work to do. At the garage, I suppose."

"I wasn't at the garage this evening."

"Paget, my boy, there's something on your heart tonight. I trust we understand each other well enough to know that there need be no secrets between us. The flesh is frail, my boy, but your father loves you. How can I be of help to you, Paget?"

"It's nothing like that, father," Paget assured him. "I have been spending the evening with Dorie Mayhew."

Matt twisted his beard thoughtfully. "Dorie—Mayhew?"

"Yes, father. She has promised to marry me."

"Dorie—Mayhew." Matt drew the name out, lingered over it thoughtfully, reminiscently. "Dorie—Mayhew. Let's see . . ." He drew out his underlip with his forefinger and thumb, his eyes narrowing in careful thought. "Yes, yes, the girl who plays the piano in that picture house at North Main. What—what was it you said about her?"

"I said Dorie had promised to marry me."

"My boy"—his voice was full of affection, paternal tenderness. The overwhelming thing about it was that his heart was in his voice—"my boy—you don't mean you want to marry the daughter of Sam Mayhew?"

"Sam Mayhew has nothing to do with it, father," Paget retorted.

"Ah, Paget—what a pity, my boy, what a pity!" He leaned forward in his chair and looked closely at Paget. "Tell me, son—she has no—no *hold* on you?"

Paget knew very well what the old man meant. "There's nothing like that, father," he said, drawing himself up in an effort to remain calm.

"I was *sure* of that, my boy. You are a Welland, Paget. Let us say no more of this to-night. This storm—we must talk about it when we can talk more quietly. In the meantime, we'll say nothing to your mother about it, eh?"

"Why not?" Paget demanded.

Matt got up and placed his hands upon Paget's shoulders. "My boy, I wouldn't hurt you for the world. But I'm your father, Paget. You can't marry Sam Mayhew's girl, my boy. She is town property."

"Father!"

Paget drew back suddenly, his face pale, his black hair falling over his brow, his eyes gray flames without meaning.

"Now, now, my boy! You would not bring that girl into your mother's house."

"That will be for mother—and you—to decide," Paget retorted. "I'm going to marry her as soon as I have settled the business with Kepler."

"Consider what you are giving up, Paget." The old man's voice was stern now. "Your mother, your sisters, your brothers—everything that has been dear to you. I—I won't mention myself, I mean nothing to you—I, your father, who brought you up in decency in a Christian home. I—I mean nothing—at last."

Matt's voice broke.

"You know that isn't true, father," Paget stammered.

Matt sat down and began turning the leaves of his Bible. In a moment his sonorous voice began, the words coming out, a slow, charmed caravan, up out of the ages, out of Egypt, out of the land of ancient kings.

". . . Thou shalt not make unto thee any graven image, or any likeness of anything that is in heaven above, or that is in the earth beneath, or that is in the waters beneath the earth . . ."

A stifled cry from Paget cut into Matt's voice. He turned and rushed to the door, flung himself toward the stairs.

"Paget, my son!" Matt's voice was a thin note of despair above the clamor of the storm. In that same moment a bolt from heaven struck the house.

Paget leaped back from the stairs. Matt was already in the hall.

"Where's Sophie—and mother—and the girls? My—my—my! Quick, Paget! Run and fetch David! Mother—girls—out of the house, all of you!"

Paget could not move at once for the spectacle the old man afforded. He wanted hysterically to laugh. What a gorgeous power, to throw the fear of something other than God into this poor old fool!

A moment only he stood, then bounded upstairs. Wind tore down upon the house now, and the din was unthinkable. Paget's mind was a senseless blank, but the reverberations in his blood told him that this was the beginning of something, some slow, eternal frightfulness.

In the upper hall he met Carla, white and speechless. "Where is Sophe?" he asked her angrily. "What's the matter with you?"

"She won't come out," Carla replied, her fingers pressed against her lips. "She's in the bath tub and says she won't be disturbed."

Paget tore past her to the bathroom at the end of the

corridor, rattled the knob violently, calling Sophie's name.

From within came Sophie's voice, "Can't you leave me alone!"

"Good God!" He ran back, pushing Carla before him down the stairs. Tom and his father had herded the family into the living room. Ruth and her children had joined Seena and hers in the center of the group, the youngsters terrified and weeping. Dave came in, drenched to the skin. It was all right, after all. There was no fire. The lightning had struck a drain pipe and had been conducted through the rain barrel and into the ground. The drain pipe on the southern gable of the house had been splintered loose. Dave had seen it clearly in the glare.

Paget turned from them all, went to his room, where for a moment he cursed the whole household in a fierce undertone, then threw himself across the bed and wept.

§ 7

Tom came in and prepared at once for bed. "Well, that was a close call," he observed.

"Not close enough to suit me," Paget snapped. "It wouldn't worry me to see the whole damned thing go up in smoke!"

Tom turned and looked at him. "What's the matter with *you?*"

"Not a damned thing! I'm getting out, that's all. I told the old man about Dorie to-night."

Tom continued his preparations for bed. "So—that's it! I thought as much."

Paget looked at his own reflection in the mirror. "I'm going to marry her—and see the old bastard in hell!"

"Easy, boy," Tom cautioned him. "Are you sure, considering everything, that she'll marry you now?"

Paget said nothing. He would not let Tom know that the same thought had flashed upon him when he had thrown himself upon the bed. He whipped off his clothes and lay down between the cool sheets and waited until Tom crawled in beside him.

"We're going to get married right away and move into the little Kepler house for our honeymoon, and start work on the vineyard together," he muttered rapidly. He turned upon his side and dug his head into his pillow. "Oh, God, what a scene! Oh, what the hell!"

As he closed his eyes, the final intoned words of his father droned in his ears, like an oracle across æons of time and space. ". . . or that is in the waters beneath the earth . . ." The mystical waters under the earth—the pulling, deadly tides of suspicion, of fear, of bigotry. He opened his eyes and stared into the darkness, saw the strong, dragging flood, and the graven image therein, and heard the voice of the original God—the free and golden soul of man.

III: TOM

§ 1

Into his cardboard suitcase, very new and very pretentious with its shiny black finish and its steel lock and leather straps, Tom packed the two crisp suits of blue and white striped cotton pajamas his mother had made for him. They would shrink, of course, as they always did when they were washed a couple of times and would become too short in the crotch and the sleeves. Tears came ridiculously into his eyes as he patted the garments gently down and arranged a half dozen pairs of socks in a row on top of them. There was a jar of jelly, too, wrapped in newspaper and tied about with a string. He would have to be careful not to let Pete Sunderberg see him unpack. Pete was by now a man of the world to whom home sentiments were derisible.

Paget, sprawled broadly in the chair beside the chiffonier, the drawers of which were all half open and empty now of Tom's things, had not spoken for minutes. Tom glanced at the squarish figure, built so much more sturdily than his own, so lean and unmanageable, and wondered what was passing in Paget's mind. Poor old Paget! He was worrying the nails of one hand with those of the other, as he always did when something disturbing possessed him. It was a full year now since he had given up all thought of the Kepler place and had kept his job in Phelan's Garage. Dorie Mayhew had refused to marry him after he had told her what Matt Welland had said. It had been futile for Paget to argue that she was not marrying the family. Dorie was the daughter of old Sam Mayhew, but Dorie was proud, too proud to become a member of a family that despised her. After that, the Kepler place had meant nothing to Paget. Tom wondered whether anything meant much to him now.

"Aren't you in a hurry to get out?" Paget asked, his eyes upon the suitcase which Tom was closing. "Your train doesn't leave till to-morrow noon."

"I don't want to leave everything off till the last minute," Tom explained.

Paget laughed. "Hell, I'd have been packing a week ago if I was getting out. I don't blame you a bit."

"I wish you were going with me."

"If Dorie would go along, I'd drop everything so fast you wouldn't be able to see me for dust, boy. But what the hell!"

Tom stood for a moment, his hands in his pockets, and looked from the window, his eyes brooding out over the lilac hedge, across the yard behind the printing office, and into the west. He tried to put the deepening loveliness of that sky into words and then, in despair, thought of what it really looked like: a strip of ripe watermelon beyond the peaks of the houses, paled upward into color as translucent as lime-juice, and deepened again to thin green glass. Tears sprang into his eyes; tears for the maddening beauty of things, and for his own ineptitude.

Tom abominated himself for his own poetic weakness, for his morbid imagination which had shackled him to the conviction that he was a victim of a predestined impotence. No amount of rationalization was of any avail. Between Tom and the image of his true soul, Matt Welland stood, a frightening mirage. Since he had left high school five years ago and gone to work in the printing office with Dave, his own identity seemed to have receded farther and farther from him, like a vanishing point of light on a dark plain, the static shadow of his father's dominance weaving across it until he doubted that it had ever existed.

He thought of Pete Sunderberg, who had gone to Chicago and got mixed up with a crowd of radicals there. Pete could get him a job on a small paper he worked for—not much of a salary, but it would give him a chance to write, or at least to find out whether or not he could write. At the thought of that test his vitals crept with horror. He would not dare to write with the eyes of the family upon him—Matt's eyes particularly—and to lend himself to any more tepid text would most certainly predicate dismal failure. He comforted himself, with a surface swagger, a sickly bravado, that it was his sensitive spirit that thwarted him at every turn; but deep down, the satyr of truth grinned up at him and told him that it was simple blood-cowardice that checked him, and from that there was no escape. He writhed, even now, when he thought back upon his lofty attitude toward Pete who had come up for a visit with his widowed mother in Thrace. "My dear Peter," he had said in what he had fondly considered a very unprovincial manner, "if I am to write, I shall do it as well here as in your more enlightened surroundings." Well, there was truth in that too, he thought bitterly, for if he went to the ends of the earth he would not be able to leave behind him that medley of self-consciousness and inhibition and adolescent fear that was himself.

He turned on Paget. "I'm going to walk out and see Ruth before I turn in," he said. "I promised Carla I'd go out and fetch her home."

"I thought the kid was doing her lessons down with Frieda Gertner."

"She went down there for an hour after supper, but she'll be out at the farm, I imagine, by this."

Paget stretched himself in his chair and yawned. "Good thing someone is taking a little notice of old Ruth. Clint has been in town all day. Phelan was telling me he's on another bat."

"Well, there's a situation that won't go along much farther."

"Why not? Everything goes along—to the end, old timer."

"This won't. Ruth is going to break under it one of these days. In her condition just now, especially, her mind won't stand it."

"Her mind! Hell, she's always been crazy, more or less."

Tom was about to speak when the voice of Dave's wife shrilled from the back yard below. Paget got up and went to the window. Sophie was sweeping the porch, paying no attention to Seena, while Mrs. Welland calmly shook out and folded the cloth that had been used on the supper table that evening. Tom joined Paget before the window.

"There's a limit to everything!" Seena announced loudly. "I ask people in for a visit and *he* locks himself in that back room in the shop and refuses to come out. He's doing it for spite, and I won't stand for it!"

She tossed her head back, her nostrils flaring with determination.

"Come indoors, Seena, and talk," Mrs. Welland suggested, glancing anxiously across the garden toward the Linklater place. "The whole neighborhood will hear you."

"Let them hear me!" Seena declared truculently. "I've got nothing to be ashamed of. People know, anyhow, whose money has been keeping the Wellands alive."

Paget struck the window sill with his fist. "Shut up, you damned fool!" he bawled down at the woman, who threw her head up with baleful surprise. Then in disgust and quick apprehensiveness, he drew the window down and strode across the room.

"Good God!" he exploded. "What keeps me around this madhouse! Where's the old man?"

"He went down town after supper," Tom said.

Matt had a curious way of cajoling Seena when she was angry, and no one else in the house was in the least effectual in stemming the tide of her abuse.

"The prospects are for a big night, then," said Paget. "Hell, I'm going to get out."

"You don't want to walk out with me and pick up Carla?"

"Hell, no! I want to get away from the family. I may go around and call on Dorie. I haven't seen her for a week."

"I think I'll slip into the shop and talk to Dave for a minute before I go," Tom said. "Seena will give mother a headache if she keeps on much longer."

He went out by the front door so as not to encounter Seena.

The heavy, purple tassels of the lilacs stooped down upon him as he slipped along the wall of the printing office, around to the little back room, where the shades were drawn. At the end of the hedge, where the low, copper-hot sun brushed the clusters, they were an undreamable loom of color; a pang of sudden loneliness struck him. These, too, he was leaving behind, cutting them out of himself together with the fear and sentimentality of his boyhood, as being incongruent to his new life as a man. He quailed a little at the thought, and told himself that after all he was not really mature, that he might be excused if at first he could not easily accept the harshness of the world that lay beyond the Welland fastness of moral and physical security. There was the old Alhambra at the foot of the garden. He thought of Sophie, long ago, afraid of the dark, bribing him on winter nights with promises of stories in return for safe-conduct there and back. Poor old Sophe! She was really the one who deserved to get away. . . . Oh, damn!

He called softly after he had knocked at the back door. Presently David opened it, let him in, and locked it after him.

The shades on the west side of the room were drawn also, and the only light in the place came from a small bulb that was fastened in a wire basket against the wall. In front of the light stood an old arm chair with a packing box as a foot stool. The room was little more than a shed built on the rear of the printing office, was littered with the accumulated rubbish of years for which Matt might some day find use, and smelt of dust, yellowing paper and machine oil.

David returned to his chair, picked up the book that lay open upon it, and seated himself. Tom saw that it was Conrad's *Heart of Darkness*. He sat down on the packing box and looked at Dave. It occurred to him that they resembled each other, he and Dave, more than any other two members of the family. And yet Dave was inexplicable to him. One day, in Dave's part of the house, Tom had found tucked away on a dusty upper shelf a tattered copy of *Treasure Island* which Dave would not permit his own children to touch. It had borne the name of "David Welland" and below it was the date, "October 9, 1906." When the United States had entered the war, Dave sought enlistment in the navy, but a cardiac condition, the result of measles at the age of twelve, had been a barrier. Seena was outraged that he should even have thought of the war—they had been married two years and had one child—and never let up in her tirade against his avid following of the maneuvers of the Allied fleets. Tom remembered his intense perusal of maps, his ink-stained forefinger following the sea lanes and working out probable eventualities. But whatever his yearnings were no one had ever heard him express them.

Why had he let himself in for this barbarous marriage, when the only outcome of it was his enslavement to a pursuit he subtly hated? Inertia—by God! A sinister inertia, bred in the bone, and fostered through a childhood of fear of reality, of reverence for the phantasms of caution and respectability.

"Seena is raising Cain with mother and the girls," Tom said.

David smiled. He had a serene, child-like smile, very reminiscent of Carla's. "She'll get tired of that," he said. "I told her this morning that I'd be busy to-night—and I *am*."

"She said something about visitors—"

"Some of her women friends, and that new bird—that Christian Scientist—Murdoch. He's been here less than two weeks and she's gone on him already. There'll be fur flying plenty in the house when Seena turns Science. Imagine the old man!"

David chuckled softly.

"Well, I'm leaving it," Tom said. "I don't see why you don't clear out and get a job somewhere. The old plant would get along just as well—"

"What's the sense in all this talk of clearing out?"

David replied. "You know how well the old plant would get along if I let go. Father hasn't done anything here for ten years except put his O.K. on the work that I turn out. Besides, I'm perfectly satisfied. I got over that stuff of wanting to go places—long ago. One place is as good as another in the end. It's different with you. You go—and get all you can out of it—and forget about us. And I mean—*forget!*"

It was a long speech for Dave. Tom looked at the floor.

"But you did have other ideas, once," Tom blurted out. "You old nut—you never say anything."

"Nothing to say, boy!" He took a crumpled cigarette out of his shirt pocket. Tom winced when he saw it. He supposed he would have to learn to smoke when he got down with Pete Sunderberg, or Pete would be ashamed of him. But even Dave didn't smoke in Matt's presence, and Seena wouldn't tolerate it in the house.

"You haven't got another, have you?" Tom said, realizing how timid and silly his question sounded.

David lifted a quizzical eyebrow as he felt again in his pocket. He drew out another cigarette, even more wilted than the first, and handed it to Tom.

Once, back of the woodshed in the autumn, when plantain spikes were crisp and brown, Tom and Paget had been caught by their father smoking the seeds in rolled paper torn from their copy books. They had been soundly trounced. But the effect of the plantain had not had the bewildering buoyancy of this. Tom rested his hand on his knee and shut his eyes. Dave laughed.

"If you can't finish it, throw it in the stove," he said. "I hope you go to hell in Chicago."

With Dave, then, it was simple inertia. The damage had been done years ago, when his dreams of the sea had been turned inward and an unbreakable seal put upon them. It was no moral sense that held him liege to Matt Welland, but a morbid conviction that he was meant for nothing better.

Tom got up to go, tossing the butt of the cigarette into the small iron stove.

"I promised to walk out to the farm and bring Carla back," he said. "I want to say good-by to Ruth, too. I'll run in on you in the morning before I leave."

"That's all right, boy. I'll probably knock off and go down to the station. Anyhow—good luck!"

Tom stirred uneasily. "I feel rotten about leaving you with it all," he said. "I'll—I'll come back if you can't make it without me."

"Rats!"

"By the way," he added with a hasty casualness, "you understand, of course, that I'm not going on the job I said I was going on. I'm breaking in under Pete. Don't spill the beans, though."

Dave looked at him with narrow surprise. Tom shifted nervously; that look said more clearly than words could have said that Dave did not believe Tom had it in him.

"I'll keep mum," Dave said, and opened his book. "You can tell Seena that I'll be over later, if her guests care to wait."

§ 2

To reach the Proles farm after sunset, one walked straight toward the promontories of flame and pearl magically there, in the west. When she was younger, Carla had often considered going on, out past the gaunt Proles farm, for beyond it there was neither tree nor stream to hold her. What fancies a person had—until she was sixteen!

It was a good thing she had thought to leave her school bag back there in the bushes at the junction with the highway. The road was full of ruts after last night's rain, and the walking hard. She hoped Tom would get out to say good-by to Ruth before it was dark or he would get his good clothes splattered in the puddles, with no moon to see by. She was glad that he was coming out purposely to walk back with her. She had been too excited with the feeling of things to concentrate on her work with Frieda Gertner, and Frieda was stupid and ugly anyhow for a lovely evening. Knowing that the family was content as to where she was, she had felt easy about slipping away early. She would get out to the farm before Tom, and would have an opportunity to visit Ruth before he came.

It would be lonely with Tom away in Chicago, and she would feel so much younger, with all the others so grown up. She never felt that Tom had outgrown her, even now when he was twenty-two. Even when he called her "an afterthought" it was only in affection. Yes, it would be strange having him away, but before long she would follow him. She would keep house for him, mend his socks—badly, to be sure—and accompany him to the theater every night. Of course he would go to the theater—father would never know. She herself had never seen a play although she had read all the plays she could lay her hands on in the public library, and she had made a very able "Portia" in the school production last year until father had heard of it. The disappointment his objection had brought was not very great, because she had continued being "Portia" in private—and many other decidedly more intriguing persons who were to be found between the covers of books. As she nimbly avoided the mud holes, she donned again the stately robes of Lady Macbeth, gestured appropriately with her hands, and proclaimed the lady's bright guilt to the bushes that flanked the road. . . . *Will all great Neptune's ocean wash this blood Clean from my hand? No. This, my hand, will rather The multitudinous seas incarnadine, making the green one red . . .*

Suddenly she paused. In a silhouetted figure reeling from side to side in the road ahead of her, she recognized Clint Proles. He was carrying something under one arm. It would not do to overtake him. He was quite obviously drunk. She glanced back along the road, nursing only a faint hope that Tom might be in sight. But there was no sign of him.

Clint kept on his erratic way, a grotesque figure in the brilliant afterglow. She felt suddenly a stirring of curiosity about him. What were a man's sensations in that state? Did the world spin, as when you whirled around and around and then came to an abrupt, dizzy stop? If so, what a gorgeous feast of sunsets he was having! Sophie said that Ruth had driven Clint to this with her nagging. Ruth wasn't content, Sophie said, with being a happy wife and mother. She wanted to go to the movies every night, and dance, and have a good time. And Tom said Ruth and Clint had been mismated from the first. Why did people get married, anyhow? Ruth had got married because father had been so strict about her getting home early at night. Ruth was pretty and feather-brained, and father had been afraid for her. Carla had heard him say to her mother that he feared Ruth would "get into trouble," if she didn't get married. That was an old-fashioned phrase, and Carla understood it with contempt and boredom.

They were nearing the farm-house now. It was odd that there were no lights in the windows. She drew back abruptly as she saw Clint do an unaccountable thing. He scrambled down awkwardly into the ditch and climbed out of it and disappeared into the tangle of willows and brushwood that grew up to the pasture's edge behind the barn. An extraordinary impulse, quite senseless and inexplicable, since all her loathing of the man rebelled against it, seized her to follow him. She stood for a moment in excited horror, then found herself, as in a dream, crossing the ditch and stealthily following him on his heavy, thrashing course. Some imponderable curiosity, pulling at the very core of her hatred of him, drove her on. It was as though she were

84

about to witness some ghastly ritual which she could not resist. Once or twice she stopped and felt the wild beating of fear in her heart, and tried to turn back, only to discover herself going on, chill rippling over her flesh.

When Clint emerged at the barn he seemed to hesitate for a moment. Carla drew a breath of relief—if he saw her now he would not wonder at her presence. But she preferred that he should not see her. She hated the glistening slant of his eyes whenever he looked at her. Since that day a month ago, when she had been out here making taffy for Ruth's children, and he had come up and playfully bitten a piece of the candy out of her mouth, Carla had not been near the farm. And yet, she stood in awe of him because he was the only person in the world whom she really hated.

While he stood irresolute, swaying a little, she held herself still. Then Clint seemed to make up his mind, and moved with a bold swagger toward the house, covering his package with his coat.

It was darker now, with a thin blueness close over the earth. Why were the lamps not lit? Strange there was none in the kitchen, where Ruth usually sat until the children were put to bed. Could she have gone into town? It would have been wiser to have telephoned before coming all this way out.

Clint was making for the heavy sloping cellar doors, which could be bolted on the outside as well as on the inside, to keep the cellar waterproof. She realized now what he had in mind. He had brought something in a bottle from Thrace and was planning to hide it in the cellar.

While Carla's eyes were fastened upon the black cellar-way, she felt her feet approaching it as if they were doing so against her will. There was at the back of her mind some rational notion that she might catch Clint red-handed and denounce him for Ruth's sake, but the immediate impulse to follow him was sheer fascinated horror. Noiselessly, step by soft step, she felt her way down the damp stairs into the black smell of the mold. Then Clint struck a match.

Years later, whenever she thought of that moment, all that came to her mind was a bloated mask that swung, bodiless, above her in the sudden spurt of light. By then, Clint Proles' curse of amazement, the dawning narrow gleam of his eyes, and the forward lunge of his body, had become unrelated to reality. Untrue as a nightmare, too, had become his thick, swinging arms as they clasped her.

She buried her teeth in the cords of his neck and Clint dropped her with a stark oath. In the tangled dark she could see Clint lurching toward her again. As she flew to the outer cellar-way she heard him stumbling after her. He must have fallen headlong, for when she was half way up the steps there was yet no pursuing sound. The conviction came to her then that Ruth was not at home, and without an instant's hesitation she slammed the heavy door shut and bolted it.

She ran, her mind senseless with terror, her body a-crawl with loathing, through the dimness of the brushwood, until her numb legs could carry her no farther. Brambles caught at her clothes, soft fern laced about her feet. She shrank at length exhausted on the moist, new-smelling earth. The thought of seeing anyone, anyone at all, even Tom, after what had happened, was horrible. Least of all did she want to see Ruth. She was glad Ruth had not been in the house after all, had not heard her or seen her running away. It was too shameful, too unthinkable. She wanted only to lie here, becoming clean and sweet again with the sweet damp newness of May in the earth. For the violence she had discovered was not wholly revealed by Clint Proles. There had been that mysterious, reckless urge that had drawn her into the cellar, something evil and obscure that eluded her now as she thought back upon it. The very beastliness of Clint had hypnotized her, and that could not possibly be Clint's fault. Rather it was the fault of something lawless within herself.

Presently, in the soft tumult of night sounds, in the opaque mist that began drifting in among the young cottonwoods and willows like something spectrally animated, the episode was improbable. In a few moments it tired her, irked her quite as something that had to do with another person in whom she was not interested. She listened to the outer sounds, and heard a bull-frog croaking dreamily in a slough, the bark of a dog on a neighboring farm, and the distant voice of a man calling across the fields.

She thought suddenly of Tom, got abruptly to her feet, and began to hurry out to the road where it joined the

Thrace highway. A few stars had budded palely above the mist in the woods, but it was still light enough to move easily. Trees at night were things of secret graces, some beckoning, some turning away—but they were never things to be frightened of.

At the junction of the two roads she found her books. She stood and looked back toward the Proles farm for a moment, then continued along the road toward town. Of course, she would not say a word about Clint to anyone, unless perhaps to Tom. In a way it did not seem fair to Clint to tell *that* about him. He hadn't known what he was doing at the time.

Presently, growing out of the dusk, Tom's lean figure came swinging along the road toward her. She called to him and waved her school bag and Tom's whistle answered her, a clear note upon the silence.

§ 3

Tom glanced down at Carla once or twice with a feeling of bewilderment at her beauty and elation in it, though he could never quite escape a sense of uneasiness when he looked at her. Her face seemed always pale and tense with some secret rapture. She alone had been untouched by the solid, unimaginative meddling that had informed the childhood of all the others. What would happen to her? Would her glowing destiny be deflected into the prosaic channels of cautious and uninspired existence down which the others were moving to oblivion? He thought, jealously loyal, that each and every one of them, from David down, had at one time or another held, burning high in their eyes, this rushlight of beauty that shone out of Carlotta. In David it had been a passion for the unseen, unheard, unsmelt sea of his invulnerable boyish dreams; in Sophie it had been a genius for love; in Jenny, a true talent debased into china-painting; in Ruth, a delight in laughter and small, sturdy joys; in Paget—the pattern of Tom's thought blurred.

Carla was unimplicated—that was the word. He had never thought of it just like that before, though he had known it, of course, for years. There was this business of her going all the way out to visit Ruth, for example, and finding her away from home. She showed no disappointment, no concern. Nothing mattered to her.

When they reached town at last, it had grown almost dark. People were still sitting on their front porches, for the day had been hot, or watering their lawns, or talking with neighbors over hedges. Peace, Tom thought, the peace and serenity of a little town late in May. That was what he was leaving, so that he might learn how ugly it was, how suffocating, how narrow, how unilluminated. They added nothing to the beauty of the imagination of the world, these people. No, but they watered their lawns, and people motoring through to Chicago or Detroit said, "What a pretty little town! Twenty-five hundred people—you don't say!"

A sharp defensiveness in Thrace's behalf presently possessed him. Then suddenly he had to grin at himself. After all, he had better wait until there was some call for his excitement.

Once or twice they were stopped by some of the church people who had heard of Tom's going away and wanted to wish him good luck in the big city, reminding him that he must not forget the home folks when he got down to Chicago. But the young bloods of the town, bareheaded youths in white flannels, strolling with their girls and airily smoking cigarettes, greeted them with a casual condescension that smarted along Tom's skin. Damn them! They had gone to college in Redlands, a Methodist college at that, while he had grimed away in the printing office, but whatever influence the college had brought to bear upon them had been shed from them like water from a duck. Once, two of them, sauntering arm in arm, had stared hard at Carla, whose regard was elsewhere. When they had passed, Tom looked at her. Her blue serge school dress was getting too short for her. Then he heard behind him the idiotic laughter of the two who had passed.

"Damned yokels!" Tom fumed aloud. "That Lee Prince was the dumbest dumb-bell that ever cribbed his way through high school."

Carla tucked her arm through his and looked up at him with amazed eyes. "But what do you care, Tommy? You're going away—and you're going to be a great man. I'm—I'm—" Her voice trailed away dreamily.

"Your chance will come, too, some day," Tom said.

She laughed. "I think I'll be a lady of delight."

"What are you talking about?" Tom demanded, frightened and inclined to anger. Then he laughed, realizing that again he had revealed in himself a grave lack of humor.

Japanese lanterns swung and glowed palely under the ceiling of the deep veranda of Cranford Reed's house. Beneath them, Cranford Jr., not long back from his trip abroad was entertaining his friends. A victrola was littering the air with some gay nonsense, and girls in the embrace of smartly cool young men gestured in the extraordinary fashion of the year—like diaphanous bobbins, Tom thought. He would have to learn to dance, he supposed, although the thought of being so close to a girl sent him into a cold sweat.

Cranford Jr. called down the broad lawn to them as they passed, beckoning them to join the party. But from behind the vine of a small arbor where a girl in white sat with a tall glass in her hand there was a burst of laughter. The laughter was quickly muffled and Tom could see that a man had passed his hand across the girl's mouth. Tom waved his hat in cheery regret to Cranford, and went by without quickening his pace.

"Would you have liked to go in?" he asked Carla, a little breathlessly.

Carla pursed her lips thoughtfully. "No-o," she said. "They laugh at us, and anyhow—I think father is right. They aren't good enough for us. The Reeds got their money through that government deal—and *we* are Wellands, even if we are poor."

"They're crooked," Tom observed knowingly.

"It isn't that, either," Carla went on. "It's that—it's

because I *feel* superior. Some day they may ask me to come to their party and—I may—and I may not."

Tom grunted. "Huh! I'd rather they didn't ask me."

Small houses with small gardens stood along the street in the evening. In the trees the locusts spun their furious wheels, a sleepy catbird called, here and farther on; crickets balanced their bows upon their own smaller silence.

"Part of my life is walking here," Carla thought, and decided to embody the idea in a poem.

§ 4

The voice of Matt Welland greeted them from the deep shadows of the porch. He was alone and waiting for them.

"Jared Gale was here until a few minutes ago," he said pleasantly. "He said he wanted to bid Thomas good-by, but I'm not so sure that was his only reason for coming. Our baby girl is growing very fast, eh, Thomas?"

The old man chuckled as he came forward and pinched Carla playfully on the cheek.

"He said he would be down to the station to-morrow to see me off," Tom replied.

"No doubt he will. He said as much when he left. He's a fine young man, is Jared. And now, my girl, you had better run along to bed and get that beauty sleep. A young girl must be careful, you know. Besides, Thomas and I would like to have a few words to ourselves on our last night together, eh, Thomas?"

Carla said good night and went into the house immediately.

"Sit down, my boy," said Matt, going back to his chair among the shadows.

"Ruth wasn't home," Tom said as he seated himself on the porch swing and permitted his eyes to move nervously toward his father.

Pity and annoyance, and a certain exasperating consanguineous understanding of the old man harrowed Tom's thoughts. If he had not been so much like Matt himself he would have gone on to college at the close of his high school course. If he had not had that same fumbling timidity which he knew instinctively lay beneath his father's passive, blighting power, he would have left home long ago and worked his way through college despite all obstacles.

"Thomas," Matt began, "you are leaving us to-morrow."

"Yes, father."

"It is a great sorrow to us—to me especially, my boy—that our business here is not big enough to include you. On the other hand, there are great opportunities in the world, Thomas, and I am happy in the thought that you will have your chance to develop them. I believe you have chosen a field in which much good can be done for humanity. The men who make our great newspapers wield a tremendous influence for good or evil. Journalism stands in need of good men, Thomas—men who will remain true to their birthright—to the best that is in them. You are going away with my complete confidence."

Tom writhed. It was bad enough to have a heroic lie on your conscience without having this suffocating, sentimental faith in you expressed with a rustic grandiloquence that struck down into the center of your being, into the very core of your personal pride.

"I am not too sure," Tom ventured sagely, "that the world is waiting for good men in these days."

"You are quite right, my boy, quite right. It has been the habit of the world to reject its good men. But the stone that the builders reject, Thomas, becomes the corner stone when the edifice is reared. It has been so throughout the ages. The good man earns contempt, but only for a time. In the end, Thomas, the world follows him, even though they may not suspect it. If it were not so, the world would destroy itself in a generation. The right will prevail, my boy. It does prevail—every day—before our very eyes—if we have but the eyes to see it."

"We hope so, father," Tom replied weakly.

"It will become more than a hope as you grow older, Thomas. It will become a conviction, as it has become a conviction to me. If it were not for that, we could not live with the forces of evil about us as they are. Mother and I will have no anxious hours over our son, wherever he may go. Our hearts and our hopes go with you, my boy, and our faith in you will never be dimmed."

An impulse seized Tom to tell the old man the truth about his prospects in Chicago. It was not that the lie troubled him. He had done right, he told himself again for the hundredth time, in lying to Matt about his job. But it was this blind, staggering trust that Matt had in him that wrenched at his scruples. And yet, good God, working on a two penny radical magazine wasn't so outrageous, except for the pay he was getting out of it, and if it was going to cost the old man a stroke to learn of it . . .

"I was in your room, Thomas, before you came home," Matt went on. "I put some little things in among your clothes—nothing much, of course—the Lord has been very good to us, but He has not blessed us with much of this world's goods, Thomas. And now, my son, I wish you every happiness, and may God bless you and keep you. We shall never forget to pray for you."

Matt was on his feet now, his hand extended toward Tom. With a feeling of keen discomfort, Tom got up from the step and took his father's hand.

"God bless you, my boy, God bless you!" Matt turned away and went slowly into the house.

Tom watched him, then followed him into the hall. In the heavy silence the clock in the hallway ticked with maddening precision, clarity. The damned assurance of a clock!

The darkness of the staircase as he trudged upward bore down upon him like a physical weight. That was just another thing he could not conquer—his fear of dark enclosed places. He had reasoned that out, too, but it did not help any to know that it was the eternal space of night within himself that he feared. He remembered when, as a boy, he had felt his hands go clammy in this well of darkness. But you did not cry out in your anguish—you prayed. He would be praying in his grave, he thought, and his hands would be like cold lard.

Paget was in the bedroom, painfully filing his nails. He waved his arm toward the bed, where Tom's suitcase lay open. "Take a look," he said.

Tucked snugly down into the corners of the suitcase were six large oranges, a package of chewing gum, a box of peanut brittle—Tom's favorite candy—and a fine, new, small Bible, bound in morocco and with gilt edges. On the fly leaf, in Matt Welland's delicate hand, was the inscription, "To my son Thomas, on the occasion of his going forth into the world. May he ever remain the boy who is known by his father, Matthew Welland."

He replaced the book. He felt suddenly hard and heavy. There was really very little point in his going away. David's look of surprise had been quite justified. He was too preoccupied with his own searching through chaos to be of any value to a cause. If he was too weak, too vacillating to take a stand in respect to his own soul, how could he hope to emerge as anything but an idiot in his address to the outer world?

In the bed he shared with Paget, Tom tossed from side to side, unable to sleep. He tried to think of Pete Sunderberg and the job awaiting him in Chicago. A cool breeze was blowing in and the heavy, sweet and disturbing scent of the May night stole in upon him. He threw the covers off him impatiently, and the dark chilled air from the window startled along the small of his back where his pajama coat was pulled up leaving a naked space. To-morrow he would be taking the noon train—away. But it wouldn't do him any good. He didn't have the guts to take advantage of his freedom. Poor old Dave! He had done his best, was doing his best, to give him his chance. The printing office—God damn it! The oath was a prayer, uttered out of the blind and bound struggle of his soul. It was of no use, Dave, old boy, to put yourself to all the trouble. It was too late, already too late, with this heritage of fear. Fear, fear, fear! Fear of living, fear of loving, fear of thinking—down in the wells of wonder—fear of the crucifying doubt of holy things. Terror of the mystery and power of self, housed in the fugitive flesh of a dream! No good, Dave, just no good! Your face, with its silent, aching pity, will follow me into the world, and I'll see you forever, setting type for birth announcements and Sunday school tracts, in the cobwebs of the printing office, and your eyes with a quaint vision of the sea in them. Yellow for buttercups on the bank of the old slough, Dave, in spring—and yellow for Tom Welland!

§ 5

When Tom awoke he found Paget sitting up in the bed beside him. Something had startled them out of their sleep at the same moment. Voices came to them from below, excited voices—Ruth's angry voice shrilling above the others.

"That's Ruth," Tom said, dazed.

Paget got out of bed. "I've been looking for something like this," he said. "She's gone off her head at last."

In the hall Tom met Carla, who was hurrying downstairs.

"It's Ruth," she said. "Something has happened."

Tom could hear his father and his mother trying to quiet Ruth, but her voice persisted, shrill, strained, unnatural.

"I told you I wouldn't stand for it. Two nights now he hasn't been home. Let him go home to-morrow, then. Let him see what I left for him."

"Ruthy, *Ruthy!* Hush, my girl! Take her upstairs, mother. Ruthy, Ruthy, hush. You'll have the neighbors—"

"Let them come. Let them all come. Let them look at a mad woman. I'll tell them all about it. I'll tell them to go and take a look at where the house *used* to be— where it *used* to be! It isn't there now. I saw it. I waited till I saw it—like a torch—like an old straw stack—like a furnace—like hell! And I did it. I took the kids out— and then I put the match to it! Ha-ha!"

Carla looked at her, fascinated and afraid. What was she saying? The knowledge of what Ruth had done came horribly, like a mad dream from which she could not awaken. Where was Clint Proles? In the cellar, in the damp stone cellar—not damp, no, a blazing furnace, under the heavy bolted door. Faces spun around her in the glare of the living room, faces of strangers. No, these were her own brothers and sisters, her own mother and father. There was her mother, sitting very still and fixed, with the two children of Ruth and Clint Proles in her lap. Sophie, biting her lips and twisting her hands—and Tom and Jenny, with her father, urging Ruth upstairs. Where were Paget and David? She felt her stomach shrinking sickeningly, into a knot, and then the room darkened.

Presently she found herself lying on the couch, the lights clear, the room steady. Tom was holding a glass of water to her lips. She drank from the glass and looked about her. There was someone standing behind Tom— a thin, dark man—the marshal, Mr. Leader. No sign of Jenny or Ruth or Sophie or her mother now. Just Tom and her father—and Mr. Leader.

"Give her a little time," Mr. Leader said quietly.

She looked clearly now at the marshal's face. He was a sad looking man, she thought. Tom was watching her curiously.

"Feeling all right now?" Tom asked.

The question surprised her. "I'm all right," she said. "What has happened?"

"Mr. Leader wants to ask you some questions," Tom told her.

Carla looked again at the marshal. He was stooping over her now. How sad he looked.

"Can you talk a little?" he asked her.

"I'm all right," she assured him.

"You were out at the Proles farm to-night, weren't you, Carla?"

"Yes."

"Did you see Clint Proles there?"

She must not tell about Clint—she must not tell about him if he were dead. Or even if he were alive. But she must say something, at once, or she would tell the truth.

She spoke rapidly, without drawing a breath. "Yes, I saw him when I was going out—on the road."

"He was walking—home?"

"Yes. I walked along behind him. He cut through the woods and I followed him because he was drunk. I was afraid he might fall and not get home."

"Where did he go when he reached the farm?"

She kept her eyes wide upon Tom's face. "He went in the cellar-way. I saw there was no one in the house, so I began to be afraid. I ran back and took the short cut through the woods. I met Tom on the road and came home."

"Do you think he stayed in the cellar?"

"I didn't see him come out. He was very drunk."

"You didn't see any fire about the house?"

"No. I saw Clint strike a match in the cellar. I could see the flame because it was dark in the cellar. But the match went out."

"What time was that?"

"About nine o'clock—maybe half-past nine."

"And Mrs. Proles was not anywhere about the house?"

"No."

Mr. Leader's face cleared. He straightened and smiled and patted Carlotta's hand. "Thank you, my dear." He turned to Tom. "It seems likely that he set the fire himself, accidentally, and couldn't get out in time. It's perfectly understandable. I'll come around in the morning

swell send-off for me, all right. Imagine Clint—dying like that!"

She would tell Tom now, quickly, so that the knowledge would pass from her to him. Then she need never think of it again. A fact like that had to *be* somewhere, and Tom would not be oppressed by its presence as she was.

"Do you think Ruth really started the fire?" she whispered.

"Of course she did," he said in a white, low voice. For an uneasy moment she was afraid he was going to cry; she could not have stood that.

"But she didn't lock Clint in," Carla continued, bending close as she used to do when, as a small girl, she had a "secret" to tell him—about what ants said when they met, or about the tiny lizard she had hidden in Sophie's bed. "She didn't, because—I did—in the cellar."

There was a long, blank instant that seemed to swing like a weight before her eyes. Then Tom had grasped both her wrists, and if it had not been for everybody in the house, she would have cried out with the hurt.

"Tell me about it, quick!"

Carla, in a rapid whisper, gave him the story, and as she drew to an end it became less and less her own possession. Finally, something that had been there, but not quite thought out because she had been so bewildered, came forward and was whispered with the rest.

"Clint wasn't very happy with Ruth. There wasn't

very much use for him to live. Sophie says Ruth drove him mad."

Then like a slide passed before the lens of her mind came the picture of Clint groping toward the cellar stairs, stumbling in the darkness and falling before she closed the door upon him.

"Forget this ever happened, kid," Tom said suddenly, getting to his feet. "It wasn't your fault—he would have been trapped anyhow, if he had gone up into the house. He probably went to sleep in the cellar. And it wasn't Ruth's fault—that part of it wasn't. She still thinks he's in town somewhere. Don't tell anyone what you've told me. Remember—you're keeping quiet for Ruth's sake."

"I'll remember."

"And now get away to bed. I'll have to go out toward the farm. I may get there before they come back, though there's nothing anyone can do about it now."

Carla went back into the house and slipped quietly to her room. Sophie was already there, sitting in her kimono before her mirror, staring at herself.

"Better get to bed, Carla," she said. "Jenny and mother will stay with Ruth. The less stir there is about the place the better."

As soon as Carla was in bed, Sophie stole out of the room and went to the bathroom. Carla heard the cautious click of the lock as Sophie turned the key in the door, and a moment later the sound of the water running briskly into the tub. Carla lay back and gazed at a crack in the ceiling until her eyes closed heavily as though there were pennies on them.

Presently Sophie came back, smelling hot and steamy from her bath, and Carla sat up in bed. She lay down again and Sophie came to her and brushed her hair, up from her neck, cool and away along the pillow, for a long time. Sophie had thrown a blue scarf over the lamp shade, and the room was like some still chamber deep at sea, lighted by a strange sea-moon. Once she heard Sophie say something, almost, but she was just on the lovely margin of a dream and she could not linger long enough really to hear what it was she said.

§ 6

In the morning, when the family came downstairs, Matt Welland was seated in the living room, his short hands gripping the arm of his chair, his head thrown back and his expressionless eyes fixed upon the wall opposite him. On his knees lay the open Bible, its blue satin marker shining in the sun.

Carla, always the last to come down, saw him thus, shut her eyes delicately, turned and entered the dining room through the hallway, and passed on to the kitchen. She went to the door and stood a moment in the sunlight. In a moment she began to sing, in her sweet, light voice—

*"My soul to my God and my body to the sea,
And the dark blue waves a-rolling over me. . . ."*

Jenny, at the kitchen table, was cutting bread for toast.

She looked up, shocked, as Carlotta turned from the doorway.

"Well, I never!" she said sharply. "Haven't you any decent feelings at all?"

"Now, Jenny," Mrs. Welland sighed, "don't make things worse, please."

She took the coffee pot off the fire and Carla drew in a deep breath of the cheerful fragrance and opened the screen door to the porch. Lulu was sunning herself pleasantly. She stretched and yawned as Carla knelt beside her.

"Come, Carla."

Sometimes her mother's voice filled her with an unease, an involving disquietude which singing or laughing or reading poetry could not quite dispel. There was foreboding in her gentleness. She was so tall and brown and kind, and her fingers were already knotted and shiny as hickory twigs.

Carlotta rose and went indoors.

Although the table was set for breakfast, no one was as yet seated. Everybody was in the living room. Paget stood beside the east window that looked out upon the porch and over the garden, where the light was still the pearly silver of a shell's heart. Sophie sat erect, only her fingers moving in her lap as she polished her glasses with a crisp handkerchief. Jenny fussed with her dress, pulling it down about her legs. Mrs. Welland sat in a rocking chair with her hands folded. Her eyes, Carla thought with a pang, looked like Lulu's when her puppies were taken from her.

Matt had not moved from his place. His head was thrown back and rested on the hard wood of the chair, his eyes were closed behind their gold-rimmed glasses, and on his white, hollowed face there was not a glimmer of expression. Carla, looking at him askance, thought that he was like a dead child who had somehow aged appallingly after he had died.

Mrs. Welland brought a cushion and sought to place it behind Matt's head. But he held up his hand in gentle protest.

"No—no, Sarah," he said patiently.

Mrs. Welland sighed and replaced the cushion on the couch.

A door opened upstairs, then closed softly. At last Ruth was coming downstairs, with Tom beside her— slowly, as if they were counting the steps. Carla saw them at last in the doorway, Ruth's narrow little face turning from one to the other with a pale, half-arrogant smile, until her eyes rested upon Matt.

She wore a cotton dress of Jenny's and it was too large for her. She crossed her arms and pulled at the flesh of her upper arms with her fingers.

"Hope I haven't kept breakfast waiting," she said, with an airy tremor that made Carla's eyes go suddenly wet. "I didn't feel like eating this morning. I haven't even dressed the kids yet."

"That doesn't matter, Ruthy," Matt said, his voice low and labored. "Sit down over here by me, my child. I've been waiting for you all night. I have not left this chair, Ruthy, waiting for you. I have sought divine guidance—and I think it has been granted me. Come—sit beside me here."

Carla could not endure the painful crackling of that voice. She looked out of the window and saw how tall and gallant the tulips grew, mauve and cool yellow.

But Ruth was talking, her voice cold and hard. It was like a small whip, snapping back toward herself. "Yes. You have been granted divine guidance, father. Well, what is there for me to say? God has told you everything there is to know. What more do you want?"

"Ruthy, dear," Matt pleaded, his voice slow and patient, infinitely tired, "we have some things to talk over among ourselves. We must talk quietly and humbly, as becoming those who stand in the sight of God, Ruthy."

"Talk—more talk!" Ruth retorted. "I talked to you a year ago, didn't I? I warned you. There's nothing to talk about now."

Matt drew himself up slowly in his chair. "Ruthy, I have waited all night—to talk with you. I want you to tell us what you did last night—everything. Won't you please come here and sit down. Don't stand like that, away from your old father, Ruthy. I want to help you, my poor child. Don't make it harder for me, I beg you."

Ruth laughed. "Harder for *you?*"

"Ruthy!"

"Well, what do you want me to do?"

"Tell us what you did last night, Ruthy."

"Haven't I told you? I burned Clint Proles' house down."

"Ruthy, what—what brought you to that?"

Ruth walked slowly toward her father, her eyes fixed upon his face. When she stood directly in front of him she narrowed her eyes and smiled, a horrible, twisted smile. I'll tell you what brought me to it. I was mad, insane. For years I have been giving this body of mine to a beast. Look at me—look at me now, father. Do you think I'm bearing this child because I want it—or because I love the man who is its father?"

"Please, Ruthy!" Matt pleaded again. "Let us talk only of last night. What brought you to it?"

"I'm telling you what brought me to it. Years of beastliness. Day before yesterday he came to town in the car. When he didn't come home, I was glad. I didn't want him to come home. I was tired, tired." Her voice now was without expression, a dreary monotone. "When he didn't come home yesterday, I was glad. I didn't want him to come home. I don't want to see him again. Last night, I went over to the Carlton farm and had supper with Mrs. Carlton. I came back late. It must have been after ten. I was afraid he would be home—waiting for me. But the car wasn't back. When I went into the house and he wasn't there, I was glad—at first. Then—I don't know—I felt I had a right to know where he was. He had no right to stay away. I sat in the kitchen and waited for him. I said to myself, if he doesn't get back by twelve o'clock, I'll leave and never come into his house again. He didn't come. I began to hate him. I waited for another hour—and then—something happened to me. I don't quite remember. I got the kids together. I said to myself, if he comes home now I'll kill him. Then I said—I'll leave him no place to come to. I'll go where he can't find me—and I'll leave nothing behind. So I took the kids outside—and I did what I did —and I came away—and I walked along the road—hoping I might meet him and tell him what I had done. And I looked back—and it was done! The sky was red. I stood and watched the sky. A car passed me and stopped—and then other cars—and someone brought me here. And here I'm going to stay. And I won't see him. Tell him that, all of you. I won't see him—I won't—I won't!"

Her eyes darted from one to the other, glazed with furious tears. But nobody moved or spoke. Mrs. Welland and the girls were weeping softly. Paget was looking from the window at the garden, worrying his nails. Carla glanced at Tom and saw him standing near the doorway to the hall, his chin quivering.

Matt's broken voice spoke once more. "My poor child! My poor child!"

Ruth's brandished laughter made Carla's blood run cold. "Your poor child, father, is free!"

"You will not be free in spirit, my child, until you have first made your peace with the Lord," he said, in the richly emotional tone he used in prayer-meeting, with the winning weariness over it. Then he got up and put one arm about Ruth's shoulders. "My poor child, our hearts are breaking for you! God's ways are incomprehensible to us, Ruthy." He was weeping as he spoke, but Ruth's eyes were dry and hard. "Ruthy, my poor child—your husband—your—"

His voice broke. Ruth looked from him to the others, questioning: "What are you all standing around for—what are you waiting for?"

Matt drew her close to him. "Ruthy—your husband has been taken from you."

She drew back from him, shaking his arm from her shoulders.

"Where is he?" she asked.

"He—was there—in the house—last night. They found him in the cellar."

Ruth had gone suddenly rigid. Her lips moved, but no words came. Matt looked quickly about the room. "Leave us—leave us together—mother—the rest of you. My poor child!"

§7

Carla fled into the kitchen, and out the back door. On the porch Lulu lay snapping at the large, sluggard flies of early summer. Outside, robins dipped their notes into the gold of the morning; crickets chirped their tiny, inscrutable challenge; leaves rustled, drooped, rustled again.

Carla tiptoed down the steps and crept along the side of the house. What she felt was piercing shame, shame for the triviality of human conflict, when life was so deep, so high, so unencompassable. What had started all the wrong, fixed thinking in the world, without plasticity, without rhythm—the rhythm of simpleness and truth?

In an hour she would have to leave for school. In less than that time, Sophie would have to take the small trolley to the Redlands district, and Paget was already late for his work in the garage.

It was impossible not to hear her father's voice now, pleading with Ruth. "You must first clear your conscience, Ruthy. You must go to Mr. Leader and confess everything."

Ruth suddenly broke her silence. She flung her desperation at Matt. "I won't! You can't make me go! I won't, I tell you. I'm not to blame! I didn't know—"

"Your first duty is to your fellow man, Ruthy. Only then can you seek for God's forgiveness."

"What do I care for your God and His forgiveness! What did He ever give me but misery! Your God!"

Sobs were shuddering through her now.

"You will go to the marshal, Ruth, or I shall fetch him here," Matt told her.

There was a long silence, broken only by Ruth's sobs. Then she spoke suddenly, incredible bitterness in her voice. "All right—I'll go. I'll have that—distinction—anyway." It was an unusual word for the simple spoken Ruth. "I'll be the first of the Wellands in jail."

Carla could hear her rushing into the hall, her sobs rattling grotesque and dry.

Then, from the sustained silence of the living room, Matt Welland's voice came, a hoarse, agonized entreaty. "Mother—Paget—Tom! Stop her! Stop her!"

There was a quick rush of feet into the hall and up the stairs. In a moment Matt's voice spoke again, this time in prayer. "Oh, God, forgive me—forgive Thy servant, Lord, for his weakness. Oh, God, forgive me!"

IV: JENNY

§ 1

In her little cubicle, flush with the bay window of Kelly's Barber Emporium, on a side street just off North Main, Jenny Welland sat before her small white-enameled table, with her manicurist's paraphernalia neatly arranged upon it. The table was scarcely ever out of order, for that matter, since an average of not more than six "clients," as she called them with a fine defensive dignity, each afternoon, left her regrettably ample time in which to keep her equipment tidy.

On this August day she was dressed coolly in white crêpe de Chine, with a blue brooch at her breast. The brooch was always lowered an inch or two after she left home, so that a space of her moist pinkish skin showed above the silk. Her indefinitely blond hair, which she had wanted to bob, but that Matt Welland would not hear of any such newfangled and unwomanly conceits, waved pleasantly about her temples in the day's humidity. Now and then she took a small powder puff from the drawer of her table and dabbed surreptitiously at her nose and chin, glancing out, from old habit, to make sure that her father was not at the moment passing by. Since Ruth's house had burned—more than three months ago now—Matt had gone out very little. Ruth's affair had been a ter-

rible blow to him. The true story of Ruth's insane act
had never gone beyond the family, and within their circle
her reckless violence had been explained and covered over
as part of the temporary insanity resulting from her condition. Ruth had been content to grant them the comfort
of her own silence on the subject. Not since that day when
the marshal had visited her—himself already convinced
that the fire had been started accidentally by Clint Proles
—had she spoken of it to anyone, within the house or out
of it. Indeed, by that strange alchemy of the mind that
converts a worthless wish into a precious belief, Matt had
regained to a serenity in which it seemed he now glossed
over Ruth's account of the events of that fatal night as the
hysterical raving of one who was momentarily, and quite
unaccountably, demented. The family tacitly indulged
Matt in his pretense, although once, in anger, Paget had
spoken of Ruth as a "firebug." David maintained his ironi-
cal silence toward the matter. Sophie had been bitter for
some time—and Carla continued mute, inscrutable.

But all feelings about Ruth had been blended magically
when her child was born within a month after she had
come to live under her father's roof once more. For two
weeks both mother and child lay between life and death,
and the family united in daily prayer for their recovery.
When they were both out of danger at last, Matt's happiness knew no bounds. He had his family about him again,
bound together by suffering and prayer. He called them
all together one Sunday morning, about the cradle of the
child, and gave thanks to a God of love, a God of right-

eousness, who fulfills Himself in many ways and chastens His loved ones that they may not forget Him.

Since those grave, uncertain days, however, life had gone along quietly enough. Jenny's spirit had been humbled, but her pride revived quickly as her fears for Ruth were dissipated. The vanities of the flesh were not to be denied. Her longing to bob her hair persisted in spite of Matt's opposition; her use of the powder puff when she was safely beyond the danger of paternal reprimand was a little unworthy, perhaps, but it yielded its delights. Once she had even made so bold as to use a little rouge on her cheeks, a touch of lip stick, and a brush of stiffening black on her lashes that made her blue eyes starry, but the result had been so remarkable that men had paused before the window to stare at her, and with a tremulous heart she had gone quickly and washed the whole effect from her face. It had done something to her, nevertheless. It had left her with an excited pride in her own potentialities, and often when she looked at her rather peaked and hungry features she thrilled with the knowledge of what could be done with them.

On a double shelf on the wall behind her reposed samples of her skill in china-painting, with small price cards braced against them. There were powder jars in two designs, black background with gold and red cockatoos, and gold background with black and red cockatoos. There were neat hair-receivers with forget-me-nots margining the hole in the cover. A set of glass bottles was rakish with butterflies unknown to any lepidopterist. There was even a sturdy shaving mug—which upbore a formidable looking elk's head—out of deference to a mode which might possibly have a still living adherent. Once in a long while someone bought something and Jenny went furiously to work to replace it.

She was wont to remark to Sophie and Carlotta that her painting of china kept her "in touch with finer things," a consummation difficult enough in a prosaic town like Thrace. Carla had looked at her curiously once when she had said that and it had given her a thrust of discomfort. For an instant she had suspected Carla of despising her art and her memory had flashed back a false glimpse of something she had had when she was very young: a glimpse of herself as she might have looked, standing before an easel, brush in hand—of colors and distances and graces in forms ineffable. How silly she had been to think that she would some day be a great artist! Artists were born out of vast chaos, fashioned from the stuff that went into the first creation, molded by the Hand that flung the shining stars out into space.

Jenny sighed, looked out of the window, fanned herself with her handkerchief, and reflected that it was pay day. Seven dollars a week, with tips bringing it up to twelve, was not bad for half time work. Half of it went to the family and was little enough to make ends meet. Poor David, only thirty-one, was already graying at the temples with worry about the spiritless shop. The sale of the Proles farm had brought Ruth little more than five thousand dollars which, carefully invested by Dave, gave her an income of about twenty dollars a month. How twenty dollars a month was going to provide for Ruth and her growing family, no one could imagine, but Matt Welland would not hear of her going out to service, the only alternative for a woman of Ruth's limitations. Matt, Jenny suspected, was in terror of having Ruth out of his sight. He had never been able to trust her since that horrible night in May.

Had it not been for the earnings of Sophie and Paget, indeed, the household would have been in a very precarious condition. Moreover, in direct proportion to the growth of the family's needs, grew Matt Welland's dreamlike, rhapsodic ineffectuality in the handling of his business. Except for Dave's prodigious, heart-breaking efforts, the shop would have been a shambles of failure long ago. It seemed incredible, Jenny thought, that her father did not realize this. Perhaps if he ever did glimpse the facts, he shut his eyes upon them promptly so that his own increasingly mystic absorptions might not be disturbed. His religious tracts, composed largely by himself, were distributed now quite deliberately gratis, in service to God and man, and to these tracts he devoted most of his time. Only once had Dave dared to expostulate with him. Jenny would not soon forget the look Matt had turned upon him, a look of wide, child-like, hurt surprise, that had hardened into glassy, fanatical fury. Then the old man had seemed to crumple and had gone off wringing his trembling hands and had shut himself up in his room for the rest of the day.

But Jenny could not dwell for long this afternoon upon the family's difficulties. She had had a post-card, safely tucked down inside her blouse, which had been sent to her in care of the Emporium, and which bore an intelligence that made her conscious of the bright burden of her heart, now floating and light, now heavy and oppressive. Milton Pierce, itinerant salesman of kitchen utensils, would bring his humble automobile to a point directly across the street from where she sat at her window—he would be there about the time she would be ready to leave the shop. And a minute later, he would be seated across from her at this table, his thin, nervous fingers resting upon her own nervous palm, ostensibly having a manicure.

On the barber shop wall, just opposite the door of her little compartment, the clock said a quarter past five. Milton should be here now, knowing as he did that she left the shop at half-past five. Perhaps she had better telephone home so that they would not keep supper waiting for her—she could make some sort of excuse that would serve the purpose. No, no, that was silly. What if Milton should not come at all? She looked out again, up and down the street as far as the window permitted, on edge with anxiety and anticipation.

To give herself the poise of confidence, she went carefully over their relationships from the beginning, three months ago. She tried to belittle him in her mind, to calm her pulses by reminding herself of her own superiority. After all, he was only a traveling salesman—a sort of peddler, in fact—racketing about the country in a dilapidated Ford. A peddler with an incongruous streak of poetry. A peddler who had no connections, nobody in the world; a peddler who had had incipient tuberculosis and had to be in the open air; a peddler who had nervous, fine hands, curiously, clingingly strong, and a winning mouth and sad, hopelessly hopeful eyes. A peddler who had told her, haltingly and with embarrassment, his life story, not wanting pity, but understanding and human friendship. A peddler who had made her cry and want to kiss him, and whom she had kissed night after night in her dreams for the past three weeks—since his last trip through Thrace. She covered her face with her hands, and the blood rushed into her cheeks at the thought of him.

With a grinding of ancient brakes, a car came to a stop in the street outside. Jenny glanced casually out, then became suddenly busy with the rearrangement of the articles upon her table.

He came in and stood for a moment irresolutely in the doorway, his straw hat in his hand. Jenny felt stifled; an expanding turbulence seemed to be pressing outward from the entire surface of her skin. She could not move. She could only sit and look at him with a fixed smirk of a smile, while within her there was an ache of rapture, fear and utter capitulation.

Now he had hung his hat on the rack and was sitting opposite her, shyly examining his hands.

"I was afraid you would be gone before I got here, Janice," he said diffidently. "I had a little trouble with the car."

"I would have waited." She could say no more, with the breath halting so painfully in her throat.

His hands darted across the table and caught hers.

Jenny looked nervously out of the window, but the street was empty.

"You hadn't better—here," she murmured, withdrawing her hands. "Do you want a manicure?"

He made an impatient gesture. "That's over, for good," he said, with more determination than she had ever heard in his voice before. "I want to marry you, Janice."

Jenny felt the blood fly out of her heart, to the farthest corners of her body, where it pounded wildly. She leaned back in her chair and closed her eyes. "Oh, Milton!" she breathed.

"You will! I knew you would. No, I didn't know, but I hoped—I hoped like the devil." His voice was so joyous she could have cried. "I haven't been able to get my mind off you for the past three weeks, Janice. I knew if I didn't say this quick—soon as I saw you—I'd lose my nerve. Can't we go somewhere and talk? We could drive out a piece in the car. What do you say, Janice?"

She almost sobbed, "My name isn't Janice—it's just plain Jenny. Oh, Milton—I don't know what to do!"

"Yes, you do!" He laughed confidently, leaning toward her again. "You're coming out of here with me. It's half-past five, anyhow. Come on, Jan—Jenny! Say, I like that name better than the other—a lot better, Jenny. That suits me. It's more like you." He smiled at her deeply, happily, showing the strong white teeth she had thought of so often. "Will you come?"

Her cheeks burned with excitement and the consciousness of his nearness. One thing was certain—they could not remain here talking like this. "Yes, yes, Milton. I'll come. You go out first and drive down to the end of the street. I'll meet you there."

Milton looked searchingly into her eyes. "You won't run away home?" he urged, so anxiously that it brought her tremulous laughter.

"I promise not to," she whispered, glancing again into the street. "Go, quick. I'll telephone home and tell them that I've been kept here a while. I have to get my pay, too, from the boss. Drive down about two blocks—I'll be there in five minutes."

§ 2

In this small hollow on the side road north of Thrace, all the massive heat of the day seemed to have gathered. The branches of a tree, dulled and scabrous with dust, brushed the roof of the little car in which Jenny sat with Milton Pierce. In shadow the road was a reddish purple, and the avenue of sky above it, between the trees, was like flushed lead. Somewhere beyond the trees the sun was sinking behind a bank of dark cloud.

It was a strange thing that now when they were alone together, as they wanted to be, there should be a shy restraint between them. Jenny's hands were tightly clasped before her, as though she were holding in leash there the too rapid beating of her heart. Milton leaned forward over the steering wheel, his arms crossed. His face was grave, with a flush on the rather high cheekbones.

"I haven't much to offer you, yet, Jenny," he said slowly. "But if you'll take a chance with me, I don't think you will regret it. I can take a steady job—any time, now—

from the company I'm with—in Chicago or some other city. I have never met anyone in my life that I wanted as much as I want you, Jenny. I feel that I could do—great things—if you were with me."

Again Jenny felt that crowding of her blood to all the surface of her body. She looked out over the tops of distant trees in an effort to steady her pulses. There were things that would have to be told—she would have to tell them—in fairness to Milton. He must know about the Wellands. He must know that her father would disapprove of him as he had disapproved of most of the friends the Welland children had tried to bring to the house.

"I have only myself to offer you, Jenny," he said, his hand moving over hers, strong and reassuring. "I am all alone in the world. I have only myself—and my love for you—and my great need of you. That's all, Jenny. You have your home, I know, and your family—and I—"

She took an unsteady breath. "I was just going to tell you about them, Milton," she said.

"Can't I drive you around there now? I'll meet your father and mother—and tell them."

"No—I'm afraid, Milton."

"What's the matter, dear?" He had reached out and was drawing her toward him, and she was weak against him. "Don't you want me to meet your family? Are you ashamed of me, Jenny?"

His anxiety, his defenseless humility, cut her through. "No—not that, Milton," she said. "Not that. My family is queer. People laugh at us in town. I don't think you would like us much."

He laughed buoyantly. "Like *us?* It's *you* I like, Jenny. Don't worry about the others."

She was silent for so long that at last he turned her face toward his with both his hands. "What's the matter, dear?"

She began to talk, slowly, laboriously. Unused as she was to clarifying her mind, the effort was dismal. Her account of the family merely served to illumine for herself the hopelessness and the confusion of their lives. Never having been obliged to think beyond the homely, practical problems of every day, interwoven with those minute, superficial problems of the Welland household which she was permitted to share, she found herself overwhelmed now and unable to understand what was happening to her. One secret thought, as she talked to Milton, did strike sharply into her brain, with a quick and sensitive revulsion of shame for herself. Why, the thought insisted, could she not have fallen in love with some strong and quite irreproachable man against whom Matt Welland would have been powerless in every respect? The answer came deplorably clear: no such man existed, or if he did, he would not be bothered with the Wellands.

She told him of Sophie, by way of explaining what she could scarcely put into words. "My eldest sister, Sophie, was in love with a man—years ago, during the war—but because he had written some articles on some new religious idea—some free thought stuff—and had lectured about it, father would not let him near the house. And so Bertram went to the front, and he wasn't even allowed to write to Sophie, and the last we heard of him he was reported missing. I don't think Sophie has ever stopped thinking of him. But it would not have mattered who he was—everybody was wrong. Now the young people in town—even the girls—think we are queer—and laugh at us."

She stopped suddenly and caught her breath as she saw the look of pity and incredulity that had come upon Milton's face. He laughed huskily and drew her to him.

"Wait—wait, Milton," she pleaded. "Father is a good man. He loves us very much—and he is awfully kind. But—"

He caught her by the shoulders and looked at her, smiling.

"Jenny—we'll have weeks and months and years to talk all we want to about that. I'll listen—to-morrow—or next week. But I'm not listening now. I have a lot to tell you, too. It will be a lot of fun, telling each other about our lives—seeing which can make it look the worst. We've both had hard lives, Jenny, but I'm glad of it. We're going to be just that much happier together, having each other. And I don't care if I never hear the rest of your story. What I want to know is are you coming away with me—now! What do you say?"

His hands were about her wrists now, and her body gave out toward him irresistibly. "Will you come with me to-night, Jenny? We can be married to-morrow, in Chicago. There's a nice old lady that I stay with sometimes—not more than two hours from here. You can stay with her to-night and I'll take you on to the city to-morrow.

Then we'll be married right away. What do you say, Jenny?"

The flush of the heat lay ominously still about them and the west was sullenly red. But Jenny was oblivious of the heat and the sky. She was oblivious even to Jenny Welland, of the heart and mind and body that had been Jenny Welland for twenty-four years. She was conscious only of the savage impulse that lashed out of her toward Milton Pierce, to possess him entirely, and in turn to obliterate herself in him so that the last vestige of Jenny Welland should be gone.

He leaned close to her and pressed his lips to her hair. She was afraid, afraid for herself, afraid for Milton Pierce.

"Oh, Milton—please—I can't stand it!" she pleaded. "Wait—wait. Take me home now. I'll come back. I'll meet you."

"You mean—you'll come away with me—to-night? It's too good to be true. You mean it, Jenny?"

She was breathless. She drew back from him and smiled. "Won't I be a nuisance to you, Milton? I could work—"

He laughed. "I make enough. You'd be surprised. And I'm going to make more. My wife isn't going to have to work. No, sir!"

"I don't care about that, Milton," she said. "I'd be glad to work—with you."

His face was all alight now. Looking at him, she adored him with a sense of something miraculous that had appeared, this moment, beside her. Suddenly she was fiercely glad that he was not a great, potent personage who would

126

be the equal of her father, or even more than his equal. She was glad that there was something a little pathetic about him, so that she must cherish him, protect him against all outer violence.

"You love me enough—to go with me, Jenny?"

"I'll go—to-night."

He laughed tremblingly, stroked her arms and hands, and kissed her helpless fingers. Vaguely she could hear herself agreeing to meet him later, as soon as she could pack a few things to take with her and slip out of the house. She would manage it somehow. No, it was out of the question for him to come to the house. Everything would be sure to go wrong then. The quiet road back of the church, that would be their meeting place. She would have to go at once now. They would be asking questions of her if she was too late. They would have finished their supper by this. No, no, she would not fail him. She would meet him—behind the church—at half-past nine.

And now the poor little car was backing, turning, heading again toward town. She would have to get out at a safe distance from home. Would anyone see her and wonder? Would the marvel and fear of what was happening to her show in her face? How would people whom she had known before, people in their dull little lives in their little dull streets, look to her now? Thoughts, bewilderingly bright and strange, wheeled unaccountably through Jenny's mind. The ground, the ashy-purple trees, the very sky seemed to lift, to pulse with inner, secret life. Even the gray fence posts of a field, and a sluggard flock of crows in the field, became sharply beautiful, a pang of hitherto unseen reality in her consciousness.

"Milton," she said, very still, like something speaking within her to herself, not to him, "I feel—as though I am just coming alive. I feel as though I hadn't seen anything around me before. It's strange!"

He lifted her clasped hands with hot impatience, kissed the palms, the defenseless wrists where the veins ran bluely. "My sweetheart!" he said. "You don't know how wonderful it's going to be—you have no idea!"

His kiss on her palm flamed down into her body. Tears blurred across her eyes, tumbling the suddenly alive trees and earth and sky into one.

§ 3

The family sat on the porch, in the pocket of heat under the Virginia creeper. Jared Gale and Carla were playing croquet on the lawn, Carla laughing heartily and tossing her mallet into the air at some discomfiture on Jared's part. Deacon Loftus, seated in a wicker chair on the porch, was craning his neck in an effort to watch the game. On the small table beside him stood a pitcher of lemonade, a plate of doughnuts and a glass. The Deacon had a doughnut poised in front of him, and was munching with a swinging motion of his jaw. The fact that he must at this very moment be digesting a meal he had eaten in his own home, Jenny thought with disgust, would not discourage the Deacon from accepting a toothsome morsel somewhere else. Matt, half facing him, had his fingers pyramided before him, and was looking out gently over his glasses and talking in an earnest tone.

He did not change his voice or his attitude as Jenny walked slowly up the porch steps. She stooped and kissed his cheek lightly, as he always expected the children to do upon their return or departure. At the slight smack of the Deacon's lips over his doughnut she felt a quick nausea, and her eyes, meeting his squarely, narrowed.

"Back, my dear?" her father said with a little contented sigh, parenthetical to his discourse with the Deacon. "I managed to save some peaches for you—unless our Lottie has filched them for Jared. . . . But as I was saying, brother, the real work of salvation comes not *during* a revival meet, but after it. The follow-up work. It comes in standing by, and praying with the convert so that his spirit, overwhelmed by the experience of conversion, does not fail. There is where your real work lies, brother—"

Her mother looked up from her crocheting. "I left the table set for you, Jenny dear," she said. "We had a cold supper—so nothing is spoiled for you. You look flushed, child. Was it very hot in the shop to-day?"

"Yes, it was pretty hot, mother," Jenny replied.

She walked, dazed and unreal to herself, through the hall to the dining room. Her hands groped at her throat, to relieve the choking there, the actual choking, as though the knowledge in her mind, the burning, violent knowledge that had come up from her body, were retreating again to its secret places and lodging in her breath. She saw the cold supper laid for her on the table, the pressed ham, the potato salad, the sliced cucumbers and tomatoes, the sliced peaches in their glass bowl. Going on to the kitchen, she washed her hands and face in cold rain water, pressed the towel deep into her aching eyes. If she removed the food into the kitchen, she thought, out of range of her father's voice, and the Deacon's breathy compliance, she might be able to eat. It was torture even to know that Ruth had to sit out there on the porch with her children about her, and listen to Matt Welland's confident talk, that had no reality. What was happening to her—Jenny? But let it happen, let it happen, whatever it was! Ruth was suddenly illumined for her, Ruth who had been down in the very depths, the dark vitals of living, and who had to listen now, day after day, to the vaporous optimism of a man who had lived always in the upper air of sterile illusion. What was Carlotta thinking, out there on the lawn, all a-shimmer with the gold of her hair and the gold distances of her eyes, Carlotta with her absent, imperious youngness? Carla, of all of them, was somehow apart, as one strange unaccountable green leaf on a dead tree seems apart. She wished she had the courage to tell Carla what she was planning to do. But the child would probably look upon it as a gay escapade. What did Carla really think of Jared, she wondered. She treated him so lightly, and yet—

When Jenny had brought her supper in from the dining room and set it on the kitchen table, Carla and Jared came indoors. Carla turned on the cold water faucet for a drink. She stood jauntily with one slim leg crossed over the other, her hand on her hip, and looked at Jared with an impish grin.

"I trimmed him beautifully, Jenny," she said. "And how he loved it!"

Jared took the glass of water she offered him, and seated himself near the window. "If it wasn't going to rain I'd take you on for another round," he said. "Then *I'd* laugh!"

"Even the gods are on my side," Carla exulted. "So you're out of luck, Jerry!"

Ignoring her, he turned to Jenny. "I had a letter from Tom, to-day," he said. "He doesn't seem so keen on the city, does he?"

Jenny was making a woeful attempt to eat. The mention of Tom did not help matters any.

"Tom expects too much," Jenny said.

"He ought to go looking for the Holy Grail," Carla observed. "That would keep him busy, at least."

Jared got up, looking faintly displeased. "It wouldn't hurt you to look for it a little," he said. He set his glass on the table.

"Don't be such a bore, Jared," Carla retorted. "You're too good-looking."

He swung toward the hall door. "Well, I've got to get over home, girls. I'll say good night to the others and slip along. See you again!"

Carla gave him a playful push through the door, and disappeared after him, and again Jenny was alone. While she washed the dishes she had used, her eyes kept wandering toward the screen door, through which she could see the sky pendulous with the gray and green breasts of clouds. Now and then sheet lightning flared between them, and she felt it curiously in her own body, in a sort of omen. But the thunder was distant, soft, only a brooding mutter. And then the rain came, surprisingly soon, almost thoughtfully down upon the garden, slow and long, and the light withdrew in gentle deliberateness, as though a hand had drawn a dark curtain over the wet glow in the west. It would rain all night, and now the family was coming indoors, with a noise of chairs prudently lifted in, and with Deacon Loftus declining regretfully Matt's invitation to come indoors and play dominoes.

She heard the family moving to various parts of the house with something of the slow and laborsome hesitancy of injured ants crawling toward their narrow chambers. Paget was moving about in his room above the kitchen on heavy, lifeless feet. He scarcely ever sat of an evening now with the others down in the living room, or if he did it was at his father's request that he be present when there were callers. She noticed that he never changed his clothes any more when he came home from the garage in the evenings, although he had once been almost like a girl in his love of cleanliness. She could remember his saying, it seemed very long ago, "There's something clean about grapes!" Had Paget known this rapid heat along his limbs, then, this knot of excitement somewhere in his body, at once sore and sweet, when he had been secretly seeing Dorie Mayhew, and hoping to marry her and live with her in a grape vineyard? Poor Paget, so true, so singly intent! He could not have stood the sorry splitting of his dream—and so the vineyard, too, had withered in the drought of his heart.

Sophie was softly playing the piano in the parlor. Infrequently, on rainy nights, she would be seated there, alone, making the keys murmur, almost inaudibly. To-night, from the dark parlor, the notes wavered like a wraith out of the darkness, the faltering wraith of *Liebestraum*. Jenny had never been greatly drawn to Sophie, but tonight the sound of her imperfect, timid playing filled her eyes with tears. If one went into the parlor, Sophie would promptly stop playing and go to her room.

Carlotta returned to the kitchen, doing a slow waltz step, her arms moving with instinctive, inner grace, with the subtle and true knowledge of motion that trees have, or wind in trees, or rain in wind. Jenny winced at the vision of her almost unsupportable loveliness. The child had no knowledge of herself; only her body had knowledge of her, and the rhythm of living flowed through her like a song.

"Careful father doesn't see you," Jenny said. But the hurt of the words was Jenny's, not Carla's. Indignation at the need of the words, at all, burst in Jenny like a small crisp bubble.

Carla paused and looked vaguely at Jenny. Her lids, so silky above the dark lashes that were blown a little sideways toward her temples, had a faintly blue shine, like the cupped petal of a pasque flower. She dropped and lifted them vaguely once or twice, but said nothing. Out of sheer exasperation for her impudent, evasive beauty, Jenny could another time have shaken her. But now, on an impulse, she threw her arm about her and kissed Carla's smooth cheek. Carla looked a little surprised, and

Jenny's eyes filled with unreasonable tears. How could the child be expected to know that possibly, after to-night, Jenny might never see her again?

To hide her feelings, Jenny stepped into the pantry to put away the dishes she had washed. But Carla, leaning on her elbows over the kitchen table, was speaking softly to her.

"What's the matter, Jenny?"

When Jenny did not reply, Carla came and stood in the pantry doorway.

"Nothing is the matter," Jenny said at last. "It's just a sort of blue evening. Turn on the light."

In rhythm again with Sophie's music, Carla swayed across the room to do Jenny's bidding. Jenny stood and watched her.

"If you wanted to be a dancer, Carla," she said in a low tone, "would you dare—no matter what anybody said?"

"I'd be anything I pleased, and let anybody who didn't like it go hang."

Carla bent over, suddenly a child, swinging her short curls forward so that the fragile white nape of her neck showed, moist under the gold-shot hair. "But the time is not yet at hand!" she added, as she straightened herself again and looked at Jenny.

But Jenny, aware of a rapidly beating heart, went quickly into the dining room, where she seated herself to read the evening paper, with a determined attempt to be casual.

David had come in from his own part of the house, and was talking with his father in the living room. Into their talk Ruth's voice broke vehemently. For weeks Dave had been coming in from the shop with an empty look on his face, a look too negative for despair. Even hopelessness had been wiped clean from it, so that it was fresh for any new heartbreak. It meant, Jenny realized, that the skeleton of the shop was crumbling under its infirm flesh of bigotry and prejudice. What was she thinking? When before had she harbored such ideas? And in there Ruth was talking—her voice like a small steel trap.

"If things are as bad as Dave says," she cried, "how can you insist on my staying here, making it that much harder to make ends meet? I can get a job at house work to-morrow—I can go out cooking for threshers. Mother will look after the children, and I can at least earn enough to clothe them!"

Matt cleared his throat, with that sound that always ended in a patient sigh. His anger, Jenny thought, always assumed the appearance of injury, saint-like grief at the defection of one of the faithful. The family was insane—no, not insane, there was something comparatively robust and healthy about insanity—it was idiotic with submission. Where had her mind been that she had failed to see this before?

"She may as well begin, father," Dave said slowly. He sat near his father's desk, with his clasped hands hanging down between his knees. "She will have to do it when the kids get a little older, anyhow, if they're going to school. The money just isn't going to stretch—"

Matt raised his calm hand, the fingers short and held close together, so that his palm looked like a trowel.

"David, this is no affair of yours," he said, not sternly, never sternly, only in gentle reprimand. "While I have food and shelter, no child of mine shall want. And no grandchild, either. I'll hear no more of this nonsense, Ruthy, about your going out to work—where there are—people—who will perhaps not respect you. You are my daughter, and this is your home. With God's help I shall see that you stay in it!"

"God's help! God, God, God!" Ruth was beside herself. "For months I've heard nothing but God's help! Show it to me, if you can!"

She laughed with a scorn that thrilled Jenny even as, from long habit, she felt herself shocked by it. Ruth, since she had come back home to live, had grown more and more irreverent, until now she seemed to take a positive delight in torturing her father. Jenny's instinctive piety had been outraged frequently. Ruth would come to no good end, she had thought, with that contemptuous defiance of the Supreme Being. But now—Jenny felt her mind wheeling in bewilderment. Who was right, who was wrong? And what of herself, and the dark urgency she had so lately discovered in herself?

"Oh, cut it, Ruth!" David said. His black rough head shook with impatience.

But it was her father's eyes, gazing up at her where she stood, those blue, child-like, wondering eyes of his that looked somehow spell-bound, that broke Ruth, as always. She sank into a chair and went small and beaten.

"Ruthy, Ruthy!" he pleaded. "Have my prayers and hopes for you been of no avail, then? I can't believe it, my child. You do not mean what you say. Tell me you did not mean it, Ruthy."

Tears stood magnifying his eyes now, and his little whitish wisp of a beard trembled. Jenny looked away, at the wall of the dining room, gritting her teeth. The clock on the wall, the silly blue porcelain clock with ducks on it, said five past nine. In less than half an hour she would have to be on the gravel road behind the church, to meet Milton in his car. Or had she dreamt all that? It seemed that it had never really happened. She felt her lips with numb fingers. It all seemed obliterated now, by this reality that was the Welland house. Ruth's beaten voice obliterated it still further, if that were possible.

"No, I guess I didn't, father," she said.

Matt was joyous. "There's my girl talking now!" he cried. "Come, let us read a little from the Book. Let us all get together. Jenny, call mother and Carla downstairs—and Paget, if he's not too tired. Oh—Sophie! That's lovely music, but come and hear some that's still more beautiful. You'll stay with us for a minute, Dave, eh?"

Dave seemed to hesitate a bit. "All right," he said, sinking back into his chair.

Anything was better to him than going back into Seena's lair, Jenny thought viciously.

Sophie silenced the piano on a lifeless note. She closed the instrument as though her hands, too, were dead, or perhaps that was just a mad idea born out of the general madness of this house. Jenny looked again at the clock. If there were going to be prayers, how would she be able to get away? She would have no time to pack, and in any case she would not be able to slip downstairs unobserved. Suddenly the desire to go, to be with Milton and have his arms about her again, came real as pain to her, overrode all the prayers and tears and sense of sin that had grown to dark bloom and darker fruit under this roof. She walked mechanically out into the hall and to the staircase, where, half way up, she called to her mother and Carla to come down.

Mrs. Welland, in a loosely crocheted wool hug-me-tight, moved softly downstairs. Jenny told her of Matt's plan to read.

"Paget has gone to bed," her mother said. "But you had better run up and speak to Carla."

Jenny, passing her mother on the stairs, had a curious repugnance toward touching her. She would be loth to touch anyone in the family now. She had become like a secret tide, with floes of ice and fire, straining to its destiny. To Milton Pierce. Milton, Milton. Her lips moved over his name as she passed through the darkness to the closed door of Carla's and Sophie's room.

When she opened it, Carla was lying on the bed with her face turned toward the wall.

"Didn't you hear me call? Father is going to read."

Carla yawned and stroked her temple. "I have an awful headache, Jenny. Please tell father to excuse me this time."

"This time!" Jenny went over to her and pulled the pillow out from beneath Carla's tousled head. A book fell to the floor. Jenny picked it up and read aloud, with the outward part of her mind, *The Crock of Gold,* By James Stephens.

To Carla's grateful surprise, Jenny merely turned and went out, closing the door softly behind her. Just as she drew it to, she heard Carla's jaunty, rippled remark, "Good night, Jenny! Don't forget to wish on the bed post!"

The others were all seated in their customary places when she returned to the living room. Matt, in his deep, thread-bare chair, had the Bible open on his knees. His eyes were closed, his chin sunk upon his folded hands. Jenny strove to keep her eyes off him as he began to read. But the beautiful words glowed in Matt's beautiful voice, shimmered and glowed and became a presence of ineffable beatitude, as a violin under a bow that knew it well.

"Seek ye the Lord while He may be found, call ye upon Him while He is near: Let the wicked forsake his way, and the unrighteous man his thoughts: and let him return unto the Lord, and He will have mercy upon him; and to our God, for He will abundantly pardon. . . ."

Matt read on and on, choosing those passages he loved best. Through a mist Jenny saw Ruth, white and small, her face like a moth, like something unutterably flimsy and destructible. But Ruth had known what it was. Ruth had had children. Ye are born in sin. It would be a sin to have children with Milton. A bright sin, white and furious as a white-hot spear run through her naked body. She was overwhelmed, she shut her eyes on the image of Milton, and saw him more wonderfully still, smiling a secret smile and closing all about her, her breasts all enclosed and the length of her body. "Lest thou give thine

honour unto others, and thy years unto the cruel . . ."
Milton would not be cruel, Milton would be tender, because he had suffered so. He had been lonely, and he would lie with his head on the curve of her shoulder into her breast, all night, all night. They were getting on their knees now, and her father was holding Ruth's hand. Ruth —ah, the hypocrite! He was praying, and rich tears flooded his cheeks. She, Jenny, was on her knees, too. The hall clock struck half-past nine.

"For Thine is the kingdom, the power and the glory, for ever and ever, Amen."

In the little offering of silence that followed, the rain stung against the window panes on the south like myriads of gnats. Everybody rose, but not too hastily. Good nights were said. Sophie and Ruth kissed their father and followed their mother upstairs. David went and seated himself at the desk and began to thumb over the papers spread upon it. His face was unreadable, but the fingers of one hand, doubling up an ink eraser, broke the thing in two. Then Matt, heartened and cheery, sat down beside David and put his arm about his shoulder. "Well! Now, then!" he said exuberantly, with a little laugh of sheer pleasure. "What seems to be troubling our David? It doesn't seem nearly so bad now, does it, my boy?"

Jenny groped for her coat in the darkness of the hall. She had no time to go upstairs now. There was a little money in her purse, so that to-morrow she would be able to buy herself at least a nightgown.

"What, Jenny?" her father asked from the living room

as she passed the doorway. "Going out in this rain, at this hour?"

"Just around the block," Jenny said laconically. "I've got a little headache."

"Mother must look after you girls," Matt remarked absently, turning back to David. "All these headaches . . . Put your rubbers on, Jenny."

§ 4

Safely in the street, with the rain slanting fine as needles into her face, Jenny began to run, praying frantically that he would be waiting still. Already, brought down in the rainy dark from the density of trees, there was the pungent smoky smell of dying leaves. An image of the years, pounding like black stallions over the fields of her youth, came to her, and terror at herself, at her own strange thinking, caught her up violently. What if he were gone, what if the rain had already swallowed him and his pathetic little car on his lonely journey to the next town, to all the other little next towns there were for him? She could not bear the thought. Now, at the church, she cut through its grounds rather than follow the sidewalk the longer way round. Dimly from a distant street lamp, she could make out his car, standing parked a little off the road.

He was very nervous, almost unstrung, when she crept into the car beside him. On his upper lip, in the light from the instrument board, she saw fine drops of perspiration. He took out his handkerchief and wiped his face, and then, drawing her toward him with both hands, he smiled ruefully. "God, what a fifteen minutes that was!" he whispered. "Oh, Jenny, I'm so glad you came!"

Jenny had never fainted in her life, but she experienced now a sensation which she thought must be like dying, a swift delicacy of pain that went out of her to him and left her hollow, entirely defenseless. Her tears ran unchecked down her cheeks, while Milton stroked her shoulders and her hair and soothed her with random endearments. At last she straightened and smiled unsteadily.

"Shall we move along, then?" he suggested, starting the car. "We can get to Mrs. Chase's by midnight, easy."

"I wasn't able to bring a suitcase," she faltered.

"That's all right," he said. "Mrs. Chase will lend you things for to-night. Oh, Jenny!"

He threw his arm about her and tucked her down under his shoulder. Jenny let herself drift into a haze of happiness.

The misty flanks of the rain slipped past them, and the darkness opened ahead to rolling, confused regions that seemed no part of the earth. For a time Jenny's mind was empty of all thought. She pressed close against Milton and breathed the delicious presence of him, listened to his buoyant voice and thrilled to the touch of his face on her hair. Then, when Thrace was far behind them, he stopped the car in a little cove at the side of the road, overhung by dripping trees.

Milton lifted her into his arms and kissed her, closely, dearly, without any violence. But now, in Jenny, there was a resurgence of terrific force of the compulsion she had known toward him. She seemed to come suddenly savagely awake within herself. Her arms drew him furiously down to her breast, her hair falling damp and heavy along her neck and shoulders, her temples moist and throbbing with the swift throb of her blood. His eyes were half closed above her eyes; when she forced them open with her fingers buried in his lids, she saw the pupils dilated and burning. She laughed wildly, and the heat of her body flung upward toward him in a fierce gust. He began to mutter words that ran together and made no sense in the storming of her being. She crushed his words out against her lips, and they fell away into a long fainting silence that rocked terribly in the pith of her body. Then her tears were streaming down over her cheeks, wetting his face, his throat, and she lay inert in the hollow of his arms and breast while time and consequences glided over her.

"My darling, my darling!" His voice shook. It was hushed with a piteous awe that reached her only remotely. Tenderly he brushed her hair back from her wet temples, where coolness and quiet had come like death. "You aren't very kind to us, Jenny." He laughed shakily, and held her limp fingers against his cheek. "Will you always love me so much, I wonder? Dear little Jenny."

For a time they sat quietly, Jenny in a sort of sleep against Milton's shoulder, almost unaware of him or herself. Even when he started the car again, and settled Jenny securely close to him, she did not rouse from her exhaustion. The rain beat dreamily about the little car, beat dreamily on Jenny's tranced heart. Her mind was a dim vacancy, an insouciant space of dimness.

Then, from somewhere, thought began creeping in. It crept slowly, with a terrifying, cold luminousness.

At length a feeling of dread possessed her, the feeling that they were being followed by something—something relentless out of the Welland house. Then, in the pearly nimbus of the rain ahead of them, she seemed to see her father's face, his gentle, lost eyes, the tears falling unrestrainedly down the withered ruddiness of his cheeks. "Let the wicked forsake their ways . . ." Oh, wicked, wicked, to triumph with this blind, sweet and blinding desire deep in your body! Wicked and shameless and abandoned! She had not cared, did not care even now, whether she married Milton or not before he possessed her. The knowledge dawned upon her like a baleful and frozen sun, like the dawn of death in the soul. Her teeth chattered as she drew away from him and sat upright.

"What's the matter, Jenny?" he asked anxiously, slowing down a bit. "Why, darling—"

"No, no, Milton," she said miserably. "Let me think a while. I don't know— Stop the car, Milton, please!"

When they had come to a stop he tried to put his arm about her again. But Jenny held herself away from him. To breathe seemed to her like drawing cotton into her lungs. She had been about to do a thing of unbelievably gross selfishness. A thing that might have killed her father. The thought of the peaches he had saved for her supper that evening came to her with quaint, heartbreaking pathos. She could almost hate Milton Pierce now for taking her away. She had been worse than Ruth—yes, she had been crueler even than Ruth, who at least had had the decency to spare their father's feelings, who had not flung his mortification at the world!

"Dear Jenny, talk to me!"

She turned upon him, icily calm. But she did not really look at him; she dared not, even now. "Turn back," she said. "I've done a terrible thing!"

He laughed incredulously. "You're kidding, Jenny!"

"I mean it!" she cried in anguish. "I must have been out of my head to do this. Oh—take me home, take me home, for God's sake!" She burst into wild tears, and when he tried to put his arms about her, tried to soothe her and reason with her, she only threw him off.

"All right, Jenny," he said in a stricken voice, and proceeded to turn the car about in the narrow road. For the moment he was too occupied with the difficult managing of the car to think of anything else. But, once they were headed back for Thrace, Jenny sitting erect and frenzied, tears of disappointment smarted bitterly in his eyes. Jenny did not look at him, dared not even to think of him.

"Do you want me to meet your family first, then, Jenny?" he ventured. "I thought that was best, all along."

"I don't know," she said, defensively. "I don't know anything—now. I just know it was wrong—selfish and unfair to father to do what we were going to do. It was wicked, and I would live to regret it. Father would never have forgiven me, never!"

Nonplussed at the change in her, back in his old lonely despair, Milton sat silent. He gave the car all the speed he dared over the wet and slippery road, and kept his eyes fixed wretchedly ahead. The lights of Thrace began to wink sleepily now, the inward-looking and rebuffing lights of a small town. God, how many of them he had seen! And he had thought, at last, that he would have to look upon them no more, approaching them alone on hostile nights of a raw spring, or heartbreaking nights full of autumn death, when he had not made a sale anywhere along the endless road. Well—perhaps he had been too impatient—perhaps things would work out all right, after all.

A half mile from Thrace a truck, without lights, swung drunkenly into the road, and Milton's car, like a blind insect, struck it full in the side. The little car hurled itself backward from the impact, turned completely over and rolled down the steep ditch at the side of the highway.

Jenny lay very still in an extraordinary lushness of pain, that swept up from her hips to the core of her body, extinguishing all sensation and then blowing it exquisitely back into a sharp point of white fire, a searing torch under her breast. Ah, it *was* pain, then. Ruth had said . . . yes, Ruth had said that this part of love was pain. First love . . . pain. Agony. Oh, God, not love! Agony! No, no, not consciousness with this agony! Mud, reeds under your hand, something crushing excruciatingly down upon your body. Not love, no. Death. Death. A wandering away into a blessed eternity of darkness, away, away.

She moaned, far beyond any knowing, when the men lifted her out carefully and laid her on the floor of the truck.

In a brief and brilliantly horrible spasm of consciousness, she heard one of the men say: "I don't think he's
hurt much. The poor devil's got friends, anyhow. He's a
Mason. Here's the emblem."

Jenny screamed with laughter and lapsed away again,
away, away, beyond the quaint sweet pain of first love.
And now there was a soundless dark in which things
faintly palpable passed and passed again, wove and inter-
wove, like a strange rain in a waste of air beyond all stars
and suns. A voice there spoke out of the soundlessness, a
voice curiously broken, like the break of water over stones.
But a voice going on, strong and smooth, like water flowing serenely beyond the stones, to the calm deeps beyond.

"My little girl! My little girl! But she was coming back
to us, mother! She was on her way back to us! Thank
God for that. Thank God!"

V : DAVID

§ 1

Another Christmas was being celebrated in the house of Matthew Welland. The parlor was wide open, holly wreaths in the windows, red candles on the clock mantel, and a symmetrical, baubled and silver-festooned tree stood before the front window. On the eve of Christmas, Ruth's children had been brought down and David's children had come in to see the tree lighted. The tiny electric candles with which Paget had decorated the tree had been turned on and for once the children had been dazzled into a moment's silence. Then, before Matt had had time to take orderly charge of the distribution of the gifts at the bottom of the tree, little Matt, Dave's eldest, and his brother met head-on in a dash for a handsome bow-and-arrow which, unfortunately, had not been wrapped in paper. The result was an abrasion in the skin above Horace's left eyebrow, where the teeth of little Matt, who had been open-mouthed with cupidity, had encountered it. Old Matt had parted the boys and had feebly striven to make peace, while Dave had looked on from his chair in the shadow near the hall door, perversely unwilling to use his paternal authority in the disturbance. Then Seena had come shouting at them from the kitchen and had her large, red and bony hand poised in mid-air to deal a blow on little Matt's head when Dave, with swift precision, had sprung from his chair and all but snapped Seena's wrist in two with his fingers.

In the ensuing violence, Jenny, from her exclusive wheel-chair—she had never regained the use of her limbs since that night when she and Milton Pierce had met disaster on the road north of Thrace—had breathed, "How vulgar!" And David, turning upon her, had found it in his heart to do murder, but had instead marshaled his progeny and his wife out of the room and into their own quarters. There, a little later, Carlotta and Tom—he had come back from Chicago for the holiday—had brought the children their gifts and a dishful of pop-corn balls which she had just made, and except for Seena, who sulked all night, harmony was restored. Little Minnie, the youngest, had begged to go back and stay all night with Carla, but Seena had peevishly said no, and Dave was too bored to participate in any further bickerings.

But now it was Christmas day and a certain measure of tranquillity prevailed in Matt Welland's house, with the entire family present. David had told Seena, calmly and without spleen, that if she so much as lifted her voice once above the ordinary requirements of speech, he would walk out of the house. When she had looked upon him with amazement that bordered upon admiration, he had turned abruptly away and catching a glimpse of his own eyes in a mirror, he had smiled satirically at himself. How much would it really matter, either to Seena or to himself, if he did walk out of the house?

It would probably matter to his mother, he thought

wistfully, and to his father—but he didn't permit himself to dwell upon that. There had been the little problem of paying the coal bill, for example, that had come up just the day before Christmas. Old Sam Greenleaf had been benevolent in his attitude to the Wellands, albeit he was a Jew, and besides had stood conveniently in awe of Matt Welland. But Sam had died some three months ago and his widow, herself a Christian, had taken the coal business out of her husband's dead hands capably into her own. Before Greenleaf's death, David had known the woman as a rather full-blown, good-natured housewife who sometimes appeared in the coal yard with bedroom slippers on her feet and kid curlers peeping out from beneath an astonishing lace and ribbon boudoir cap. She had always professed a gay disregard and a child-like ignorance where her husband's business was concerned, but David had observed that her mouth was short from corner to corner and her teeth small and sharp. It had not surprised him much when he had received from her, one immediately after the other, two notices of the long-overdue Welland coal bill, with the peremptory foot-note, "Kindly remit at once." To his telephone call about the bill, however, Mrs. Greenleaf had responded graciously enough. Yes, she would be delighted to see him about it, and wouldn't he please come in the afternoon when she was at home— to-morrow afternoon, since she was staying at home for Christmas—as she did not wish the office help to know how she conducted affairs in which she had a sympathetic interest? David said he would drop in on Christmas afternoon, and recalled wryly the arch eyes she had once or twice turned upon him in the coal yard office before her husband had quit this life.

Dave sat in the living room, where the pale sun flashed the faint blue of china-smooth snowdrifts in through the window. Paget, after the Christmas morning service at church, had gone for a walk with Tom and would probably not come back to the house before it was time to sit down to the table. Dave was pretending to read one of the scant dozen of secular books which Matt permitted on his shelves—it happened to be Livingstone's *Through Darkest Africa*. But what he was thinking was that there was a time, a preposterous lifetime ago, when his imagination had insatiably gluttoned upon it. And that when he had timidly proposed to his father that he should like to emulate Livingstone by exploring the jungle's heart, Matt had told him kindly that there were jungles of sin in our midst through which he must struggle, and that this was the moral Livingstone had set for little boys; it was unnecessary, even a bit impudent, for little Davey to contemplate the physical Darkest Africa.

Matt was softly reading aloud to Jenny the latest chapter of his book, which he had called *Travelers Through the Dark,* a small guide to spiritual rectitude which he was compiling with generous quotations from the Bible, with ancient and terrifying prints depicting the wages of sin, with little awkward parables—original with Matt—that brought involuntary tears of pity to David's eyes. This grotesque handbook was to have a pasteboard binding and was to be printed in the Welland shop and sold broadcast for ten cents, although the actual cost of manufacture was very nearly that amount. Against this under-taking David had protested to his sorrow. Matt had dis-covered his life's mission, and though the house fell, *Travelers Through the Dark* would take wing and carry its message of salvation to the erring.

The children sprawled idly on the floor, bored and im-patient for the morrow, when they would be permitted to play with their toys—and few enough there were on this lean Christmas. They had listened captivated while Carla read them the story of the Nativity, until Horace had spoken up and said, "Gran'pa, didn't they let little Jesus play with the presents the wise men brought Him on Christmas? Did he have to wait till the next day, too?" Matt had frowned at him through his glasses, and Carla had replied brightly, "Silly, He was too young to play with anything." Then Horace, still unsatisfied, persisted, "But the next Christmas, didn't they—" And Jenny, with the asperity that was growing in her daily, rank as nettle, had interrupted him with a word to David about the man-ners and reverence of his children. At that point Carla had risen gracefully and gone out to offer her services with the setting of the table.

Seena was with the other women in the kitchen, prepar-ing the vast Christmas dinner. The smell of the roasting turkey brought a little curl about David's nostrils, but it was not one of olfactory pleasure. Two days ago he had told his mother that the family could not afford the luxury of turkey this year, and Mrs. Welland had pensively rubbed the back of one hand with the knotted fingers of the other, and had said, "Father will be so distressed,

Dave, to find that out." David had snorted and had thought of the bill he had received from Mrs. Greenleaf, but the turkey, in order that his father should be spared a jolt in the beatitude of his occupation, had been purchased.

Dave sank lower and lower into his chair, his book before his face.

"Lovely, father . . . simply lovely!" Jenny was exclaiming, transported. Her voice had that feathery softness which it had developed recently in all her conversations with Matt. In fact, their voices of late had become almost indistinguishable, Matt's growing more and more feminine in his solicitude and his tireless preoccupation with Jenny. It seemed he was building a wall of mystical preciousness about her, enclosing her from the rest of the family; their voices came from behind that wall, rarefied almost to extinction and dedicated to the magnifying of mysteries.

"I think you could make that even stronger, there, father," Jenny interrupted a little later, as Matt read. "People are so stupid, you know. I'm afraid they might miss the point just there."

"Well—yes—maybe so, maybe so," Matt conceded, his voice full of gratitude for Jenny's sharp interest. "I'll just mark that passage."

"It would be interesting to know," Jenny observed after a moment, "just where Tom and Paget are all this time. It's a little unnatural that Tom should want to go chasing around town on his first day home."

David looked across the top of his book at Jenny. His

eyes narrowed to a dark line of contempt as he saw her uplifted face, hard with intolerance and suspicion. In the four months that she had been a cripple, the jealousy she bore toward the chance that anyone else might find happiness had actually changed the contour of her face. It was bitten with invidious spite, hollowed out and stark with resentment. Only when Matt read to her from the Bible or from his own writings did a certain relaxation appear on her features, a mark of exaltation which to Dave was more repellent than anything else.

"Oh, now, Jenny," Matt protested in his mild way, "boys will be boys, and you can't blame Tom for wanting to take a look at his home town."

Jenny sighed. "Of course, father, you are always so lenient. We who are helpless, I often think, see more than you who are normal and healthy. Not that I want to add to your anxiety, father. I shouldn't have spoken. Ah—I am so tired!"

Matt rose quickly and lowered the back of her chair and rearranged her pillow, smoothing her hair back with one of his nervous, diffident hands.

"There, now, Jenny," he said. "You rest a little while before dinner, and I'll pull down the blinds. I'm afraid I've worn you out with my reading, poor child. You're always an inspiration to me, and I thank God you are safe here with me—every hour of the day I thank Him."

He carefully drew down the blinds and Dave took his book and went into the parlor, the children following him listlessly. In sudden exasperation and love for the unhappy troop, and with a glance back into the living room at his father, Dave murmured to them to go out behind the Alhambra and throw snow-balls, for God's sake! With glee in the conspiracy, they dashed into their coats, hats and mitts, which had been hung with unusual neatness in their grandfather's hall on the return from church. Dave stood and saw them bound out, and felt a stirring of desire to go with them. His children, not his, at all—the fruit of his father's patriarchy and Seena's possessiveness! But instead of going out with them he dropped his book, stole out through the front door and around by way of the veranda to the east entrance, went into his own domain, and lay down on the couch.

§ 2

Two extra leaves had been set into the Welland table, and about it were gathered all the Wellands, except Jenny, who sat a little apart in her wheel-chair, beside her father, a tray strapped to the arms of her chair. Paget and Tom sat on either side of their mother at the other end of the table, with Sophie beside Paget, Carla on Tom's right, then Ruth with her baby in his high chair. David sat between his wife and Sophie, drawing his wry analogies between Jenny in her chair and Ruth's infant in his, while Matt said the long, archaically elegant grace of his own childhood.

Then, after the discreet pause in which Ruth's child dinged his spoon lustily on his plate and in which a choking sound came from the small table by the windows where David's three children sat with Ruth's two eldest, Matt began to carve the turkey.

"Well, son!" he called jovially down to Tom. "White meat for the prodigal, eh? And lots of dressing, if I remember right. Now this is something like it, isn't it, mother, having 'em all around us again! Merry Christmas, everybody!"

Everybody laughed, because it was one of Matt's familiar little jokes to bid a hearty Merry Christmas a half dozen times or more during the day, as though each time were the first. Seena laughed heartily, obsequiously, and David looked across the table at the thoughtful smile upon Carla's face.

Plates were relayed down the length of the table from one to the other, until they reached Mrs. Welland, who dished up generous portions of potatoes, vegetables, gravy and cranberry sauce. Then, with everybody at the large table served, Mrs. Welland attended to the children's table in the window nook. At last, when she had seated herself, the sun shone in upon her and you could see the infinitesimal beads of sweat on the fine down of her upper lip. There were faint liver spots in the dark skin about her eyes, and down the cords of her throat. David wondered what had gone on through the years behind those patient dark eyes of hers. Her hair was graying reluctantly about the temples, as though it had only lately relinquished the hope of a youth foregone. Had she had any pleasure, he wondered, out of conceiving a single one of these children for whom she had cooked, scrubbed, washed and ironed for over thirty years? Or had it all been one long anxiety lest any of them should turn out to be a disappointment to the husband whom she adored? For his mother did love Matt, in a strange, humble and self-effacing way which David found hard to understand in a woman so capable, so really intelligent. Poor mother! He remembered her saying once, years ago, that her one ambition had been to go to Niagara Falls on her honeymoon, but since there had been no money for such a trip, she had not gone then or since. Good Lord, if he had any stuff in him at all, he ought to be able to grant his mother that little wish before she died!

The girls were plying Tom with questions about Chicago, as though it were two thousand miles away instead of two hundred. Now and then Matt would interrupt benignly with some more specific question about Tom's work, and David would hold his breath until Tom got over the difficult moment. But what David noticed about Tom's attitude was not so much a guardedness as it was an inner dissatisfaction with himself.

"I suppose you have a good chance of promotion to something better than just reporting, Tom?" Matt asked, his eyes twinkling. For he was not a little pleased with the thought that his son was, in however humble a position, on one of the dailies of the great metropolis.

Tom threw his head restively to one side in the manner that had marked him from childhood, like a horse with a fly bothering him.

"Yes, I guess—if I keep it up," Tom said noncommittally.

Dave, looking across at him questioningly, caught his

eye, but at once Tom's gaze moved uneasily away. Dave exclaimed under his breath. So, somehow in his months away from home, Tom had failed. His elaborate deception of Matt had been just so much wasted energy. Dave recalled his conversation with Tom on that night before the boy's departure, and realized suddenly that he was not surprised at this result of his exploit. But he was curious to know in just what way his predestined defeat had come about. Paget, eating his food in studied silence, probably already knew, although Tom was not likely to go into any fine analysis of his experience for him. David resolved to get Tom alone and sound him out. After all, his visit to the city must have had some effect upon him. It was curious—except for a certain obstinacy in his silence Tom seemed not to have changed at all.

"Oh, you'll keep at it, my boy!" Matt replied confidently to Tom's remark. "We Wellands don't give up just because a job seems hard at first. You have great opportunities for good in the field you have chosen, Tommy. There is plenty of room for reform in our press, you'll admit!"

Matt was expanding under the effect of a good dinner, with all of his own about him. David, noting that expansion, felt depressed and knew that presently what he had eaten would disagree with him. Suddenly the sacred institution of the ponderous Christmas feast, which must be upheld at all costs, revolted him, and refusing the slab of fruit cake and hard sauce which was passed to him, he fell into an ascetic vacancy of thought which separated him from the rest of the family.

The talk of Seena, Jenny and Matt made up most of the conversation. Seena, with mock timidity, was citing examples she had heard of which proved the efficacy of Christian Science in seemingly hopeless cases of paralysis and kindred ills. Jenny, with her interest in her own disability, which was now the one healthy thing about her, would listen avidly only that she might refute all that Seena had said. Matt, resolutely generous toward the faith of others, so long as it was founded on acceptance of the Trinity, strove not to show too strongly his disapproval of Seena's cult, though he privately thought it a bit presumptuous, feeling in a vague way that it identified itself intimately with Godhead to a point of impudence. To David the talk seemed entirely fantastic, built upon shoals of insanity.

Carla was talking to Tom and eating her dessert with undiscouraged relish.

David leaned across the table and said, "The fairies are lucky—they can eat the cream without understanding the language of their hosts."

"What sort of nonsense is that?" Sophie demanded.

"Lovely nonsense," David said, but Sophie was not waiting for a reply. She had turned abruptly in her chair to urge the children not to make so much noise. That was Sophie, only half present at any time, anywhere, and then only when some sensory impression disturbed her.

Carla laughed. "Dave," she said, "let's you and Tom and Paget and I go for a walk in the woods this afternoon, with Lulu. Lulu," she looked down at the lazy old dog lying in the parallelogram of sun on the floor behind her chair, "you would love a walk in the woods, wouldn't you, darling?"

Lulu got up obligingly and stretched, then pointed her ears to make sure that she had heard aright.

"Go ahead," Dave said. "I have some work to attend to."

Carla made no reply. She was handing Lulu a tidbit of fruit cake which the dog took delicately, discarding the tiny piece of candied orange peel when she found it. Later, Sophie, who never noticed anything, ground the orange peel into the carpet with her heel, and Jenny, being moved into the sunlight in her chair, discovered it and remarked that Carlotta was very selfish and inconsiderate of the work she made for others. It was Ruth who scraped it up with a knife, while Jenny sat looking serenely out upon the steaming roofs of houses where people lived and probably loved in a highly improper fashion.

§ 3

It was possible to walk in almost any direction from Thrace and come upon wooded country, although there might be a small field or two to cross, or a fruit farm to skirt before the woods were reached. But Carla's favorite haunt was where the great oaks grew, east of Thrace, and half way to Redlands. Paget and Tom were amenable to her choice and in a little while the discreet, Christmas-conscious, better homes of east Thrace faltered behind them and they entered upon the silence and white dignity of winter earth with trees upon it.

The day was mild and no winds moved under the remote blue purity of the sky. There was a faint rustle and drip of thaw in the underbrush, with glistening threads of wet down the great trunks of the trees and narrow dark troughs at their bases. Here and there on the branch of an oak a congress of leaves still clung, rigid as flakes of bronze. At intervals an evergreen stood, somber and firm, with its shelves of snow, white to the sun and darkly blue to shade. Naked bramble-bushes, like snarled whips, threw delicate webs of shadow on the snow, and where there was an old nest there would be a knot in the web. A flock of strident crows took their dark passage across the sun to the fields beyond, and after that the stillness was deeper than before.

Now and then Carla stopped to touch a frozen rose-berry, ripe as blood against the snow, or Paget shied a snow-ball at a tattered crow's nest. Tom looked straight before him into the dazzling, polychromatic wash of almost non-existent colors, mauve reaches where the tall tree shadows fell, and thought of the cool virtue of trees.

They had come to the open ribbon of snow which had been an old logging road; beyond would be the creek, frozen over now, but warm beneath with memories for them all.

Tom looked back. "Shall we go and sit on the bank for a while?" he suggested.

"Let's," Carla replied. "Could we build a fire?"

"Might try," Paget said.

From the rocky, high bank of the creek the snow had blown clear and the sun slanted across it like a rosy lance. All three seated themselves and Lulu threw herself down at their feet, tired and excited. Below them the creek was a gentle cradle of white, with silverish dogwood, wild gooseberry bushes, and chokecherry branches, all bare and shallow, leaning over its opposite bank. All the Welland boys, but only Carla of the girls, had stolen away here in their summers, to swim in the pool downstream, or upstream to slide frantic with delight down the moss-slippery rocks which were olive-green and suave as dolphins beneath the glassy water. It had been great sport, at times of high water, to go rushing past the overhanging winey dark clusters of chokecherries and try to pull one off before the current carried you away. Of all this their father had known no part, since in such pastime resided not only the risk of drowning but also of meeting with bad company, to say nothing of the waste of time which could be put to profitable use.

Paget had been rummaging in his pockets. He had found some old letters and a small box of matches.

"Let's see what we can do about a fire," he said, rising and avoiding Lulu's gently pluming tail.

Carla watched her brothers build the fire, on top of a flat rock. In the stillness the blaze climbed smoothly against the sun, flamed to paler flame, and the snow below the rock darkened from the reflected warmth. The cradle of the creek hung in dim amethyst, and the shadows of the trees reached strong and dark across the snow.

From his pocket Tom drew forth a small anthology of English poems, well frayed, the cover wrapped in brown paper.

"This is what Pete's crowd laughed at down in Chicago," he said. "I had the nerve to bring it to one of his poetry meets, and they howled me out of the place."

"And you went, I suppose?" Paget remarked.

"No, I stayed. But I shut up about Matthew Arnold, and these fellows. It seems they never lived and wondered about anything. I wrote you about that red-headed girl who called Browning a lumbering, bow-legged infant. They roared at that, and somebody went and wrote it down. A fellow from New York read one of his latest masterpieces that started out, 'Why are the potatoes resolute, and standing upright on their crystal pinnacles?' I thought it was a joke, and laughed. They were outraged and some of them even pitied me. Then the red-headed girl told me there was more than 'One Way of Love' and offered to sleep with me. That broke them all up."

Paget put more brush on the fire. It snapped and sparkled up in a brief constellation within the smoke.

"Read *Dover Beach,* Tommy," Carla requested.

For a half hour, then, Tom read from the old favorites, and some of the tightness seemed to be leaving his voice. At last, when the light became difficult with its encroaching blue, he closed the book and put it into his pocket.

"Say, Paget," he said hurriedly, "I've been thinking that I'm needed at home now, with Jenny the way she is, and everything. It wasn't quite fair in the first place for me to go away."

Paget's sharp eyes sought him out and a crooked smile played about his lips. "Crawfishing, eh?" he said.

Tom reddened angrily. "Well—I've stuck it as long as I can. It doesn't cost Pete's friends a twinge to knock down God and morality and the whole works, and they don't bother looking around for a substitute. They laugh at me for worrying about humanity. They call me the Missionary from Mudville. That was after I suggested that there was something in Christianity that ought to be saved. They told me I was a little late to do the saving unless I could raise something from the dead. I can't stand their shallow smartness any longer."

Carla gazed at him wonderingly. "Do you want to be a minister, Tom?"

Paget chuckled. "There ought to be one in the family."

Tom looked away with embarrassment. "No," he said impatiently. "But something ought to be done or everything that's beautiful is going to die. Of course I can't do anything about it." He jerked his head irritably to one side.

"Why not?" Paget asked.

"A man has to be educated," Tom replied, "and know what he's talking about. You can't argue with these intellectual fools unless you meet them on their own terms."

His sneer was bitter. Paget got up and stamped on the

embers of the fire, scattering them with his foot. "It would be hell for you to try to live in the same house with Jenny these days. She's worse than the old man ever was. But you know best what you want to do." He buttoned his coat and made his muffler snug about his neck. "I guess Dave could use you in the shop all right, the business couldn't be any worse anyhow. Let's get along home. We can talk about it later."

He gave Carla his hands and pulled her to her feet.

"Why do you worry about things so, Tommy?" Carla asked when they were once more on their way. "Why don't you just live? A tree gets beauty in every season just by standing still. You try too hard, Tommy. I—I am going to stand still—and grow upward—and the rain and the wind and the sun will come to *me*."

"And hail and snow and lightning and perhaps a forest fire—if you're going to be poetic," Tom said.

Carla laughed with delight. "I'd love those, too," she said, and ran ahead with Lulu frisking about her, tossing up the snow.

In the falling twilight her red tam signaled to them through the trees, and Tom's heart was wrung by her fragile buoyancy. Somehow—somehow, the family blight would destroy her, too.

He took Paget's arm. "What do you think of the kid?" he said. "She's developing, isn't she?"

The air smelt raw now of frosty evergreen needles and snow in old leaves. The chill bit down into the body, down into the frozen dark of the earth, which the body would one day share. What did it matter, after all, whether Carla survived in triumph this ordeal of living? There was but one end, and the great trees, with their roots in the knowledge of oblivion, knew it.

"What do you think of her?" Paget asked.

Tom smiled. "She's in rhythm with some comet, I think. She's a true pagan. She never takes more than she can use—but she'll use a lot, or I miss my guess."

§ 4

It was snowing as David walked down the street. Little soft bouquets of flakes faltered down and plashed into a white mesh on the sidewalk. He blinked against the weft of the snow, and looked down the little huddling street through which he was making his way, and thought how, except for the growing of the trees and the burning down of old dead Trudy Gallop's house to the ugly hollow of a decayed tooth, the street had not changed since he was eleven. He was eleven years old still, unreceptive to any of the modern phenomena that had come with his maturity. In a sense he was an anachronism, a sort of full-rigged windjammer, sailing the mythical seas of lost illusion. He had never come into any port of manhood from those dreams he had pursued when he was a boy. The thing that disturbed him— though very rarely now—was that he did not give a tinker's dam!

He had read something about glands of late, and he was inclined to think, in a detached way, that probably his whole trouble was glandular. It was true enough that until he was twenty-one, and married, his father had controlled him as the pole controls the needle of a compass, but after that, if he had had any guts at all—or glands, probably—he would have swung free. For a resentment such as he bore toward Seena should have inspired any normal man to achieve his integral freedom. But a profound inertia had governed him, had usurped the place of the motive power of his being, until it had at last become a part of him upon which he looked inward with a detached and perverse interest, as upon some physical organ functioning abnormally. The years had passed over him and he had looked spell-bound upon their meaningless coming and going. He liked to think of himself as a boulder in a slow midstream, whose gray top the floods of turbulent seasons never quite reached.

To go almost begging for commissions, or, as to-day, to be seeking the generosity of a coal dealer whose last bill had not been paid, pierced his dull, armor-deep apathy. It really amused him to think that his paralyzed soul was still capable of feeling something.

He quickened his step and looked ahead at the Greenleaf house standing beside the coal yard. The house was the color and somewhat the shape of a maltese cat, with a high cupola in front, and sloping haunches. The blinds, since Samuel Greenleaf's death, had remained drawn, and for this reason Thrace adjudged Mrs. Greenleaf a pious and properly grieving widow, albeit a Christian widow of a Jew.

He mounted the lean steps of the porch where the

snow lay like great white porous caterpillars along the top of the narrow balustrade. Underfoot it was soft, damp and secret. David looked at the drawn shades of the windows. They were like eyes that looked through you without seeing you.

Mrs. Greenleaf herself opened the door to his ring. She was of about his own age, but determinedly girlish in her dress, and dauntlessly Titian as to her hair. She smiled up at him with a baby-like widening of her eyes, which were a not unpleasant blue, and her mouth went into a little cusp.

"Oh!" she cried blithely, looking past him into the snow. "Christmas just isn't Christmas without snow, is it, Mr. Welland? Come right in."

She stepped aside for him to enter, then closed the door behind him and gently turned the key in the lock. He heard the little, soft, witnessing snick of it, and for a moment an unspeakable confusion covered him. But Mrs. Greenleaf proceeded airily into the living room, a cozy place, with a reddish purple floor lamp with silk fringe, a piano in one corner, and a deep fire-place where coal—the Greenleaf coal—burned rosily.

David followed heavily, self-conscious as a boy. The house fairly sighed of bodily comfort. A bleak feeling struck him somewhere in the region of the diaphragm. It was odd that he should think just now that his mother and his wife had been unable to put up preserves this year because Jenny's accident had taken every penny that could be scraped together. Perhaps it was because the house reminded him somehow of damson plums.

But Mrs. Greenleaf did not seat herself in the living room. Instead, to his surprise, she waved a well-fleshed arm about the room and said, "How do you like the way I've redecorated this room?"

"Why," David stammered, "I don't know what it was like before. It looks very cozy."

"Well—I've had the whole house done over since—ah—since Samuel passed on. You know, Mr. Welland"—she turned full upon him, with a little frank and yet hesitant gesture—"you know I don't believe it's right to go on moping all your life just because you've had sorrow. Life is not meant for that. Or what do you think, Mr. Welland? Do you think I seem—er—"

"Unsympathetic? No," David said.

"Well, I'm glad you don't," she said, relieved. She flicked a speck of dust off the piano. David began to wonder when the coal bill was to be discussed, when she turned upon him again with one of her piquant, three-cornered smiles. How well-fed she looked, he thought.

"Wouldn't you like to see the whole house?" she suggested. "I've had the upstairs papered, and all. I keep the curtains pulled down because the people across the road are so inquisitive." She chuckled. "I'm just letting them stew a while before I let 'em see a thing inside here. Come on. There's nobody but me here so you've nothing to be scared of. Not that you would be, anyhow, of course. Ha, ha! How silly I am!"

"But," David protested, stammering again, "what about the business I came to talk about? Hadn't we better discuss that before—"

"Oh, dear!" she interrupted, and brushed her hand through the air as though to dismiss a trifle. "Let that wait. I really want to know how you like the way I've fixed the place up. Not another soul has seen it. Come along! Here's my dining room."

She led him through the house, downstairs and upstairs, until they came at last to the little cupola which, from the outside, looked like the head of some arrogant animal. It was a room with window benches all around, heavy draperies, low chairs and low tables, and huge cushions on the floor. It was unlike anything David had ever seen in his life. He found it difficult, somehow, to attribute the genius of this room to the woman who stood triumphantly surveying it from the doorway. One small amber light illumined the place softly. It came from a bowl in the center of a low, black-lacquered table.

Mrs. Greenleaf stepped into the middle of the room. David followed her, unsure and strangely ill at ease. For the past ten minutes she had become more and more pointed in her manner, as though he were making advances to her against which she was modestly protesting. In the bedroom downstairs, he had been of half a mind to turn and go abruptly home, but it had really seemed too ridiculous to do so.

"David," she quivered in a dramatic whisper, throwing out her arms. "You will let me call you David, won't you? Let me talk to you here."

She motioned him to one of the low chairs. He sat down a little weakly and looked at her. Rather, he looked at her black silk dress, which flowed close as water over her full breast and hips.

"From these windows, David," she continued, "I have watched you come and go many, many times. And you never guessed, did you, David?"

He was at a loss for words. But, back somewhere in his mind, the cold rationality of expedience was asserting itself. He was, it was true, a little appalled, and he could have laughed aloud at the ineffectuality of the fundamentals of that dour religion in which he had been raised to awaken in him any conscientious scruples.

Mrs. Greenleaf came toward him, swinging her silky and aggressive hips. One hand confidently caressed a marcelled puff of her hair. She smiled down at him, a little inimically, a little wistfully, and with a coarse resentment of her David slipped an arm about her waist.

§ 5

"Most men like both cream and sugar in their tea, I believe," Adeline Greenleaf said, cheerily bringing to the kitchen table the silver cream pitcher and sugar bowl. "They aren't afraid of getting fat, like us poor girls. Ah, dearie me, it's a hard life! Is this strong enough for you, Dave? I'll have to learn how you like it, eh? Ha, ha! I never was good at keeping such things straight in my mind. There! Have some jam on your bread and butter. Oh, I think this is jolly!"

David helped himself to the jam. "Thanks, Adeline," he said softly, treacherously. "Did you make this, too?"

Adeline laughed modestly. "Oh, it isn't so awfully good!" she deprecated. "I'm afraid I'm not much of a cook!"

He raised his eyebrows and smiled at her, inwardly jeering grossly at himself. She giggled and dropped her own eyes to her teacup.

"Hadn't we better talk business now?" he suggested, breaking his bread and butter in two. He kept his face down as though embarrassed, although what he felt was a grotesque hilarity.

"Oh, *Dave!*" She was really hurt. "Let's not talk about that. It's such a little bit, anyhow. If you get a lot of money some time, you can pay me, but not now. I won't let you. I know how hard it is for you. And I'll have the men send you another load to-morrow."

"That's too much, Adeline," he protested. "I can't let you do that."

"Nonsense," she said firmly. "If I can't do a little something for a friend once in a while, it's just too bad. Don't you dare say another word about it."

They sat for a moment in silence, David looking down and listening to the heinous laughter of his own brain.

"Oh, this *is* cozy, isn't it, Dave?" she said finally. "You know—it's nice being with a Christian again."

"Is it?" Dave could not check his laughter from coming right out this time.

"What are you laughing at, Dave?" she said, a little piqued. "Oh, you're just teasing me. But you can't hurt my feelings—you're too nice."

"I couldn't hurt your feelings," he said, leaning over

and patting her hand. "Only—I don't see what being a Christian has to do with it."

"You seem to forget that I was married to a Jew," she said. "Though it never turned me away from my church. Nobody in Thrace can say I'm not a good church member."

He stared at her absently for a moment, then looked away. He had a glimpse then of the real nobility of asceticism. It spared you the trouble of even trying to solve the labyrinths of the human mind.

"Let's not talk church, for God's sake!" he pleaded. "I'm fed up with it."

She clicked her tongue and frowned roguishly. "Bad boy!" she said. "He mustn't say such things!"

Adeline lisped a little when she was happy, David had discovered. And Seena laughed with an adenoidal vibration. So, in one way or the other, the fabric of the flesh presented itself. It took a dog to wag his tail with classic restraint.

"Tell me, Dave," Adeline said after a while, leaning forward on her pink bowls of elbows. "How is poor Jenny? Is it really as bad as they say? Isn't she ever going to be able to walk again?"

David grinned bitterly. Adeline was talking now as though she were one of the family.

"The doctor says not," he replied. "The injury to the spine seems permanent."

Adeline uttered a soft little moan. "Oh, I'm *so* sorry," she said. "Jenny was so pretty. Although I think your little sister Carla is going to be the family beauty."

Something in Dave's mind went cold against the woman. He had no intention of discussing Carla with her—Carla with her tree-top aloofness, her aloneness that was as pure as a cloud. For all that anyone knew of her she might be as innocent of virtue as she was of vice.

"Jenny's able to get around in a wheel-chair," David said, clearing his throat. "And she keeps busy with her china-painting."

"I must buy some of it," Adeline said, briskly charitable. "And I'll tell people about it. Poor dear, it must be terrible!"

"Oh, no," he said. "It's really not so terrible as you might think. You see, Jenny has her religion—she has become very devout—and it's a great comfort to her."

Adeline looked at him half dubiously, then sighed complacently. "Yes, I can believe that," she murmured. "But the young man, this Milton Pierce—he recovered quite nicely, didn't he?"

"He was out of the hospital in a couple of weeks," Dave replied. "All in all, he was very lucky. Worse things can happen to a man than running into a truck and being laid up for a few days."

Adeline eyed him curiously. "Why, Dave! What do you mean?"

With a glance at his watch David got to his feet.

"Great Scott, Adeline!" he exclaimed. "You've bewitched me! I had no idea it was so late."

She walked to the front door with him. It was going to be awkward saying good-by to her. She would build her little bridge of promises from now until the next time, and he would have to walk very carefully across it.

"You'll think of me, won't you, Dave?" she whispered, touching his arm in the semi-darkness.

There was something almost pathetic about her now, something plaintive, and David in a momentary relenting of his resentment, stooped and kissed her. "I will, Adeline," he said, and added, tactfully, "if you'll think of me."

"Oh, Dave!" she exclaimed, reprovingly. "Call me up sometime, won't you? Here—not at the office. They're all too nosey over there."

David agreed, and with a cheery good night for anyone who might be passing in the street to hear, she let him out of the door into the flickering white dusk of falling snow.

§ 6

Under the harsh and comfortless stuff of his cheap old coat, David's shoulders heaved with cruel mirth. Then at last there were tears in his eyes, and angrily with the back of his hand he dashed them away.

Main Street was in reality two thoroughfares which sandwiched a strip of park, the railway track and the depot. About him the snow fell in a concentrated silence that was the soul of sound. There, at the station, the evening train groaned and sobbed, steam clouding from its engine up into the nimbus of the lights on the platform. But to Dave, passing almost within arm's reach of it, it was unreal; its blatancy had not penetrated the crypt in which he moved. When he was a boy he had walked in the snow inviolate, proud, hand in hand with his dreams, secreted and happy. Now he walked in the falling snow and it was the revelation of silence, the blank din of irony in the human heart.

With a distaste for meeting anyone he knew, he kept to the inner edge of the park and came finally to the street that led homeward. Here he came upon Paget and Tom, with Carla walking a little before them, her face atilt to the snow.

David fell into step with her, but for a moment she seemed not to be aware of him. He laughed and took her arm. She started vaguely, glanced up at him, then continued looking with half-shut eyes into the upper tumult of snow among the bare trees.

As he looked down at her he wondered how it was that she always gave an air of gentility to whatever she wore. Her gray coat, with its snug little collar of squirrel, was one her mother had made over for her from an old coat of Sophie's. Her scarlet tam Mrs. Welland had knit from Angora wool, and on Carla's head it looked gayly, gravely royal. Under a street light it sparkled with its incrustation of snowflakes.

"What are you thinking so hard about, young one?" Dave demanded.

"Oh," Carla said readily, "I was just making a poem."

"A poem? What's it about?"

Carla modulated her voice confidentially.

> *"I buried my heart at the root of a tree;*
> *Wormwood, they said, and I laughed, and now*
> *When I lift my eyes from the earth I see*
> *An apple of gold on a silver bough."*

"Not bad," Dave said, pleased. "But what do you know about wormwood?"

Carla turned enormous, shadow-lit eyes upon him. "It's a lovely word," she said, withering him.

They had reached the Welland terrace, and the lights from the living room twinkled out upon the snow.

"When did you start writing poetry?" Dave asked. "I didn't know you were taking that line."

"We don't always tell the world what we think—or what we do. Some things are like dying. They're nobody's business."

The burden of Dave's knowledge of Adeline Greenleaf moved forward from its noxious darkness at the back of his brain. Like dying. A private affair, this business of thinking the body into humility, sordid and haphazard and infinitely ridiculous. And yet Carla had seen golden apples on a silver bough! She was being spared for something—he knew it suddenly with illumined conviction. Genius protected its own.

When they entered the house they found that Matt had already gone to the church to help put the finishing touches to the decorations for the evening's program. The Christmas tree, which Matt had selected, was one to strike awe in the hearts of the congregation, with its silver star soaring to the ceiling of the church. He took a touchingly childish interest in this responsibility of his, and glowed with pleasure each year, in the effect achieved.

A visitor sat in the living room. David looked in, and saw his mother talking with him. She was obviously nervous. Her hands were clasped together in her lap, and she spoke with more than usual diffidence. Jenny was leaning back in her chair, two bright flames in her cheeks. Seena and Ruth were in the kitchen preparing supper.

The man was in profile to David, but memory hurtled back to the long ago and with a telescoping of his thoughts Dave knew suddenly who it was.

Carla was asking the question with her eyes. David grinned. "It's Uncle Felix Welland," he whispered. "He's got fatter, but it's him, all right. I wonder where father is?"

Sophie was coming down the stairs, dressed gracefully in black chiffon with long, trailing sleeves. Her dark hair was swept back from her forehead, and her widow's peak showed startlingly beautiful. She sailed elegantly, almost dramatically, into the living room, and David heard his mother introducing her to Uncle Felix.

They all knew there had been a Felix Welland and that he had gone to some foreign country where he had presumably died, since he had never been heard of again. David could remember a certain terrible morning in the house of his grandfather when his Uncle Felix had returned from a distant city and there had been violent words between Felix and the old minister. Matt had been there and had tried to stop the quarrel. But Grandfather Welland—David had never forgotten a detail of that awful scene—ceased abruptly his stormy denunciation, turned suddenly white, and sat down, clutching his heart. A moment later he was quite dead. A week afterward the Wellands had removed to Michigan and Uncle Felix had never been mentioned again, except as a beloved brother who had gone abroad and there had honorably died.

"Better go in and be introduced," Dave said, amused at the situation as he anticipated the drama of Matt's return for supper.

Paget escaped to his room upstairs, in no hurry to put in an appearance for the sake of a visitor. Dave entered the living room, followed by Tom and Carla. At the same moment Ruth came in from the kitchen, no tidier than usual, her baby clasped in her arms. Uncle Felix rose mellowly to greet them.

He was a tall man, a little pompous, a little splendid. He was perhaps a year or two older than Matt—Dave seemed to remember that he was the elder brother. But his hair was scarcely gray and there was about him an overwhelming fleshly vitality, as though he still had his eye not backward but forward upon the pleasures of living. He stretched both hands out to each of them in turn, kissing the girls heartily and without ado, and standing the boys back from him to look them over.

"Well, I'm dog-goned!" he exclaimed. "To think that old Matt could produce such a fine, upstanding bunch of offspring! With your help, Sarah—I'll grant that! This is jolly! My word, but this is jolly!" He said the word, Dave thought, as though it ended in *eh— jolleh*. Whether that went with his slight corpulence or whether he had spent some cultural time in England, it was hard to say.

He seated himself gustily and continued to survey one after the other of the family. "And this"—he bent forward with sudden fixed interest toward Carla—"this is the Michigan edition that I didn't know about, eh, Sarah? H'm!" Then he sank thoughtfully back into his chair and continued to look at Carla, pulling his under lip out with his thumb and forefinger. One gesture in common with Matt, David thought, resenting a little his staring at Carla. Then Felix looked at his watch, a slender, elegant thing with a case of platinum, David judged.

"We expect Matt back at six-thirty, eh, Sarah?" Felix observed. "Well, let's all have a good time while we may. Ha, ha! Old Matt may throw me out, bag and baggage, you know, when he finds me here. Figuratively, you know, Dave! I took the precaution of putting up at your hotel down here, just in case. A good pigskin bag, you know. Matt might not pay it the respect due it. Well, now! That leaves us half an hour. By Jove, you've not changed a whit, Dave! The same little boy with the fine straight eyes. And you're a printer, too, Sarah says. By the way—" He lapsed into thought again, and Mrs. Welland asked in the lull if he'd like a cup of tea while he waited for Matt. "No, no, my dear! I can wait. But—there *is* a matter—perhaps now the rest of you would let me have a word with Dave before Matt gets here. Just the two of us. Would you mind?"

He stared beneath heavily lowered eyebrows across the room at Carla, who got up and looked at Dave with mirth-compressed lips, and passed with her floating movement out into the dining room, and to the kitchen. Tom wheeled Jenny's chair out, the others following.

The attitude of Felix changed a little. He passed his fine long hand across his brow and David thought he saw it tremble. "Dave," he said, "I've made a bit of money. I don't know whether Matt ever told you kids anything about me, but I was the one that got the breaks in our family. Matt wanted to enter the ministry, but father spent his money giving me an education. I was the old man's favorite. But the best he could make of me was a portrait painter. I began to make money, though, and then I went agnostic. That's what broke the old man's heart. It killed him—you remember. Oh, there was a little more to it than that. I fell in love with the wife of a man in our town—and father got wind of it. We had it out one day—you remember the day I mean. Matt turned me out and swore he'd kill me if he ever saw me again. Poor Matt—he didn't mean it, of course. But I never did see him again, although I've thought of him a good deal, and I've quietly kept track of him. My wife—we were married, finally—died within a year. I never married again. I couldn't. We had no children, and I'm alone. So there you have it, Dave. I've got a little money, and I'd like to help Matt, only I know what he'd say to that. The notion struck me that Matt's youngest might be just about ready for college now. And I thought—well, it's Christmas, Dave—and, hell, boy—you know what I mean. I'd like to make up to Matt a little for what the past has done to us."

He paused after his long speech and drew an unsteady breath. Dave had thought quickly, more quickly than he had ever thought in his life before. If this were one of the signposts pointing to Carla's destiny, he would be the last one to shut his eyes to it. But he foresaw Matt's reaction to this belated generosity on the part of Felix. He saw more. The whole, desolate, frustrated panorama of his father's life rolled out vividly before him, and suddenly there were tears of understanding in his eyes. But it was too late for recriminations now. Had Matt not suffered the bitter defeat of his dreams, things might have been very different for them all. But now—the expedient thing for Carlotta—the last card in a curious deck. The joker, maybe. David almost laughed aloud.

"You noticed Carla?" he said softly.

"Who could help it? An extraordinary looking child! Is she in school?"

"Yes, and would go to college if we could afford it."

Felix got up and walked nervously to and fro. "Will you take—look here, Dave! You and I don't need to beat about the bush. You know there's no sense of going into this with Matt. He'd just raise a row. Your father, Dave, was always an old fool. Will *you* take what I can give you, and see the girl through?"

Dave's mind was grinning at itself like a satyr. After

all it was only fair to give the devil his due. Here was Carla's destiny, of course, and she should be permitted to follow it, but Matt should know of the generosity of his brother.

"I'll speak to father about it," Dave said securely. "And there won't be any trouble, either. I think I'd better walk down to the church and meet him. Then he'll be prepared to see you."

"Well, just as you think," Felix sighed, and as he leaned back in his chair, David saw that he was really an old man, spent with the pursuit of life.

The moon glittered through the bare branches of the trees, the white, dead world, so much deader in winter, in the sacred Christmas season. David formed the sentences he would use on the way back from the church with Matt, who would be happy as a child in what he had accomplished for to-night's Christmas program, when the children would speak their pieces and forget them and blush and cry, and sing, and perform their touching tableaux of the Manger, the Wise Men, the Star, the Shepherds, the Sheep. No, not the sheep, of course. Felix was here, he would tell Matt, sent by heaven itself. Well, he wouldn't put it quite so strongly as that, perhaps. But he would tell Matt that things had come to such a pass in the printing shop that nothing but a miracle could save them. The money that Felix offered would tide them over—tide them over. How many times in his life had he said that? Matt, rather than suffer the disgrace of insolvency, would swallow his pride and accept Felix's generosity. For Carlotta, of course. And he would accept Felix, too. But David, grinding his teeth, swore that the money should be for Carlotta, though the heavens fell.

§7

He met his father in the churchyard, where the light shone through the stained-glass window and tinted the snow in a lovely shimmer of ruby, sapphire, and lemon yellow—a vivid monument to the memory of one of Thrace's dear departed. The old man came happily to meet him, with his springy, brisk step, the snow crunching sharply under his feet.

"Why, Dave!" he greeted him. "This is a pleasant surprise! Are the girls getting impatient for supper? We had a little trouble with the lights—"

Dave took his arm and fell into step with him as they emerged upon the sidewalk. "Listen, father," he interrupted, "I came down to warn you. Uncle Felix has come. He's waiting for you at the house."

Matt's arm stiffened beneath Dave's hand. His step grew slack, as though sudden weights had been tied to his feet. Under the street light, Dave, glancing at him uneasily, saw his face go dead, quite dead. In quick pity, Dave lifted his other hand and patted Matt's arm in its poor, thin coat. Damn it, anyhow, it was unfair!

"Cheer up, father! He hasn't come to kill anybody."

Matt made a curious sound in his throat. "He did that long ago," he said, "long ago."

David could have kicked himself. "Now, listen," he

said, and his voice sounded harsh and unnecessarily loud with emotion. "That's all in the past, father. We won't talk of it. Besides—this is Christmas"—oh, hypocrite!—"and we'll all feel better if you receive him. He wants to help—to make amends. He—"

But Matt had stopped in his tracks. He seemed to be sagging at the knees, and David, looking at him in alarm, saw that one hand was clutched over his heart. Then, without a word, he sank to his knees in the snow, like something grotesque, something old and discarded —like a ragged gunnysack. David lifted him as he would a child, tenderly and with a hot and choking throat, and carried him home.

In the house, after Matt had been laid on the couch and Doctor Mertz had been called, David stood back with folded arms and looked about him. It was remarkable how quickly the Wellands adjusted themselves to any new situation, he thought with grim appreciation. Sophie, Ruth, Seena, rushing up with hot water, cold water, woolen blankets, spirits of ammonia, God knew what, his mother seated calmly beside Matt, chafing his hands. Tom and Paget were at the door watching for the doctor. Jenny was enjoying a collapse, complete and detestable, was weeping stormily in spite of Sophie's absent-minded and angry protests. Sophie, David observed acidly, didn't care what happened, so long as there was no noise about it; death, for instance, was decently quiet. Poor Felix moved in silent abstraction about the room, running his long fingers through his hair. Carla alone seemed to have no part in this, where she sat with her feet curled beneath her on the floor of the dining room, old Lulu anxiously gazing up at her with her head in Carla's lap.

Matt stirred, and everybody in the room seemed to cease breathing.

"Felix," he asked faintly. "Is my brother Felix here?"

Even at the portals of death, David reflected, the Wellands would not fail in dramatic effect. Then he hated himself for his cynical detachment. Poor Matthew Welland, a shabby, broken dreamer, a poet with a misdirected passion, lying there, old, out-of-date, defeated, in the presence of his own brother, who had trampled over him and his dreams, and who was large with worldly increase! Suddenly Dave hated Felix, and wished he would get out of the house, with his money and his good-humored patronage and his cosmopolitan accent. Suddenly he wanted the Wellands he knew, the Wellands who had been crushed and sealed up in a vessel of bigotry and fear, to be left alone in their poverty and obscurity, their divinely ordained doom.

But Felix was at Matt's side and his eyes were brightly wet.

"I'm here, Matt, old boy," he said, and took the hand that moved slightly above the blanket.

Then Matt did a most remarkable thing. He smiled, the ethereal smile of a sick child. His lips moved a little, first without words, then with barely audible articulation.

"Let us forget everything, Felix," he said. "Our time

at best is short in this world. Thank God you have come."

Felix said nothing, but took out his handkerchief and vigorously blew his nose. David relented a bit toward him.

"I was stubborn with you once, Felix," Matt went on, almost in a whisper, now. "But—I have had a vision."

He closed his eyes and for a moment there was a fearful silence in the room. David felt the great heartbeat of the family, felt the life, the blood and bone and sinew that were all part of its common body—and it was unbearable. His being screamed against the horrible bulky unity of this body, its blind and smothered existence, its purposeless design.

He looked at his father again, and he knew now what was happening to him. The old man was afraid he was going to die. He could not go without first making his peace with the world. That, to him, was second only to making his peace with God. It flashed coldly through Dave's mind that if it had not been for his fear, nothing on earth would have moved Matt to accept the bounty of Felix. In a curious manner, then, Matt's stern God was smoothing the way for his pagan child Carla, who sat removed and strange with eyes full of necromancy, like a lovely, adolescent sphinx. If it had not come about in this way, David thought, there would have been another way.

The doctor came in, and Matt Welland lifted his eyes and looked at him and spoke. The family breathed deeply with relief, as a tree breathes after a storm.

David turned away and left the room. He felt the need of breathing freely in the open air. On the way out he paused briefly beside Carla. "I'll not be back for supper. I'll see you to-morrow. Tell Uncle Felix I'll drop around to his hotel in the morning. And you might just tell mother it's all right about the coal. Mrs. Greenleaf will wait for the money—and she's sending another load to-morrow."

VI: SOPHIE

§ 1

Sophie Welland was thirty years old. Her birthday, falling in October, gave to that month a special significance. It was as though she caught up with the year then and made an end of it. Birthdays in general held a fascination for Sophie, and she was given, in secret, to the reading of horoscopes that were to be found syndicated daily in the newspapers. On the birthday of any member of the family, she might be found in a small state of excitement, baking a cake on which she placed candles, decorating the table with flowers of the season, and surreptitiously giving such warnings or assurances to the subject as the horoscope justified. In these matters she was impartial, granting as much attention to her own birthday as to those of the others, although on October Ninth she was obliged to content herself with a table center of autumn leaves and the last of the late flowers.

The *Thrace Advocate* the evening before had informed her that those whose birthdays were to-morrow might expect a year of great happiness in affairs of the heart. Sophie had experienced a skeptical flutter at this prediction, and had lain awake for a long time beside Carla wondering how and when and where the prophecy would be fulfilled. Now it was morning, but the commonplace bustle of the household beginning a new day did not dispel her growing mood of anticipation.

She made her toilet with unusual care before the dresser mirror, parting her hair for a change on the side instead of sweeping it directly back in the broad dark arrow from her forehead. Three times she combed it back in order to get the part precisely straight. Then she permitted it to curve frivolously forward at the sides, and the effect was most pleasing. From the depths of a drawer she removed a tiny vial of lily-of-the-valley perfume, which she put in her handbag to be used after she left for school.

Glancing up, she saw Carlotta paused in the act of drawing a stocking over her long slender leg. The girl had a disconcerting way of watching her whenever she did anything out of the ordinary, a way of looking up from beneath her eyelids so that her lashes seemed to sweep more than ever sideways toward her temples. Suddenly Sophie felt that Carla was lying in wait for her, with some uncanny intent. An unaccountable chill passed down Sophie's spine, but it might have been nothing more than the sharpening of the October breeze which blew in through the open window from the false fever of the copper beech outside.

"What on earth are you staring at me like that for, Carla?" she demanded, nettled. "Hurry up and get dressed, if you expect to take the same car with me."

Carla whistled thoughtfully beneath her tongue, her lower lip drawn in. "I was just thinking it's your birthday," she said, "and I haven't enough left of my allowance to buy you anything. But I'll save some money next week, if you can wait till then."

"Allowance!" Sophie sniffed. "Don't start putting on airs just because you happen to be the first one in the family to go to college. I could have gone, too, if I had thought only of myself. I could have worked my way through. I wouldn't have depended on some uncle to turn up and make it easy for me. But some people seem to be born just at the right time!"

A deep white organdy collar pinned to her blue serge dress restored Sophie's good humor. She looked a little contritely toward Carla, and saw to her chagrin that she was unconcernedly hooking her garters to her stockings. Sophie saw the white bloom of her bare shoulders, the shadowed troughs of the gold waves of her hair, the impudent, firm curve of her small breasts, and did not know whether to hate her or love her. As she ran the buffer hastily over her nails, her old preoccupation with the matter of age set in again. Carla was seventeen. A young woman, really, but you would not suspect it to look at her. In fact, you would probably be wrong whatever you suspected of her. Just when you thought you had her, she slipped out of your fingers like a goldfish. Jenny, who since she was crippled had assumed certain pretensions to clairvoyance, thought she knew. Jenny had made some remarks lately about Carla's unseemly habit of walking in the woods alone. *Did* she walk alone? Jenny had asked. Jenny heartily reprobated the whole idea of Carla's enrolling in the Methodist College at Redlands, or any college, which would make it possible for her to be away from home all day and to get into who knew what mischief with those she met there. Dave had told her succinctly to keep her mouth shut, and poor father had been in confusion, believing of course that Jenny was right but being obliged to keep a word that he had made when he thought, last Christmas, that he would die. Sophie had contemptuously kept out of the wrangle. She was already sorry that she had expressed herself as she had to Carlotta just now. But it was amazing how circumstances favored the child. It was almost as though Carla were a princess being fitted for the throne. Time alone would tell what this special dispensation of Providence would bring her.

Carla stood up in her scant muslin underwear and stretched. Sophie, on her way to the door, with an involuntary burst of affection flung her arms about her in a violent hug. Carla gave an inelegant little grunt of surprise, and Sophie let go of her quickly.

"Hurry up and don't keep breakfast waiting," Sophie mumbled over her shoulder as she went into the hall. "You know how Jenny frets."

"Oh, Sophe!" Carla called after her. "I just found two dollars under the bureau scarf. I forgot I put 'em there. I want to get you some stockings. What color do you want?"

"Oh, any kind," Sophie said carelessly, but secretly touched.

In the parlor, where a couch had been placed for her to sleep on since her accident made it impossible for her to get upstairs, Jenny was being moved by her father and mother into her long wheel-chair, on which her helpless limbs were extended. As Sophie passed the door on her way outside to gather her birthday bouquet for the table, she could hear her father's gentle voice bestowing upon Jenny its usual bright morning cheer, and then his "Careful there, now, mother. Over we go! That's a girl, Jenny. All set! Smell those pancakes? There's Canadian bacon for you, too. . . ."

Sophie was out on the porch, and down across the lawn. The fading grass glittered with its myriad points of cold dew, like old silvered brocade. When the wind thrust across the stillness it had a blade of searching steel. Had last night been windless, Sophie thought, there would not now be a single aster or dahlia sturdy and un-blackened. Other years, when there had been an early frost, it had not mattered, she had simply taken it for granted along with the other disappointments of her life, but this day was shaped for symbols, and she could not have tolerated finding the garden a ruin of withered death. The dahlias were strong and dusky and rich, like Amazons, and not at all sensuous. The asters were soft and coquettish, but a little brittle, too—like a young girl who has never been roused. Although she gathered an armful of each of these, it was in a burning branch of the maple tree at the extreme eastern side of the garden that she found a true counterpart of herself. These flamy leaves—a rush of beauty and their lives were over. Sophie stood for a moment with her harvest in her hands, her spirits drooping. It was true. She would never find love again. Those horoscopes were idiotic, and she was idiotic ever to have read them. She turned back slowly, heavily, to the house, her stockings darkening in the wet grass. Dave, when he had reached thirty-two a few months ago, had laughed at her when she had warned him against doing business with any women, and had said, in his sarcastic way, "Have you been following me around, Sophie? My business with women has been most profitable." She had believed that he meant his wife, Seena, of course. Dave was curious, unfathomable. Because his life had ended at his marriage he had never been in love. After all, even after marriage, and such a marriage as David's, there should be something for a normal person to go on with. In her own case, she had gone on after Bertram, and Bertram, living in her, had never really died. Bert—Bert—O God, somewhere beyond the porcelain cold clarity of the sky, what is Thy divine purpose?

The family was getting seated for breakfast, but Sophie took the time to place her flowers in a bowl and set it on the table before she sat down in her chair.

"Many happy returns, Sophie, dear," her mother said. "You look very nice this morning in that white collar. It laundered well, didn't it? That organdy usually gets out of shape so."

The talk about the table was cheery this morning, since Matt had already been to the post-office and had discovered fifty more orders in the mail for copies of *Travelers Through the Dark*. Sophie, with her private superstitions that had nothing to do with the religion of the family, had always had rather a vague idea as to the contents of that small book, but this morning she felt called upon by the demands of decent sociability to congratulate her father upon the success of his enterprise, which, it seemed, had gone far beyond anyone's expectations. In fact, according to Dave, they would about break even on the thing.

"I was thinking, father," Jenny spoke up, "that if you had a few copies specially bound, in good leather, you could charge a higher price and see how they would go, and if they went well it would be worth while to bring out more. I might"—she laughed deprecatingly—"I might even make some drawings for you, if you think they would be good enough."

Matt patted her hand. "Well, I should think so!" he beamed. "We'll see what David says. It's a splendid idea, but you know what a tyrant David is. Bless him! But we'll see, we'll see!"

Then, with his heartiest smile, he raised the bacon platter to see whether anyone wanted more. "Sophie!" he exclaimed merrily. "Now that you're thirty-one you ought to eat more!"

"I'm thirty, father," Sophie said severely.

"She'll never be thirty-one, I'll bet," Tom observed.

Everybody laughed at his quirp, except Carla, who looked thoughtfully across at Sophie. Sophie stared into those bottomless gray and gold pools searching her own eyes, and was aware of a faint, apprehensive chill.

"What are you all laughing at?" Carla asked, suddenly coming out of her revery. "I didn't hear the joke. I was thinking of something else."

"What were you thinking of, baby?" Tom asked, pulling a spun lock of hair on her shoulder.

Sophie listened with the fearful eagerness of one about to hear her fortune told. But she busied herself with her food and did not look at Carlotta.

"Why, I was just thinking," Carla said, "what I'd use for my original composition this week. I think I'll bring Chaucer back in modern clothes."

It was a small, ridiculous anti-climax for Sophie. She felt disgusted at Carla, and angry at herself. There was nothing psychic about the girl at all; she was a fraud, with those eyes of hers.

"Chaucer?" Matt queried uneasily. Chaucer was no more than a name to him, but in every new study that Carla brought home he smelt danger to the mental, moral and spiritual security of this child of his who had by a deft trick of fate been snatched out of the family pattern.

"He's middle English, father," Sophie said, a little tartly. "He can't hurt anybody. If Carla started to use that language nobody would understand her."

Matt looked humorously down the table to Sophie. "If you say it's all right, Sophie, I'll be content," he said. "With one thing and another I haven't time to go properly into what they're teaching our Lottie over at Redlands. To be sure, it is a respectable school. All I can do is trust that she won't have her little head turned by so much learning. But I guess it's screwed on pretty tight, eh, Lottie?"

A lightly pointed laugh came from Jenny at Matt's side.

"I'd say it was screwed on tight and at a pretty uppish angle, if you asked me," she said. "Mrs. Peebles came in yesterday for her tea set, and she said she met Carla on the street downtown with Jared Gale and Carla had her head in the air and never even looked at her, although Mrs. Peebles spoke to her. Of course Jared and Carla are both going to college, Mrs. Peebles said, but Jared is working his way through, and when you think how poor he and his mother are, there is really nothing for him to put on airs about, she said. What she meant was that Carla was putting on airs. Nobody thinks that of poor Jared."

"You ought not to snub Mrs. Peebles, Lottie," Mrs. Welland said, in rather ineffectual rebuke, since she was unable to like Mrs. Peebles. The undertaker's wife was notorious for her sharp dealings, even with the bereaved poor. "She gave Jenny a large order, you know, in that tea set—and she bought a good many copies of father's book."

Carla took a deep drink of her coffee. "I don't remember seeing her," she said without interest. "And anyhow, she smells like dirty money out of a dirty pocket. And I haven't time now to go to her awful basket socials. Casket socials, they ought to be called."

"Lottie, Lottie!" her father chided softly. "Do not be irreverent, my dear. And how is Jared doing? He has some years yet, I understand, before he takes his doctorate. And then he hopes to teach theology at the college, isn't that so? Brother Willsie was telling me they think highly of the boy over in Redlands, and that there's no doubt of his being put on the staff. Well, well! I suppose this fancy learning is useful in its place, if you put it in the *right* place. But don't forget, Lottie, that God gave you your mind. Don't let ideas enter there that are hateful to Him. Arrogance of the mind is as great a sin as any evil of the body."

At the last words, his face lit up, and Sophie saw him glance eagerly toward the living room. Promptly after the family rose from the table he went in and sat at his desk, and Sophie knew that he was writing down his last remark to Carlotta.

These mornings of taking the trolley with Carlotta to Redlands were a delight to Sophie. For the first time in years her cheeks were freshening with color, and the shine of her eyes was not the ghostly shine that came from looking out of the somber glimmer of the past, but one that came from the pleasant contemplation of immediacy. Her resentment toward Carla's good fortune was a superficial thing, aroused occasionally by some irritation in the Welland house. It never appeared on their journeys together to or from Redlands.

With Carla beside her in the electric car, Sophie felt acutely conscious of the gaze of their fellow travelers. It amazed Sophie that Carla seemed so unaware of this attention. She found herself guilty once or twice of suspecting that her sister knew all about it and took it as her just due, only to have Carla immediately afterwards upset all her conjectures by outstaring some over-bold drummer and putting him to rout in a cloud of blushes. Sometimes Carla talked in her half-absent but wonderfully adequate way about various aspects of her new life; again, she sat looking intently out of the window at the colored fields and woods as they flew by, saying not a word. But whatever the younger girl's mood, its effect upon Sophie was a perilously gay one, of that sort of gayety that is as frangibly thin and venturesome as a blown bubble. Usually, as soon as she was at home again after the day, she was the old Sophie, aloof and remotely contemptuous.

Very often they were on the same car with Jared Gale or Frieda Gertner, but these two serious-minded souls were always deep in some book and rarely had time for conversation. It was true that Sophie had caught Jared more than once looking up across his book at Carla with grimly burning eyes, but whatever his impulses were, he never seemed to act upon them beyond a decent lifting of his hat. Sophie thought it odd that a boy who had virtually grown up with the Wellands should have suddenly become so self-conscious. When she mentioned this, Carla said that he seemed to have very little to talk about these days, and that she suspected he was working out logarithms in his head all the while.

To-day they got a later car, and except for an old farmer at the extreme end of it, they were alone. Sophie was glad.

"Carla," she said, with a little diffident laugh, "do you ever feel that something exciting is just about to happen to you—I mean really feel it in your bones? I've got that feeling this morning."

"Quite often," Carla replied gravely, "but usually I

feel that I'm going to happen to something, rather than that something is going to happen to me. It's funny."

Sophie felt a bit balked, but was not given to the analyzing of other people's feelings. She went on: "If this car started right across the field there, and up in the air, I wouldn't be a bit surprised. Look at that sky, Carla! We could go sailing right up through it and into eternity, and I wouldn't think it was strange, to-day. Isn't it a marvelous blue, Carla? I had a dress just that color, when I was twenty-one. . . ."

" 'The long savannahs of the blue,' " Carla quoted dreamily, her eyes holding for an instant the pale mane of a cloud.

"Is that your own phrase, Carla?" Sophie asked humbly.

"No. It's from 'The Hound of Heaven.' Don't you remember?"

"It's so long since I read it," Sophie said.

"Tom and Jared were reading it aloud the other night," Carla said. "Oh—Tom!"

Carla said his name with such angry vehemence that Sophie was startled. Carla and Tom were quarreling constantly these days. No, it could scarcely be called quarreling. Carla maintained a silently jeering attitude toward him for his return to the shop, an attitude that made him furious.

"Yes, poor Tom," Sophie agreed lamely.

"Poor Tom!" Carla stormed. "Weakling!"

An avenue of light opened in Sophie's mind, and for an instant she saw her life disappearing down it. In the panic of a second she knew she must overtake it, bring it back, and make it her own again. Her pursuit would begin to-day. Yes, this day was marked. Something would happen. She was on the very brink of something happening.

They had come to the stop a little better than half way to Redlands, where Sophie had to get out to walk the quarter of a mile or so to her school. Carla agreed to meet her after four o'clock, and if the day held fine, they would walk part of the way home. Sophie started diagonally through the small spread of woods which let out upon her school at a cross-roads.

§ 2

Sophie noticed the boy first when she raised her eyes after she had polished her glasses and put them on. It was her habit, though it had no significance whatever, to permit her gaze to roam idly over the class before she called the roll. A strained silence on the part of the pupils always greeted this moment, and somehow started Sophie off with the upper hand, although before the day was done her authority was frequently put to more than one severe test.

Among her eighth grade pupils to-day sat one whom she had never seen before. He was older than the others, perhaps sixteen or seventeen. Glancing calmly down the row of seats, her eyes stopped in a complete blank when they came upon him.

How long she had been staring at him when from the back of the room a faint titter rose, Sophie could not tell.

What she knew, with a dull surge of warmth, was that she beheld before her eyes a startling resemblance to Bertram Seiffert, Bertram of the lean, searching dark face, the unruly hair, brown and soft to the touch, Bertram Seiffert—back beyond the dead forest of the years. Sophie blinked rapidly behind her glasses, frowned and caught her breath before she spoke. There was a wavelike movement over the room, and she knew that for the day her complete command over her young charges was gone.

The boy, who sat in the light from an open window at the side of the room, gave his name in a low voice with a prefatory and self-conscious clearing of his throat.

"Lawrence Parr," he said.

She had half expected him to say "Seiffert." Lawrence Parr. The name meant nothing to her. Crisply she called the roll, keeping her eyes studiously averted from the new boy. But she would have to ask him later why he had begun late in the term, and why he had not come to her first, and what his age was and where he lived. Her eyes fell upon a tuft of hair that stood straight up on the crown of his head like a feather. . . .

A May evening of aquamarine purity—herself and Bert Seiffert seated on the river bank north of Thrace—herself stroking Bert's hair and laughing tenderly—"Bert, you may as well keep that bit shaved. You'll never make it lie down." Bert's articles on his humble agnosticism—his loss of his position in the Redlands High School—Matt Well- and patting her hand and telling her gently that it was all for the best, that no happiness would come of her consorting with an unbeliever.

202

In a daze she took out of her desk a sheaf of test papers of the day before, but her eyes moved unattentively over them, and her cheek under her nervous fingers was burning. A terrifying voice back behind her temples was crying at her: "Sophie Welland, are you going crazy? Sophie Welland! Stop! Stop!" Things like this happened to old-maid schoolteachers. No, no! She was not to blame. This was a shocking coincidence. Anyone would have been similarly moved. It would be all right after a while, when the likeness began to wear away, and the boy was just a spindling boy, gaunt and hungry looking. Gaunt and hungry looking. . . . Bert, Bert, in turmoil of the spirit, shut out, rejected, alone!

Nellie Cadman had scored the highest in the test. Yes, Nellie had got ninety-three. But on the whole the class had made a very poor showing, Sophie told them. Would Nellie and Claude Johnson please distribute the papers? Nellie and Claude, old rivals, came with alacrity. They looked eagerly down at the red figures topping each paper, later to gloat over their own superior marks. Little vultures, hateful little vultures! Sophie abominated them, consigned them in her mind to an eternity of eighth grade history examinations, looked along the line of windows and met the brooding eyes of Lawrence Parr.

She learned during the morning recess that the Parrs had just moved up from the southern border of the state, and had bought the old Loomis farm two miles south of Redlands, less than a mile from Sophie's school. Also she learned that Lawrence was seventeen, and had been retarded in his schooling because of illness; but here, at his hesitancy, Sophie guessed the old story, that of the farm boy who had been kept at home to work. To conceal her own unspeakable nervousness, Sophie questioned him rather severely, and to her dismay at the end of the interview his hostility and his dislike of her were manifest. She tried feebly to make amends by suggesting that he remain after school a few evenings every week to catch up with the others; that she would be glad to give him this extra attention. Lawrence was evasive, shy, awkward, and obstinate by turns, and in the end she dismissed him and felt completely defeated.

The day dragged itself miserably to a close. At intervals so brief they threw her into a panic, Sophie would find herself staring at the new boy, and unfailingly his moody eyes would be upon her, resentful, guarded, full of distrust. Toward the end of the day Sophie's obsessing superstition had the better of her, and she was convinced that in some way Bertram Seiffert's spirit had got behind the boy's eyes and crouched there, accusing her, hating her for the betrayal of her own life and his. Finally, when at four she dismissed the class, she was so distraught that she forgot all about two miscreants whom she had commanded to stay after school for the customary punishment of writing out chastening mottoes one hundred times. She got into her hat and coat, seized an armful of composition papers, and left the building, hurrying into the deepening bronze and crimson of the autumn woods without so much as a glance behind her.

At the trolley line, Sophie sat down on the crisp, whitening grass of the bank that ran alongside, removed her hat and felt the wind blow sheer and cool along her temples. The torrid throbbing in her head seemed to ease a little, and at last when she permitted her eyes to seek out the farthest distance upon the horizon, she found a slumbrous radiance lying under the sky and bemusing into a dim gold dream the painted trees, the blanched fields, the distant toy-like farmsteads, and the timid, disappearing little roads.

She must get some more interests in her life—it would not do to live so utterly within herself. She would join the book club in Thrace, whatever her father thought of its discussions. Since affairs seemed to be going better with the shop—perhaps because of Carla's windfall from Uncle Felix—possibly she could afford week-end visits now and then to Detroit or Chicago.

But what would such visits be, alone? She and Bertram had planned such wonderful journeys. At the swing of her mind back to Bertram, the boy Lawrence returned with frightening vividness. She stood up in agitation and began to walk to the small platform where the car must come to a stop. To her mortification she had begun to calculate the years until Lawrence would be a man—four or five, at the least. She would be in her middle thirties. Such things had been known to happen. . . . Suddenly, in a flood of shame, she clutched her lips with her fingers, as though she had given voice to the wanton shape of her thoughts. With deep relief she heard the din of the approaching trolley, descending like a boisterous plaything into the quiet.

She was chagrined to see that Carla did not get off the

trolley alone. Jared Gale was with her. He sauntered up to greet Sophie, his rather ruddy, agreeable face set in its usual lines of determination, his blue eyes sober and straight. He removed his hat and spoke unsmilingly. Sophie thought: "What stubborn, crisp brown hair he has! And what a solemn young donkey he is! What's between him and Carla, I wonder?"

"We missed the first car just by an inch, Sophie, dear," Carla explained. "I'm so sorry you've had to wait. And it was all over a silly argument, too. Jared wanted to carry my books, and of course I couldn't let him!"

Jared laughed emptily. It was plain that he was annoyed.

With small talk they got over into the field where the short stubble had become spikes of pale rose in the low and enormous sun. Sophie noted how thin and tawnily transparent the skin of both Carla's face and Jared's looked, and the fragility and preciousness of their youth touched her with a pang. But then Carla linked her free arm in hers, and began to sing in her oddly plaintive and not altogether true voice, and Sophie, thinking she was like some belated and wistfully ridiculous lark, adored her and let her own better voice slip unobtrusively in with Carla's. Jared masterfully took Sophie's brief-case from her hand; Sophie felt a little glow at his chivalry.

> *"In a cavern, in a canyon, excavating for a mine,*
> *Dwelt a miner, forty-niner, and his daugh-ter,*
> *Clementine! . . ."*

206

Carla finished the song in a lusty burst of animal spirits, and began again:

> *"Softly and tenderly Jesus is calling . . .*
> *Come home, come ho-o-ome!*
> *Ye who are wear—"*

Sophie had screwed up her courage and broken sharply into the gusto of the song. "Carla! They'll hear you over at the Taylor farm!"

"Well, what of it? They always come to revival. They'll enjoy it." And she went on and finished the song, drawing it out in intense pathos and actually following the tune.

Sophie glanced sideways at Jared. He was frowning with disapproval, but she could see that he was troubled and pained, too.

"I don't see any need of that," he remarked, hitching his broad shoulders angrily. "There's one of the Taylors over in the pasture there. He's listening, too, and looking for all he's worth. You wait and see if your father doesn't hear about it."

Carla whistled her indifference. "What happened in school to-day, Sophie?" she asked at once. "Anything funny?"

"Funny?" Sophie repeated the word vacantly.

The field they were in had dipped into a little hollow, and now the hilly land lay ahead, wan on the uplands and on the stripped slopes of the vineyards, with pools of dusk where the little valleys lay. Here and there were islands of woods, bristling scarlet and ocher in the empty land, under the empty, green-cool sky, with its lonely strip of autumn yellow in the west. Lonely, lonely bulk of earth, lumbering massively around and around, day after day, season after season, age after age, knowing doom and life and doom again. Sophie thought only in pictures, never in words really, and the picture she saw of the solitude and forsakenness of the earth in the void of unthinkable space ached inarticulately in her mind. For the moment she was the earth, ponderous and misbegotten, in a radiant universe of spectral immaterial stars. Then, from a distance her own voice seemed to echo back to her, and she was saying something to Carlotta, something unbelievably casual as though she were not Sophie Welland at all.

"Yes, something funny did happen," she said. "A new boy came in to-day, and he looked so much like Bertram Seiffert that he might have been his brother. I was quite startled. But it turned out he was no relation at all."

They were walking through a shallow stand of poplars now, and the little trinkets of yellow leaves made a sound in the light wind like an elfin music-box. Carla had glanced at Sophie in quick amazement at what she had said, and then had looked away. Sophie was too bewildered at her own words to feel either regret or relief, and to recover herself she plunged on into what she knew of the boy's history, and of his people.

"If his folks have bought the Loomis place, they're due for a disappointment," Jared volunteered. "Old Loomis killed himself trying to raise anything on it."

Sophie felt a quick twinge of anxiety. Young Lawrence would be, in his turn, then, made a slave to barren soil. But why should she trouble herself about that? But why shouldn't she? She swerved from self-criticism to self defense, and back again, in confusion.

"How old is he, Sophie?" Carla asked.

Always Carla had an unerring way of touching with her light and careless finger the very quick of any situation. Sophie found herself recklessly prepared to lie about the boy's age, in the fear that Carla might divine the disorder in her imagination. But, if common sense did not dictate her telling of the truth, abhorrence of a lie did.

"He must feel awful in amongst a lot of youngsters," Carla said, when she had learned Lawrence's age. Then she abruptly changed the subject.

Sophie heard Carla exclaim softly, as though to herself, upon the great, evening-hung gallery of the world into which they had come from the close poplars.

"Jared! Wouldn't you love to stay here all night, and keep awake and watch what goes on? It's magic. Can't you just *hear* the stars coming, far away? It's a silver sound."

"They crackle in winter," Jared observed eagerly.

They had come within sight of a car stop, and Sophie, out of her abstraction, suggested that they discontinue their walk. The air smelled of the thin bloom of frost. By morning the garden at home would hang limp and blackened, and the stalks of the flowers would be slimy to the touch. Sophie drew her collar up about her throat and shivered.

Home again, and they were bidding Jared good-by at the corner where their ways parted. Sophie noticed that as Carla looked up at Jared her eyes moved speculatively over his body to his face, where they continued their curious, aggressive search. Carla's lips were sweetly curved, but her eyes were inscrutably narrow. To Sophie the performance was subtly shocking, although she could not have told why. Jared looked uneasily down at Carla, and then moved away as though he had been frightened.

Self-absorbed though she was, Sophie was disturbed. Carla, however, as they moved down the darkening street, swung her school bag and remarked that she hoped there would be something especially good for supper.

§3

A little more than a week had passed, in silent and unresolved conflict between Sophie Welland and Lawrence Parr. The boy, although he did his work faithfully and well, remained antagonistic to a degree which Sophie feared would soon become apparent to the other pupils. He never voluntarily spoke to her or looked at her.

At last on a Friday afternoon, baffled and humiliated until her nerves were on edge, she determined to face the issue boldly and have a talk with Lawrence, as she should have had to do with any other difficult pupil in her charge. At the recess in the middle of the afternoon she stopped him on his way out of the room, and, far more embarrassed than he was, she bade him remain after four so that she could have a talk with him about the work he had missed. Lawrence tightened his mouth; then, his head inclined to one side, he murmured an almost inaudible, "Yes, ma'am."

After four o'clock, when the others had filed rapidly out, Lawrence sat in his seat by the window, a solitary, lean and troubled figure, with his large hands opening and closing before him on the desk. For minutes Sophie remained bent over the papers in front of her, sorting them out with a deliberate air. How on earth should she start to talk to him? His back work—that was all a pretext, and she felt that he knew it. He was not a stupid boy. He knew that she resented his surliness, his monosyllabic responses, and that she was indignant and helpless while he took advantage of her reluctance to treat him like one of the younger children. Yet the state of affairs could not continue if she were to keep her self-respect at all. Somehow she would have to begin.

He shuffled his feet beneath his desk, and cleared his throat. Sophie looked up brightly, almost startled, as though she had for the moment forgotten about him. She produced a strained smile, and removed her glasses, polished them carefully and replaced them in their case, which she closed with a soft little snap.

"I've got work to do at home, soon, ma'am, if you don't mind," Lawrence said heavily.

Sophie used the friendly but clipped voice which she reserved for school hours. "Will you come here, please, and draw that chair over? I won't keep you long, but we must have a little talk, Lawrence."

Lawrence pulled his long ungainly legs out from under his seat and slid into the aisle. Standing up in the empty room he looked even taller than ordinarily. As he came toward her Sophie felt like cowering down and hiding her face. But instead, quite without previous calculation, she drew two books out from a drawer and laid them in front of her.

"I've decided, Lawrence," she said, with inspiration, "that it's too bad to limit you to the reading the others do, and so I want you to improve yourself in your spare time by doing a little more than they do. Now here are two books that you will find interesting and worth while. Pick them up whenever you have an hour free, and you'll be surprised how much you will know about them when you go to high school."

Lawrence picked up the first, the abridged plays of Shakespeare, then the second, a history of Europe.

"High school!" he said, with a sharp laugh that was anything but young. "I'll never be going to high school, ma'am."

Sophie pressed her palms together. In another moment she would be in tears. She battled bravely for self-control and stood up, laughing a little giddily.

"Nonsense! Your father has a big farm—you live close to town—why, of course you will go to high school! You can do anything you want to, Lawrence."

Lawrence got to his feet too, his eyes moodily upon the books. Then for a black instant Sophie experienced complete oblivion, and a moment later Lawrence was blundering backward toward the door, his eyes upon her in fixed horror. Sophie had seized him by the shoulders and kissed him fiercely on the mouth.

She stood now, rocking a little on her feet, her hand fumbling up along her temple, down her neck, and to the back of her head. Then Lawrence was gone, and turning automatically as a figure on a revolving disk, she looked out of the window and saw him plunging across the school yard, running, running, his cap in his hand. But at the road he stopped suddenly and clutched his hair, for there he met another boy of his own age, who had risen from the grass where he had evidently been seated waiting for him. With dull, unwinking eyes she saw the other boy wheel and look toward the schoolhouse, and then she knew that in his excitement Lawrence had blurted out what had happened to him.

Numbly Sophie turned to her desk. At a light voice from the doorway her hand frantically grasped her breast. But it was only Carlotta. Only Carlotta? Why was she here? What had she seen? No, no, she could not have seen anything. She was coming happily forward, she was throwing her arms about Sophie. But she was not kissing her, in her warm way.

And she was not really looking at Sophie, either, for her eyes were suffused with bright concealment. From her earliest childhood Carla had looked like that when her thoughts were withdrawn, out upon their own exclusive pilgrimage. Sophie was suddenly afraid. She moved to her desk and with shaking fingers began to tidy it, while Carla sat talking gayly about this and that of her day at Redlands.

Sophie was not in the mood for their usual Friday afternoon walk. She was in a fever to get as far as possible from her school in the shortest possible time. Carla did not try to prevail upon her to change her mind, and now Sophie was more than ever convinced that Carla had witnessed her insane act. On the ride home Sophie struggled to keep her mind on the girl's talk, but not really for an instant did she cease to wonder with anguish as to what the coming week would bring.

§ 4

It was at the lunch hour on Monday that a daughter of one of the school trustees brought the story to Sophie. She was a little girl of thirteen, with a quaintly maternal manner. In the midst of her recital she broke into indignant tears, and Sophie was obliged to put her arm about her and comfort her.

"There, there, child! Of course it's all a terrible falsehood, but I'm glad you have come to me about it. Did you say—Lawrence Parr—told this story at recess?"

All through the morning there had been an unwholesome stillness over the room. The children, when they had been called upon to answer questions or to read, had been self-conscious and unnatural. More than once she had caught wide young eyes fixed in awe or repulsion upon Lawrence Parr, who had seemed to sit the whole time in a kind of paralysis.

"No, ma'am," the little girl said tearfully. "It wasn't Lawrence. It was Tim Lester. He said his brother, that doesn't go to school, told him. But us girls don't believe it, anyway, and I think Lawrence ought to be expelled. Don't you, Miss Welland?"

The little girl was becoming interested purely in the merits of the case, and Sophie saw with relief that her woe was drawing to an end. Sophie thought with a cool precision and speed that she had never believed herself capable of.

"I don't know, my dear," she said calmly. "Lawrence has been a very disagreeable boy from the first. Perhaps you and the others have noticed how rude he always was to me. It isn't very likely that I would—kiss him, is it, Pearl? Now, I must have time to think a little while. You run along and play outside, and don't worry any more about this. Everything will be all right."

She stroked Pearl's hair, and the little girl, with a grateful and important sigh, took herself off, no doubt to hold a long and outraged conference with her chums in defense of their beloved teacher.

At the beginning of the afternoon period, Sophie took a desperate grasp of the situation. She called upon Lawrence Parr to stand. The boy got to his feet, trembling, and red from throat to hair.

"Lawrence," Sophie said clearly, "I understand that you have been telling someone stories about me. I could have you expelled from school for that, but I am going to give you another chance. You will apologize now, to the whole room, and to me, and say that the story you told the Lester boy was not true."

Lawrence's chest seemed to heave. For one hideous second Sophie feared that he was going to burst out in defiance of her. Had he done that she would have crumpled, perhaps died on the spot. But then the boy's shoulders sagged, and with his eyes staring widely at the blackboard across the room, he began to mutter something.

"I apologize, Miss Welland. It was not true."

Silence ached in the room. Sophie fought back her tears. She saw in a glare of self-revelation how cowardly her strategy had been. With dry lips she managed to tell Lawrence to be seated. She managed to tell the room that she hoped there would be no more of that nonsensical talk of the morning, and she also compelled the Lester boy to stand and apologize in turn for his part in spreading the slander. The Lester boy did so readily enough, although he looked a bit dazed as he repeated the words.

For the remainder of the day the schoolroom churned with industry. But if every child had vanished from before her eyes, it would have affected Sophie not at all. The fact that blazed in her mind was that for the second time in her life she had betrayed something fine, something earnest and sweet and enduring. For the second time in her life she had betrayed Bertram Seiffert. The boy Lawrence had suffered injury to his very soul. But to Sophie Welland something worse had occurred. The stark cowardice of her being had been revealed to her, and she was destroyed in the revelation.

How utterly destroyed, she was not to know until two days later, when the father of Lawrence Parr, a grim, iron-armed man whose face was bitter with a life-time of defeat, came to the school at the end of the afternoon, beside himself with rage at the story that had reached his ears concerning his son's villainy.

The man stalked into the schoolroom with a horse-whip in his hand, throwing the children into pandemonium, seized Lawrence by the collar and dragged him, white and silent, out into the yard. There Sophie, with all the other children cowering about, saw him flail the helpless boy with terrible reports from the whip, until Lawrence was on his knees and a hacking sound came from his throat. Sophie stood like a statue, the blood freezing in her veins. At length the man jerked Lawrence to his feet, and shouted two words at him that made no sense whatever to Sophie. She was past hearing, seeing or feeling. But now Lawrence's terrifying eyes were looking at her across what seemed to be miles of space, and she heard his voice, shrill and awful.

"I apologize, Miss Welland, for what I said about you."

That had been his father's shouted command, then. Sophie's hand groped out toward the boy. But now father and son were stumbling away across the grassy lot to the road, and the children in the school yard in various stages of hysteria were moving to go indoors, to get their things, for Sophie had dismissed them for the day.

Sophie was seated at her desk, alone. Her eyes roved vacantly over the knickknacks upon it, saw an ink-well, a fountain pen, several pencils of red and blue lead, an ink eraser and a piece of art gum, a bottle of glue and one of library paste, a stack of copy books, a theme paper with errant scrawls upon it, a calendar, a note pad, a schedule chart, three jack-knives and a wad of chewing gum on a card with the offender's name written below it. Back and forth across the desk her eyes moved, otherwise her body was entirely motionless.

"Sophie!" It was Carla, and she spoke almost in a whisper. It was a frightened whisper, but Sophie did not stir.

Carla knelt beside her, put her arms tightly about her waist, and leaned her wild bare head against Sophie's shoulder. "Sophie!" she cried softly. "I saw it all from the woods. I ducked down and watched, and I nearly fainted. What was it all about, Sophie? Speak, darling, for goodness' sake, say something!"

Sophie's eyes struck Carla vaguely in their roving, then continued again on their course over her desk. Her lips moved dryly. Then she spoke. "The boy told somebody that I had kissed him," she said. "His father whipped him and made him apologize."

Perhaps it was the sound of her own voice that broke Sophie's trance. Perhaps it was Carla's compassionate eyes. Sophie fell forward with her head in her arms, and wept terribly. Carla sat on the floor beside her, waiting, saying not a word, only reaching out now and then to touch Sophie's knee, or to pick a bit of lint off her skirt.

At last when Sophie raised her head, Carla's white face and pitying eyes told her more clearly than words that Carla knew.

§ 5

They walked for a mile or two through fields and woods, until Sophie was too weary to go farther. Before they cut through the brush to the highway they sat down for a moment to rest on a fallen tree. The silence was pure and untenanted, even of birds, now; once the single tinkle of a cowbell dropped like a thin coin into the thin bowl of the silence. Carla sat listening, half smiling, and Sophie knew that she was crowding from her mind the ugliness of what had happened, and filling it again with the things she loved.

"We won't mention any of this at home, Carla," Sophie said reluctantly. "Unless—I have to."

"Have to?" Carla said.

"I may be forced to resign," Sophie explained in a dull voice. "Even though they all know I was not to blame. The trustees may not think it will be good for the morale of the children to have me stay. That's the way it goes."

"Well," Carla said stoutly, "we all know it wasn't your fault, anyway, and if it comes to that you can get some other school. You've been there long enough, anyhow."

Carla would maintain that pretense, then, Sophie thought, of believing in her blamelessness.

"Yes, I've been there a long time," Sophie said, looking away.

Time—what a strange thing! Tom said the concept of time was a fallacy, created within the limitations of man's mind. In that moment, her brain spacious and light with exhaustion, Sophie thought she glimpsed what he meant. What she had been, what she was now, and what she would be, were all together in the present locked up in a tiny cubicle of sensation. In the flash of an instant she saw that third little bauble of the future, although there were no words quick enough to describe it.

On the following day Sophie received a discreet letter from the trustees, suggesting that although she was beyond reproach in what had occurred, in the best interests of all concerned, including herself, it was advisable that she resign. Lawrence Parr, incidentally, was to be sent to town to school, that the unfortunate episode might be the sooner forgotten.

Sophie packed her belongings into her brief-case, and set a fruit jar full of colored autumn leaves where the sun would shine directly upon it in the mornings. As she passed her desk for the last time she placed the three jack-knives in a conspicuous row near its edge. The card with the gray pellet of chewing gum upon it she tore in two; then she dropped it into the waste basket.

VII: RUTH

§ 1

It was the night before Thanksgiving. A damp wind, presaging snow, patted along the window panes, along the old walls of the house, like a lost ghost. Ruth, putting her youngest to bed in her room upstairs, tried to close her ears to that other sound in the Welland house below, that was the sound of a ghost, too, a ghost gone mad with merriment. It proclaimed in grotesque hilarity to Ruth's tortured sensibilities, the success of her father's children's party. Children's party! The family knew only too well why Matt had planned the occasion, with elaborately engraved invitations to those families in Thrace whose esteem he prized. She herself had noted with disgust how eagerly he had received acceptances to those invitations, and how relieved he had been when no one had declined to come. He must be doubly reassured now, she thought, by the high spirits of his guests, both old and young, that nobody in town harbored any doubts as to the guiltlessness of Sophie in connection with the deplorable Redlands school affair of some weeks past. How convenient it was, Ruth reflected bitterly, that she and Dave had children for whom Matt Welland could give a party!

Gay and quick came the notes of the piano from below, a sprightly tapping under the floor, a tapping on the air, a fugitive tapping in the dim reaches of the mind. Sophie, whose eyes had become like blue torches in the white mist of her face, was playing for the game of musical chairs. Sophie, innocent or obscurely base, of whom nothing was known, who had moved in her pale silence through all the days of the autumn, was training her fleet fingers over the keys so that specters of children—children who would never be hers—might scuffle for a place before the music made an end.

Ruth looked wildly about the room, seeking release from the obsession of Sophie. But here was no release.

The room held still the girlhood mysteries of herself and Sophie and Jenny. The old rosewood cradle, which had lulled to sleep all the Welland children from David to Carlotta, holding now in its fragrance Ruth's own last born, seemed oddly out of place in this room with its aroma of innocent memories.

In shelves that Dave had built under the windows still stood the girls' school books. In Jenny's there would be pencil drawings of ladies' heads prodigious with the puffs of that era, heads in profile and full face, with vast eyes. In Ruth's would be idle scrawls or half-erased names in pairs, one above the other, her own and that of some boy in the class, with the letters common to both crossed out, and then, alongside, the word hatred, or friendship, court-ship, or love or marriage. If she looked, she knew she would find between their pages little notes passed daringly by some school girl friend, or oak leaves so thin and wan that the veins stood out upon them like webbed fingers, or four-leafed clovers dim with wishing long ago; a pressed violet would be there, and sealed in its tiny paling crypt all the rainy rapture of dripping April woods when she was twelve and Sophie fourteen. With a twinge at her heart Ruth gazed away from the books, about the four walls, where in the symmetry that was instinctively Jenny's, were hung the innocuously sentimental prints that the girls had collected in their teens, and some of a still earlier time when a magazine and a pair of scissors had supplied endless delight. There were mild pastoral moods and sunsets blandly insipid as a soft drink; framed calendar-ladies with scant handfuls of waists and high, boned collars and enormous muffins of hats that spurned their heads; a tinted and haloed Christ-child in the manger, which had been a Christmas gift to Sophie from her father, and over which she had cried because it was not a teddy bear. There was also a map of South America brave with crayoned pampas and jungle, with which Jenny had won a prize in the eighth grade. These, and not the rosewood cradle or the children's shoes or toys scattered about, dominated the room still. And although Jenny had not been over the threshold for months, her fingers, striving in their small way for beauty, felt still along flowered wall and cretonned window seat, or arranged a chintz cushion thoughtfully in a wicker chair. And Sophie, who maintained mostly now a strange secrecy in her room and Carla's, drifted still in the dark pool of the old mirror, a frail, tall girl of seventeen.

The baby slept sweetly, unknowingly, in its bed. Ruth's mind fumbled weakly for some meaning in that little offshoot of herself apart from the involuntary love which it had animated within her. Henceforth, her father said, she must live for her children, and hope for them. But she was only twenty-eight years old, and not yet had she lived for herself. She got up and moved vaguely to the dresser mirror, where she stood for a long time looking at herself with eyes that grew harsh with despair. Where was the foamy prettiness that had once been hers, where was the springy impetuousness of her breasts? Only her eyes had a wild and arresting hunger in them. Hearing the laughter of the people downstairs, she parted her lips in a little panting execration of them. Stupid, stupid and cruel, to be enjoying themselves so, and never guessing that they were in the house of capering death!

With the futile anger of a caged animal, Ruth moved about the room. She picked up the children's clothes that lay here and there, placing them absently on a chair. When she came to the baby's shoes she held them for a moment in her hand, and thought with a dim agitation of the man at the Bon Ton Shoe Store who had sold them to her. Andrew Milbank had been in Thrace a year or so, and had bought a half interest in the store. He was a sturdy man, upward of forty. Two weeks ago, when Ruth had taken little Helen and the baby into the store to buy shoes for them, she had noticed that he had shy brown eyes that winked rapidly when she looked at him. Helen had taken to Andrew in a way that was almost embarrassing, beginning by fingering the neat crease of his trouser leg and ending by kissing him enthusiastically after he had laced the new shoes upon her feet. Andrew had blushed, and Ruth had laughed self-consciously, and had blushed, too. She could remember that as she passed a mirror on her way out of the store she had looked almost pretty again with that pink glow still in her cheeks. The Sunday following, Andrew had been at church for the first time in Thrace, and after the service he had come up gravely to shake hands with Helen. In the church a week later, Ruth caught him looking toward her across the pews. That day he had walked as far as the Welland terrace with Ruth and Sophie, and had paused to speak with Matt, who had come up behind them. Although Matt had been cordiality itself to Andrew, Ruth had not failed to catch the sharp glance he turned upon her and Sophie. Later, at the dinner table, his eyes had twinkled mischievously. "Sophie," he had said, "he's a fine fellow, isn't he—that Andrew Milbank? Why don't you ask him in to supper some evening?" Sophie, startled out of her preoccupation, had retorted with asperity, "What makes you think it's me he's interested in, father?" In angry confusion Ruth had felt her cheeks growing warm. Matt had forthwith begun to speak of other things, and later, after dinner, he had kindly patted Ruth's arm and stood for a moment looking at her with his searching gaze, had said softly that it was perhaps not wise for her to encourage Andrew Milbank's friendship, and then had gone to write at his desk. Ruth had been too furious to make any reply, but now, as she thought back upon the incident, it seemed only absurd. As though Andrew Milbank—or any other man, for that matter—would think seriously of a drab little wisp like herself!

It was time now to bring her two eldest upstairs and

put them to bed. She could hear, from below, the sounds of people leaving, the outer door opening, louder voices, the voices of people beholden to Matt Welland, full of good will toward him. The soft step of Sophie came, trying the outer darkness in the hall to her own door.

Ruth held herself quiet, listening to the pause and waver and pause again of Sophie in her room. Not knowing fully its meaning, Ruth had felt within herself a gathering of fear for Sophie. And because no one, not even Dave, had commented upon Sophie's indifference to securing another school, it was as though a secret of fear were spreading through the house, the drift and presence of it hovering over all.

The hours passing, the house became still with the alert stillness of a person in hiding. The party was over, the family retired. Ruth sat beside the cot in which Norris, her six-year-old, tossed fretfully from excitement and an over-plenty of sweets.

As she sat still, her mind vacant with weariness, Ruth thought she heard a sound come through the closed door between her own room and the one Sophie and Carla shared. It was rather the strangeness of the sound that startled her, the exclaiming breathlessness of it. Tiptoeing to the closed door, she stood for a moment and listened. No voices came. Still wondering, she peered through the keyhole. If the girls were asleep she had no wish to disturb them. But the light in the other room was on, the blue shaded light, and just within the range of her vision was the shoulder and left side of Carla in her yellow dressing-gown. Pressing her ear to the keyhole, Ruth was able to mark Carla's curious, broken whisper, and now and then the sharply drawn breath of Sophie. In a small mystification, she was about to tap on the door and ask if either one of them was ill, when some obscure instinct stayed her hand. Then, slowly, cautiously, she tried the door knob. Through a narrow parting, she saw what at first made her want to laugh. But at once a cold pang of understanding passed through her. They were operating a ouija board—she recalled talk of such things in Thrace of late—and Sophie, Sophie Welland, was taking the experiment seriously! And Carla—the unscrupulous little wretch—it was unbelievable! Carla was getting the messages. Ruth opened the door wide and stood within the room.

"What on earth are you two doing?" she demanded, a bravado unsteady over her qualm.

Sophie stood up, tall and seeming to flow upward, her dark hair all about the white of her loose robe. Ruth shrank away from the brilliance of her eyes; a tremor governed her central being.

"Put it away, Carla," Sophie said. Her voice was distant, but pure, without anger. "Nobody invited you in here, Ruth."

Ruth burst into thin laughter; perhaps the Welland roof was tumbling over their heads. "You don't really believe in—in that, do you, Sophie?" Her voice broke in a brittle way. She looked at Carla, but Carla only returned her gaze with a faint smile curving out from beneath her heavy lids, and moved to put the board away.

Sophie sat down before her mirror and began to brush

her long, blue-black hair. And Ruth, catching a gleam of her eyes in the glass, felt a narrow thrill of pure horror course down her spine. A cry came from the boy's cot in the other room, and Ruth hurried away, closing the door behind her.

Time passed, a shaking period through Ruth in the night. And under her fear ran a perverse amusement. Matthew Welland held that ouija board operating and like practices were a consorting with devils and an abomination in the sight of the Lord. How droll that something so odious to Matt should be going on in secret under his own roof!

In bed with the child, Helen, beside her, Ruth lay pondering what had occurred, and puzzling chiefly over Carla's part in it. But again came the fear for Sophie, blurred and difficult of discernment, a wraith moving down the shadowed aisles of sleep.

§ 2

The white scythe of winter swept across the earth and cut its final harvest of death. After the blizzard not even a dried stalk was left standing in the garden, nor a leaf clinging to the flailed trees. Tom and Dave shoveled a path from the front porch to the sidewalk and around again to the door of the shop, so that Ruth, looking out from the living room window, thought that it looked like a worm's cradle in a white nut.

But it warmed her to reflect that despite the severe weather, Andrew Milbank had continued coming to church, looking unattentive to all that was there of sermon and singing, but kindling to a deep eagerness in his few words with her in the entry afterwards.

Shortly before Christmas, a niggardly thaw set in, and the snow was shabby and pitted with chimney soot on the Welland lawn. Ruth came out of the house early one morning with Jared and Carla, who were leaving for Redlands. She had a purchase to make in Andrew Milbank's store, and thought of the coming encounter filled her with a small panic.

Jared, Carla and Ruth paused for a moment on the walk, while David, who was shoveling the blackened snow away to one side of the lawn, spoke to them. "Ha!" Dave said, laughing as he rested on his shovel. "The blot on my escutcheon, folks!"

"What do you mean, Dave?" Carla called back to him, the others moving on.

David's laughter followed Ruth. It seemed a free laughter of boyish enjoyment. His jokes had always been obscure to her, involved in words.

Carla and Jared went their own way, Ruth contemplating their fine, arresting appearance together. But quickly they had passed from mind, for there was the shoe store on the corner, wearing its jaunty holiday air with its two small Christmas trees flanking the entrance, and its large red-ribboned wreaths hanging in the windows. "Merry Christmas" in red and green lights flashed on and off above the door. She hesitated a moment, thinking to go elsewhere for her shoes. But now Andrew had seen her from within, and was coming eagerly forward to open the door for her.

"Good morning, Mrs. Proles!" he said, and she warmed toward him as she noticed that he stumbled a little on the name. "It's getting milder, isn't it? Maybe we'll have a nice Christmas, after all."

"Yes, it's nice to-day," Ruth said, loosening her coat. She looked in at a show case that faced the front of the store.

"Something in shoes for the children?" Andrew inquired. Ruth felt irritated. Couldn't it possibly occur to him that she might once in a while need something for herself?

"No," she said sharply. "I want some oxfords. Black, please."

Andrew's face became suffused. But recovering himself he led her to a bench and drew up the foot support and seated himself to take her measurement. He unlaced her shoe and drew it gently off. Ruth looked critically at her stocking. As his fingers lightly encountered first her heel then the point of her toe, Ruth felt a wave of sensation rise through the back of her knee and up over her body. While Andrew was away making his selection, she let herself sink back against the bench, and the suspended breath rushed up out of her tightened lungs. Then he was back again with two shoe boxes under his arm, and he was fitting a sober black shoe on Ruth's foot.

"Now, that's neat, Mrs. Proles," he said with authority, quite at his ease again in the familiar phraseology of his trade. "But"—and he opened the other box and drew out a brown shoe of alligator skin—"here is something very new and much smarter. That's the shoe I—I'd like to see on your foot."

Ruth knew that she was blushing. It was a blush of pleasure in the discovery that a man was once more interested in what she wore. But it was more than that, too. It was pleasure in the warm brown eyes of Andrew Milbank as he looked up at her in an appeal that had nothing to do with a pair of shoes.

The brown shoe was tried on; it fitted perfectly. "I've been wearing black, you know," Ruth faltered. "But —these are awfully nice. How much are they?"

"Seven eighty-five," Andrew said promptly. "Cut down from ten-fifty for the holiday sale. There isn't a better pair of shoes made. You'll get more wear out of these and more comfort than out of two pair of those."

"I'll take them," Ruth said hurriedly. In another moment she would have reverted to the conservative black. As it was, she had certain misgivings, since the brown cost more and would necessitate a brightening of her entire costume. But she enjoyed a feeling of having been bullied into her choice by Andrew, of having been swept out of herself if even for a moment.

He escorted her to the door, opened it for her and gave her her parcel. "Will you be at the Christmas program at church, Mrs. Proles?" he said, in a voice that she judged to be lower than ordinary.

"Oh, yes," Ruth said. "Helen and Norris are going to recite."

"Oh!" Then his eyes brightened. "I might help you

home with them afterwards, perhaps. Children always get so tired at those things, don't they?"

"Why"—Ruth felt a deep tremor—"that would be awfully nice of you, if it wouldn't be boring for you."

"Boring!" He laughed. "You know I'm just crazy about those kids. I'd—if you'd let me—I'd like to come and call for you—all."

He added that "all" in a way that gave her a rush of feeling. Oh, he was so kindly, and so sensitive, too. But behind these externals of his character there was a strong voice that woke the sleeping life within her. She permitted her eyes to rest in his for a moment that was just perceptibly long, then her gaze fell to the parcel in her hand. No, it was best that he did not call, because the family would all be going down together, and the others would help her with the children. He was faintly disappointed, but he smiled at her hopefully enough as she said good-by.

On the street, the street that had become full of a lifting light in the gray squalor of the snow, Mrs. Peebles met her. Mrs. Peebles, with her forward-peering eyes, as though in the offing she could see a profitable death. . . . "Have you heard, Ruth! Just imagine! That little minx Dorie Mayhew . . . ran away with the telegraph operator at the depot last night! Yes, sir, eloped! And him such a nice young fellow, too, you wouldn't think . . . That will show Paget just what she was, won't it! He was well quit of her, I'll say. . . ."

Ruth passed on, dim in thought of Paget and Dorie, of herself and Andrew Milbank. Dorie, gone forever from

Paget, now. Poor little Dorie, desperate from living and waiting in Thrace. Mrs. Peebles and her kind, damn them, damn them into eternity!

After supper that evening, Carla sat in the dining room reading Latin poetry. Paget was also in the room, mending his leather belt with needle and heavy black thread. Ruth had offered to do it for him, but he had waved her sullenly away. She wondered that he wore that old belt still, which he must have had for years, and when Paget broke the needle and got up to look for another, she picked up the belt and saw that engraved on the inside of the silver buckle were the words "To P. W. from D. M. 1924." Carla said softly, "Have you heard about Dorie Mayhew, Ruth?" Ruth nodded, her eyes blurred. And Carla said, "Paget knows, too." Ruth dropped the belt hastily as she heard Paget returning from their mother's room upstairs. When he seated himself again to his task, she looked up at him narrowly over the edge of the *Thrace Advocate* and was appalled at the hollowness of his face. Paget was—how old? A year younger than herself. Twenty-seven. He might be taken for ten years more than that.

§ 3

On the last morning before Carla's Christmas vacation began, the household was astir early. Tom and Dave had an uncommonly large amount of work to do in the way of Christmas window cards for the stores, and last-minute invitations, and Matt was printing, free of charge as was his wont, the announcements of the Ladies' Aid sale of cooking for the benefit of the church.

Tom had bolted his breakfast and asked to be excused so that he could get over to the shop, when Carla looked up at him over her coffee cup. Her concern was not really with Tom, or any mortal being this morning. It was with the dog, Lulu, Dave having carried her, sick and trembling, to the warmth of his room back of the shop, where he could look after her during the day while Carla was absent.

When Carla spoke to Tom, it was only from the distance of her anxiety about Lulu, with no malice in the words.

" 'Go speed the stars of thought, Tom,' " she said.

Tom, half way to the door, wheeled back upon her. His face twisted with wrath, his black hair tumbling down over his forehead in an angry mass. His fingers spread, closed and spread again at his sides as he stood there laboring in inexpressible fury. When his voice finally came it was high as an hysterical child's.

"I've had enough of that stuff from you, you puppy! You go mind your own business and quote your poetry where they'll understand it."

The hall door shut to in a lively way behind him. Matt pushed his glasses up above his brows, and looked at Carla in puzzled consternation.

"What's this? What's all this?" he asked. "Dear me— dear me! What in the world did you say to upset Tom so, Lottie? You mustn't be impertinent with him. He's working very hard these days, poor boy."

Carla passed her cup to Sophie for more coffee. "I was only wishing him luck, father," she murmured. "He seemed to misunderstand me."

"I guess he understood you, all right," Jenny said with a thin laugh from her exclusive place beside her father.

But Carla was already away from the narrowness of the moment, resolving to run over to the shop for a visit with Lulu before she left for Redlands with Jared.

Through the window she could see Jared coming across the lane to call for her. Carla veiled her eyes quickly in the excitement of her feeling for him, which was confusing and sweet and familiar over long years of growing, but which held in its center a resistance, a dread. Ruth, too, had seen him coming, rapidly, against the cold.

"There's Jared," Ruth said. "Is there a cup of coffee for him, Sophie?"

"By all means," Matt said heartily. "There must be a cup of coffee for Jared. There's a fine, upstanding lad for you. And one who'll go far, I'll wager. Ah—"

There was a knock at the kitchen door, and Matt himself sprang up to let Jared in. Jared entered the dining room, his hat in his hand, and said good morning to everybody, took a clean handkerchief from his pocket and turned slightly away as he delicately blew his nose. Sophie poured him a cup of coffee.

"Well, Jared," Matt said warmly, "looking forward to a pleasant respite from your labors, I presume? I guess a vacation means more to you than to most of the young people going over to Redlands, eh? You must be pretty tired when you come home from the restaurant at night. Your mother was telling me that sometimes you lie awake all night just too tired to sleep. That's a shame, Jared, a shame!"

Jared muttered into his cup. When he set it down again upon the saucer, Carla saw that his hand was trembling. "Oh, mother worries unnecessarily about me, Mr. Welland," he said finally. "A cashier in George's hasn't much to do at night."

"That's like you, Jared," Matt replied approvingly. "Belittling your difficulties. I wish we had more young fellows like you these days. I remember when I was young, and life wasn't as easy as it is now, we used to pride ourselves upon not murmuring when things were hard. But now—the young people expect everything in return for nothing. But mark my words—trials like yours build character!"

Carla thought of Jared seated at the cashier's desk in George's Restaurant, at eleven o'clock, when the motion pictures next door were over, and the smart younger set of Thrace began thronging in, girls and boys, to loaf about the tables and sing and laugh and cheerfully play the fool, until past midnight. It was not until after this crowd had left that Jared could go home to study. Carla was moved by compassion for him, and by irritation at her father's assumption of a value in his difficulties. But her feeling swept at once into a desire to be away, to be with Lulu, with Dave, anywhere but here.

"I have time to run in and look at Lulu, Jared," Carla said. "She's sick, poor darling. Dave's taking care of her in the shop. You drink your coffee and I'll meet you outside."

Jared said: "Would you mind if Carla came skating with me, to-night, Mr. Welland? It's my night off duty."

Matt beamed, waving his hand. "Go and enjoy yourselves, by all means."

Once out of the door, Carla had a sensation of escape. There was a weaving about her, in the Welland house, of things out of the past, weaving in the present, and reaching out for the future, herself caught in the design. She shut Jared out from her thinking, and went to Dave in the shop.

David had placed the dog on an old quilt beside the iron stove. The stove's cheeks were red from the coal fire within. Lulu's tail wagged feebly as Carla, seating herself on the floor, gathered her close. David sat in his old chair, looking on, his head bent.

"She'll get better, won't she, Dave?" Carla said, veering away from her quick-coming fear for Lulu, denying the voices of change in all living. "It's just a little cold, don't you think, Dave?"

"I guess so, kid," David said, reaching out to feel Lulu's ribs. "She's a strong old girl. We'll try to pull you through, eh, Lulu, old lady?"

"She's going on thirteen. I can remember so well when you brought her to me, Dave. You were such a *round* puppy, Lulu!"

Carla's eyes widened stiffly upon the window opposite, where she could see the snow deep and shining on the lawn in the sun, after the ice storm of the night. Perhaps

—perhaps Lulu would frisk and plume her tail no more in the snows of any winter, nor sense with her soft lifted muzzle the first faint hovering of spring. Tears welled hot and dazzling in Carla's eyes, trembled over her lids, and then welled again, as though they were the same tears running up from her very heart, making the space of her body all one unbearable ache.

"Don't take on like that, Carla," Dave said gently. "We'll bring her around all right. Listen—I want to tell you about Tom."

But David's voice was insecure. Out there, under the old crab-apple tree, a tree of dark glass, now, Lulu would lie deep in the grave David would make for her. When you threw apples for her to retrieve, she used always to bring them back delicately, not caring to bite into them.

"Tom is thinking of going away again," Dave continued. "He mentioned Detroit as soon as he came in this morning." He slapped the back of one hand nervously against the palm of the other. "That's Tom, though. He'll probably always be like that."

David was talking now as though to himself. Tom was going away again, he had said. Carla tried to examine the thought, to know whether she was sorry or glad. There was a wink of shadow as an icicle fell past the window from the eaves.

She was gone from David again, with Jared to Redlands, the day passing heavily in its presentiment of the impermanence of beloved things. At home again in the evening, and Carla found Lulu unchanged, David there giving her medicine, talking to her, reassuring her. After

David's urging, Carla went reluctantly to skate with Jared on the river where it flowed westward of town, but thought constantly of Lulu, until Jared became angry and they had words that grew into resentful silences in the icy moonlight.

On their way home Jared, almost as though he sought jealously for a grievance, brought up a subject that was infinitely boring to Carla. "You told your folks that you were staying with that girl in Redlands to study for exams the other night," he accused. "I found out to-day that you stayed with Jane Rhodes because she was giving a party. Pretty shabby, I think!"

Carla set her teeth.

"Jane Rhodes smokes," Jared persisted, "and I heard they served cocktails there. And the way that crowd dances is—is disgusting!"

They were walking through tall silvered trees, away from the river. Carla turned on him and beat her fists against his breast. "Will you shut up!" she panted at him. "The party bored me sick, but you bore me to death, Jared Gale!"

Then, flashing her skates away from his shoulder, she was apart from him, staring at him in a fascination of rage, the thought of how it had been to beat at him so, his body tight and resistant under her fists, overtaking her fearfully. Carla turned and ran through the woods, over familiar ways in the moonlight, not looking back. The town came close, streets opened up to her, and she walked with a sure and steady tread in the way that Jared would not follow.

A vacant lot lay before her now, and beyond it stood the Greenleaf house, where the coal dealer's widow lived. The house cast a patch of shadow over its rear garden, the moonlight rimming it in a live way. Carla cut across the vacant lot. A man was coming down the back steps of Adeline Greenleaf's house. Carla fell back, letting him swing out ahead of her. A little later, walking behind him, she saw by a street light that it was David. Darkness again, and as she looked blindly up at the sky the naked antlers of a tree stood against the moon.

She was home again, David having gone ahead, unknowingly, all the way. He turned first in toward the shop but Carla had no wish to follow him now. She entered the house and found the family gathered about in the warmth. Her father, resting on the couch in the living room while Jenny read to him, greeted her in a voice of contented weariness. Paget and Tom were drinking hot milk and munching cookies in the dining room, Ruth seated near with a book. Her mother rose at once and laid aside her needlework.

"Let me get you some hot milk, child," she said. "And sit over here by the register so you'll get the chill out of you. You look frost-bitten."

"Thanks, mother," Carla said. "I can get the milk myself, though."

"It's little enough I can do for you, my dear," her mother replied. Carla looked after her, and beneath the heavy upper folds of her mind where the knowledge of Dave lay hidden, there passed a wonder at the silent, brown woman who was her mother.

The hot milk brought, Carla rose to go to the kitchen. She returned with some soda biscuits, which she proceeded to crumble and drop into her glass. From the other room came the sound of Jenny reading, reading, from some book on pioneer life in the West, the pages sharply flicked. Jenny's hands had become marvelously deft and active, all of her activity going out through them now. Carla felt the need to seize upon something immediate, away from David.

"You should eat crackers, Tom," she suggested, as she stirred the pulpy mass with her spoon. "They would inspire you to bigger and better linotyping."

Tom said nothing. His face seemed to shut tight.

"Oh, lay off Tom," Paget said. "Let's see what you will do with your chances before you talk. You'll probably wind up by marrying Jared Gale and have half a dozen kids. I wouldn't be so lofty, if I were you."

Tom ate a cookie with a good deal of noise, and Jenny, from her chair close by the dining room doorway, remarked upon it. At once Tom took another and crunched it with even greater determination.

"Marry Jared?" Carla mused. "Marriage with Jared would be awfully permanent."

"You'll never marry Jared Gale if I can help it," Tom burst out. "You aren't worthy of his little finger. I'd like to see you working in a restaurant at night and going to college in the daytime. I would!"

Carla's eyes widened and then closed as though she had been struck. "I know what you mean, Tom," she said steadily. "And you remember I told you last fall that if you wanted to go into divinity I'd be glad to give up college so you could have your chance. And you just sneered at me and said I was making a noble gesture so I could congratulate myself. I never said anything about it to anybody. But I'll stop going to Redlands right now so you can start in. It isn't too late—is it, Paget? Tom is only twenty-three. He can begin after New Year's. I—I can get along with what I have already."

Tom pushed back his chair and rose distractedly. "Oh, cut it!" he cried angrily. "You know darn well I didn't mean that!" He paused for a moment as though he were going to say more, but then Matt stood in the doorway with a look of puzzled dismay, his hand lifted for peace. Tom, grimacing bitterly, turned and swung from the room. They could hear him stamp upstairs to his bedroom, where he closed the door with a great noise.

Now Sophie came down from her room, and stood like a dark wraith in the hall doorway. She had on a loose-sleeved black silk kimono, and her arms moved agitatedly in the sleeves. "I can't stand this racket!" she said.

Then, abruptly, as though she had abandoned all thought of the family, Sophie turned away, and her soft footfall could be heard again on the stairs. A great pity went out from Carla toward her. It came to her mind how her father had explained to people that it was his wish to have Sophie remain at home for a much-needed rest this year. Whatever misfortune came, he was always able to meet it by refusing to recognize it for what it was. The benign will of God was behind every seeming catastrophe. The only inconsistency, Carla thought, in his humble acceptance of the Lord's designs, was his habit of apologizing for them to his fellow men.

Paget had been talking, not looking to the questioning on his father's face. "You're wasting sympathy on Tom, Carla," he said wearily. "He doesn't know what he wants, and never will. The ministry would disappoint him as much as everything else he's tried. All that appeals to him are his unattainable dreams—and he isn't quite sure what they are."

Carla looked at her father standing in the doorway, his glasses pushed up on his brow, his hair a little disheveled. There was a timid light on his face that hurt something within her which had never been touched before. She could foresee a day when he would be out of touch with all reality, when his strength would lie in his appeal to their pity. In him was finality. And that finality of all life was reaching out, inexorably, to gather them all in. David —slinking down out of Adeline Greenleaf's back door— Carla's mind cowered away, sick from the image. And after David's course was run, he would be gathered in. One after the other, they would all be concluded in oblivion, and they would be standing as their father stood, uncertain with happy wonder, with piteous surmise.

"Paget"—Matt reached out a hand eagerly, uncertainly —"does Tom want to be a preacher? I never guessed, Paget. We can manage it, can't we? We must ask David."

"Yes," Paget said, his voice dulled now, his interest going. "Tom has toyed with ideas, too." He got up, as though the room had suddenly become irksome to him. "But it would make your hair stand on end to hear him preach—if he were to preach. So for your peace of mind you had better not urge him to enter the ministry, father. He's really in sympathy with Christ—not with churches."

At first Matt frowned, then his brow cleared as he removed his glasses and polished them. "You enjoy paradoxes, my boy," he smiled indulgently. "Paradoxes, eh, Paget?" His voice became increasingly gentle as he went on, his eyes grown absent, away on some vision, some blessed thought. "And now, let us all to bed! We have a hard day to-morrow. Mother, Lottie, Ruth!"

"I've got to look in on Lulu first, father," Carla said.

There was the sound of the back door opening, and David stepped in. He beckoned to Carla, but an oppressive heat had come all over her, making her powerless to move. She could not go to David. Even over the sudden knowledge of Lulu's death spread the knowledge of David's shame. He stood by the table, looking down at her.

"Lulu is dead, Carla," he said.

Carla rose. She could not speak, but moved quickly into the kitchen, to the door. She felt, rather than heard, Dave following her.

Over her shoulder she said, forcing out the words, "I'll go alone."

§ 4

Ruth had watched the Christmas season come and go, her heart building its dream of Andrew Milbank. She had watched the tightening of winter, a white vise on the earth, and then its sudden breaking. Now, late in March, there was a false renewal of that bondage of the cold. It was, for all the bitterness of the day, another Sunday morning in the Welland house, and although Ruth prepared for church with the others, her mind ran ahead in excitement to the evening, when Andrew would come to her here, for all to see. The stir and activity in the house was separate from her own inner activity, so that when her mother asked her to go in to see whether Sophie needed anything, Sophie ill in her bed with a cold, the request seemed almost strange to her.

Ruth lingered for a while in the room, attentive to Sophie's sleeping, glancing at her now and then in apprehensiveness. From time to time she would look out of the windows upon the low scudding gray clouds in the west with their baleful white under edges lashing up from the horizon. But the sinister under-glare of those snow clouds could not destroy the warmth of her mood.

Only last night had Andrew escorted her home to her door, from the supper party after Elmira Beckman's wedding. They had talked closely on the way, Andrew telling of his invalid sister for whose sake he had remained unmarried, and of her death a few years past. They had come suddenly close in understanding, and then, the Welland house drawing near in the darkness, a silence had fallen between them. But Andrew had held her hands for a long moment, and she had consented with a towering of her courage to his calling on her in her father's house.

To-day he had telephoned and Ruth had talked low to him, although Matt Welland was not within hearing.

Through those moments she could feel Jenny listening through the open door of the living room, and knew that Jenny's paint brush would be poised in resentful wonder. But turning away, she had not so much as deigned to glance at Jenny. She kept her anticipation proudly away from the family, as being none of their affair, and all thought of Matt she shut resolutely from mind.

Ruth was suddenly eager to be quit of this room, Sophie's and Carla's, that breathed hostility toward her. She looked at the locked door to her own room, locked always now on Sophie's side, and felt her skin rippling again with a return of dread.

A crumpled piece of paper lay on the floor beneath a chair. Upon it Ruth found Carla's small, difficult handwriting, a thing to puzzle over. "Aristotle—founder of scientific logic. Logic—the science of correct thinking. Epicurean—happy. Epicurus much maligned. Stoics—school founded by Zeno, about 300 B.C. at Athens. Descartes—Meditation III—argues to prove the existence of God. . . ." Ruth knit her brows, her lips forming to whistle. "Berkeley—Kant—Jared says I must beware of false prophets. But I shall find out for myself. To-day I have read this, *'For all reasons I should prefer to think that in mysticism the needs of sex, together with all other needs, are understood and satisfied; that all the hundred voices of human desire are here brought to unison.'*"

Argues to prove the existence of God! A fortunate thing that it was she, Ruth, and not Carla's father, who had picked up this scrap of paper. It was access to this very kind of thought that Matt Welland feared in education.

Ruth had no conception of the meaning of the notes, but it was clear that Carla would not stop at the limits of the college curriculum in her search for knowledge. She would not have a moment's hesitation in striding over Matt's prejudices to satisfy the hunger of her mind. While Ruth stood tearing the paper into small pieces, the image of her father came before her, grown small and pathetic and fantastic in his religious and moral zeal, while Carla seemed to soar above him, spacious and free as the Greek goddesses whom Ruth dimly knew. And the line about sex, too. Ruth turned guiltily toward Sophie, but Sophie was sound asleep, and her face wore a look of extraordinary serenity, not unlike Carla's own.

The hours passed over Ruth and her being projected itself to Andrew's coming.

The Sunday afternoon came, the evening nearly at hand. Ruth sat with the family in the living room, listening to the hymns Sophie was playing on the piano in the parlor. A while ago, Sophie had risen and drifted downstairs, against the anxious protests of her mother. While she played, Carla sang the old songs that their father loved, and Ruth, hearing her sisters, saw the design of their withdrawal from the family. Sophie had no heart in her music; it was away elsewhere, so that sometimes the words were wrong, or the notes faltered. Carla, who had never given evidence of really being present, sang only for the love of singing, taking no account of the matter of the song. Ruth listened in increasing uneasiness for Sophie, feeling horror at her father's contentment, his look of blessedness with his family about him.

When they had ended a song, David's wife spoke, with a lightly deprecating laugh. "I met Mrs. Peebles on the street yesterday," she said. "She said she thought Sophie looked awfully poorly. She thought she looked *haunted*, she said. I never heard anything so silly!"

"Mrs. Peebles should be told to go to hell," David said softly.

Matt regarded his eldest son with a pained look, and Seena squirmed, her smile squirming, too.

"Out of respect to your mother and the girls, David," Matt said, slowly measuring his words, "I wish you wouldn't use such language in the house, even though you cannot do without it elsewhere."

"There, there, father," Jenny soothed. "David means nothing by it. It's just an outlet for his nerves, poor dear. He has so much to contend with, you know. He's not big and strong and healthy like the rest of us, and he hasn't a comfortable home with three lovely children or anything. Poor David, his lot is a hard one!"

The acid sweetness of Jenny's voice seared the air. Ruth perceived, however, that Matt was in some way placated by it. In time, Jenny becoming more and more intolerably and intolerantly sweet, Matt would grow into senility, the fatuous, happily maudlin slave of Jenny.

In the parlor Sophie was closing the piano. The brushing quality of her voice, speaking to Carla, moved along the air. Sophie's voice, too, was becoming attenuated to a dream substance, or was it so only in Ruth's fancy, her own mind bemused by shadows? Her thinking fled to

Andrew Milbank, and saw him, strong with health and life-power, taking her close and away from all this.

She found herself presently apart again, behind her locked door, where she sat down boldly with some sewing and thought of all the monotonous Sundays she had lived through in her father's house. Even the Sunday papers were put conscientiously away until Monday. In Andrew Milbank's house there would be no such harsh observance of outworn religious customs. Living would be easy and happy, and the hereafter, whatever it was, would take care of itself. Her eyes dreamed out over the cold roofs of houses, where thin flounces of snow slid and whirled bitterly in the wind, out to the icy gleam of the sky. Somewhere out there Paget was walking in the woods, crushing his heart down into the snow under his feet, in the silence of the trees. Behind the locked door of the room across the hall, Tom was brooding, probably, over the insoluble mystery of himself, doubting and hoping and doubting as to what would come of his next venture into the world outside. In the room next to Ruth's, Sophie was moving vaguely about, the door locked between. Locked doors, locked doors! Sharply exclaiming her impatience, Ruth threw her sewing down and went to stand beside the window, looking out over the back-yard.

There was Jared Gale crossing the lane from his own home. How red his cheeks were in the stinging light! As red as the scarf his doting mother had probably tucked so snugly about his throat. He was coming to see Tom, and Carla, Matt Welland having put upon him his long approval.

The afternoon folded down into evening, Ruth waiting. Waiting through the early supper, through the church period. She was glad that Andrew was not at the evening service, for the morning in church had been difficult with Andrew a great distance from her and so many searching eyes between.

At home again, she was in her room alone, the blue-flowered silk dress which Andrew had admired fresh about her. Her hair was done in a soft way, a wetted comb run through it to make it curl. In the mirror she saw her color deep and clear in the small petal-shape of her face. There were new distances in her eyes, and when she closed her lids she seemed to see down long bright distances of her own heart.

The evening came and went like a dream in which she appeared naked on the street. Matt Welland assumed that Andrew had called on the family, shutting his eyes blandly to the sudden livened beauty of Ruth with her softly done hair and her soft dress. He seated himself with Andrew in a corner of the living room, and discussed local politics, business, the prospect of an early spring, and the profound benefits of prohibition. After an hour or so, Ruth, as from a great distance, heard him ask her mother to make coffee. Coffee, sandwiches, and cake were brought in, and afterwards Matt invited Andrew into the parlor to hear Sophie play. Here the others joined in the courteous entertaining of Andrew, and Ruth sat smiling tensely near the hall door, as far as possible away from him.

When Andrew rose at last, he threw a glance of consternation toward Ruth. She smiled at him with a quick drawing together of her brows. Then, darting into the hall, and making sure that no one saw her, she snatched down from its hook the muffler he had hung above his coat, and slipped it under the cover of the hall chest. Andrew, putting on his things, did not seem to notice the absence of his scarf. Matt saw him right to the door, and it was only over her father's shoulder that Ruth caught a glimpse of Andrew's harassed face. But the moment he had gone, when Matt had returned to the living room and was removing his shoes to get into his slippers, Ruth caught the muffler up from its hiding place and called out casually that Mr. Milbank had left his scarf behind. She tossed her coat about her shoulders and was out of the house before anyone could reply.

Andrew was already swallowed up by the flurried darkness when she overtook him. They stood together in the concealment of the snow, perhaps for a brief interval only, perhaps for a golden æon flung into the interval. Ruth did not know, in the swift courage of his arms about her, in the swiftness of his question. She could not answer now. To-morrow, yes. She was away from him again, running home. The warmth of him surged through her, the cold of the night flying off like arrows that did not touch her.

Matt kept Ruth up and talked with her a long time, after the others had gone to bed. He talked solemnly, with a grandeur of sorrow. But he was gentle, too, kindly and understanding. And in the end he said that if Ruth decided, against his wise counsel, to marry Andrew Milbank, she must make a clean breast of her story about the burning of her house. It was curious, she thought dully, seated with her hands inert in her lap, that Matt could so conveniently juggle with ghosts, laying them or resurrecting them as he saw fit. As in a dream, she heard Matt say that if she was not strong enough to tell the truth, he would be obliged to tell it for her. An honest man like Andrew Milbank must not have his honesty betrayed. And, he pointed out, with hesitant sadness, it were not fantastic to suppose that Andrew would draw his own conclusions as to what had happened to that unfortunate man, Clinton Proles.

Ruth heard herself scream her defiance, knew that she was standing in the middle of the room, her hands pressed close to the shrilling in her head. And then, in the doorway to the hall, she saw David stand suddenly, his hat in his hand, his overcoat on. She recalled with a part of her mind that she had heard the outer door open. It must have opened to let Dave in.

Matt gestured faintly with his hand. "Leave us alone, leave us alone, David," he said wearily.

Dave's eyes went to Ruth, a sharp, long look.

"What's happened now?" Ruth heard him ask.

Her father's voice came up from a depth of weariness, with great care in the words. "We will not discuss it, David," he said. "Ruth will see the wisdom of my advice to-morrow, when she is herself again."

"She wants to marry Andrew Milbank, I suppose?"

Their words ran across Ruth's hearing, seeming to echo and reëcho.

"It is strange that you should know so much, David," Matt said softly, "when I knew so little. But we will not talk of it."

There was about David then an insupportable look, a look of electric and destructive aliveness. A word moved stealthily in Ruth's mind, a word light and purposeful. Murder. The feeling from David was murder. Everything was coming together, knotting softly, in a soft, purposeful web of death. Then David passed from the room.

Sometime, after an age of night seemed to have moved over her head, Ruth lay pressed against the door between her own room and Sophie's and Carla's. It seemed only natural that she should lie here, since this, too, was part of the madness that possessed the house, the world, the storm-mad sky. Wind and harsh snow clamored at the windows, and in the room next to hers Carla was talking audibly enough for her to discern the words.

"You see, Sophie . . . Bert is there. He tells you to be happy. . . . He will wait for you, till time and times are done."

Ruth began to laugh soundlessly, and laughing, she crawled on her hands and knees to her bed, where she knelt, her face buried hot and wet against the piece-quilt, and prayed that she might become the mistress of Andrew Milbank.

§5

Spring came, through feathery last flurries of snow, drowning, rich rains and the murmurous sway of winds in trees spiked with buds. On the wooded uplands where

253

Ruth walked sometimes with Carla and Jared, or of a rare Sunday with Dave, there was a sense of the upward surge and break of the earth out of darkness, a sound, almost, startling to awareness the somber trees, the stilled and waiting underbrush, the narrow rills that hurried as though in fear, running amber over old leaves with shoals of ivory where dead grasses were. Presently there was a mist of green under the sky, shimmering to the paler mist under the depths of the trees, where the tiny lights of wood violets burned, and anemones frail as rain.

Letters come to the family from Tom in the city of his new dream. Matt Welland read them aloud, his contentment and his pride growing. Tom wrote of Brant Hixby, the ordained preacher, who was organizing a mission for workmen, to the cause of which Tom had pledged himself. Tom's remuneration in the office of secretary would be very small, he wrote, but the work would be inspiring. Ruth saw the pleasure in her father's face, and smiled ironically, knowing that David had had other letters from Tom.

To Dave Tom wrote that Hixby had developed radical notions of his own as to the purpose of religion in the world. His mission would be a sort of study club, a refuge for the minds of the workmen as well as for their souls. Those letters sounded a violently socialistic note, Dave said, reading them privately to Ruth and Carla, or Paget. In them he spoke also of a certain John Kingswood, glowing accounts of him filling the letters. "John," he wrote, "is great. He comes from out west, where his father had a

large ranch until he lost his money in some wild specula-
tion. John took a year out of college when he was nineteen
to have a look in at the war—then when the scrap was
over he came back and finished. He's that sort of a fellow.
He goes after what he wants. But the war gave him some
queer ideas on society in general. He couldn't stand the
ordinary routine of existence after that, so he began
knocking about the country, working in mines and mills
and docks and factories and God knows what. It has given
him a fine perspective on the working man, and now,
when he isn't at work in the factory he spends his waking
hours writing articles on labor, and he has no trouble in
selling his stuff. He has a brain like a dynamo. He says
that one of these days he's going to write a play, and there
won't be any parlor furniture in it."

Ruth heard David read Tom's letters, but since the
vivid part of her living was now outside the family, they
meant little to her. Of Carla and Sophie she took no further note, save now and then when she smiled at the
sound of Carla's pitying deception of Sophie, murmured
beyond the locked door of their room. With indifference
she learned that Carla was writing, late into many nights
of spring, poems which she sent to Tom, and which he,
in turn, gave to the man Kingswood. Carla had a look of
transport about her these days, and it became known that
Kingswood had sold some of her verses to an editor he
knew. But captive words were purposeless to Ruth now,
in the awareness of the swinging journeys of her heart,
in her waiting for a discreet time to pass so that Matt's
vigilance over her might end.

In her urgent feeling for Andrew she felt little regret at the necessity to deceive him. He had believed her, when, at a brief meeting in the store, she had told him that her father objected to her marrying so soon again, and that it was best that for a time they keep apart. In bewildered disappointment, Andrew contented himself to wait, and then, swiftly, before her caution overtook her she had murmured that one day soon she would come to him, wherever he would be, their meeting a secret between them.

With the coming of April, Ruth guarded her outer being with rigid care, and saw that Matt's concern for her was falling away into a confidence that all was well. Then, on a day that made its stir softly and irresistibly in the blood, a day of bloom on sky and earth, Ruth made it known to Andrew that she would meet him in the evening, at an appointed place on the wood road east of town, Andrew to have his car there.

On this morning of her anticipation, a Saturday, Ruth, Carla and Sophie, were cleaning the attic above the old part of the house.

Sophie had washed the small dormer windows and had begun to hang up crisp polka-dot curtains. Ruth and Carla had opened up an old trunk and were laughing and crying over the shabby ghosts of the past that rose up out of them, when Sophie came over from the window. They found old lace hats, bulky corsets with yellowed laces and rusty stays peeping through, valentines that fell to powder when they were touched, post cards from girls who had married and gone away, sulky-looking baby bibs, and family photographs stonily still and solid as the whole mass of the past itself. Carla held up a picture of Sophie at the age of six, Sophie with a pained smile on her chubby face.

"What on earth was the matter, Sophe?" Carla laughed.

"Oh, that was the time she had a pin sticking her," Ruth remembered, and Sophie bent her head over the picture and smiled.

"Look at this!" Carla lifted out a wisp of a bird's nest, with the fragile blue shell of an egg in it. "Oh—I remember! That was the egg Paget brought home. I must have been only about five, then. He kept it warm in his hand, and put it under one of our setting hens. Don't you remember, Ruth? He found the mother bird dead—it was a robin. Somebody had stoned her, and Paget thought he could save one of the little birds. Poor Paget!"

Sophie carried the picture of herself to the window to look more closely at it. Ruth, on her hands and knees, washed the floor where the raftered ceiling angled down to it, while Carla continued chuckling over her discoveries in the trunk. Across the floor, Ruth could see Sophie also on her knees before the open dormer window; over the pane on the right hand side the curtain was already hung, and fluttering lightly in the sweet drawing-in of the wind.

Ruth stretched her body out to the darkness under the eaves, her scrubbing brush pressing down strongly under her hand, a feeling of litheness and health going through her. The evening would come quickly with activity filling the day.

When Ruth straightened and glanced toward Sophie again, she was not there. Ruth did not look at Carla, standing transfixed beside the trunk. She found herself in an instant beside the window without any consciousness of having moved; she found herself picking up the photograph of Sophie, of long ago; she heard to the heavily beating rhythm of her heart, the quick words of her mind. To-night she would not meet Andrew Milbank.

The curtain fluttered primly in the wind, like the short skirt of a little girl.

VIII : CARLOTTA

§ I

At the foot of the garden, where the earth was wet and dark, and the smell of it was a sweet bruise on the air, the irises stood blue and tall. Gallant and frail flags of irises, blue as Sophie's eyes had been blue! Carla stood and looked away from them against the hollow, windy, violet-colored morning where a flock of blackbirds skimmed the sky with the swift blades of their wings. Sophie's hair had had that swift and lovely gloss of a blackbird's wing, too. Three years of Sophie's being dead, or ten times three years, could not erase from mind the legend of her loveliness.

Carla walked aimlessly through the garden, brushing her hand lightly along the tiny yellow spurs of the forsythias, or stepping aside to avoid treading on a wild shooting-star, come so bravely to this ordered place. Life was here, at her hand, or under her foot, creating and re-creating again, storming up through the dark earth-spaces with its small lightnings of blue and yellow and green, and its faint murmur of bursting buds. This was the assurance she had come to know in a world of change and contradiction. Sophie, who had surrendered herself to the unknown which she peculiarly knew, lay deep beyond the reach of the larkspur's roots, or the fibrous underwebs of friendly grasses. Carla lifted her face and listened to the faint cadence of the wind through the poplars, and the sound of it entered her own heart and became the voice of the aloneness which she had come to know and would always know.

Twenty-one years of living had set her apart from those about her. She was remote from them. On this same wheeling earth she had lived with them, but her intimation was one only of great loneliness, and a simplicity within herself. She was apart from all. Somewhere, sometime, man had been cumbered with the burden of immortality and now his ways were complicated and full of unease.

Robins were freshening their breasts in the dewy grass, and on the white froth of a plum branch a bluejay shrieked in joy or anger. Under the arches of the orchard she could see Tom sealing with cement the scar in an old apple tree, and she thought of how he covered these days of his defeat with irrelevant activity. He had been home for some weeks now, the mission given over long since to nonfulfillment of hopes. His failure had been painfully clear, although he had been evasive about it. His father, however, would always be proud of having had a son whose health broke in the Lord's work. For Tom was hollow as a reed.

She remembered how he had come to her in the orchard on another morning, grave and soft as this, three years ago. He had been home then for Sophie's sake— Sophie dead. On a day after all was done and put by, he had found Carla here, and in his hand there had been a newspaper with a small notice of the death, in a Western city, of Bertram Seiffert—Bertram Seiffert who had long been listed as missing in the war. Tom had looked pale and shaken. "Only a day between Sophie's death and Bert's," he had said. "Coincidence," Carla had replied, very low. A kind of rapture had seized Carla. No one need ever know that Sophie had risen, tall and smiling, on her last living night and had spoken to Bert, one spirit speaking to another across the infinite reaches of darkness. Ah, how earnest Carla's deception had been! But all was smooth and still now, the mosaic of two lives lying bright and firm, pattern embracing pattern.

The sun came through the clouds for an instant and made a live path across the tops of trees and houses. The moment seemed vivid and true. The sky moved, and there was the violet half-light of low clouds again, and houses hushed under them, and the earth below, in its purpose.

Tom lifted his head to look at her as she came toward him. His face was pale, and narrow from cheek to cheek.

"What's on your mind this morning, Tom?" Carla asked.

"Must I always have something on my mind?" he said, irritated.

"Oh, all right," she replied. "I just thought you might have had some bad news in that letter you got this morning. You got out of the house as soon as you'd read it, and you've been down here ever since."

"I don't suppose I'll ever be old enough to keep my own affairs to myself when you're around."

Carla smiled and said, "Is it a girl, Tommy?"

He turned impatiently back to his work on the tree, then swung about toward her again. "No, damn it, it wasn't a girl! The letter was from John Kingswood. He's motoring up to the lakes to visit some friends of his, and he wants to stop in here on the way to see me."

"Well, what's wrong with that?"

"What's wrong? Can you see John Kingswood mixing with the Wellands?"

"Of course I don't know your friend John," Carla said.

"But you do know the Wellands. John has written a play—that's enough, isn't it?"

Carla tossed back her head in amusement. "I'd like to see it," she laughed.

"The play?" Tom said.

"No, Tommy. I'd just like to see a man who has written a play step into the Welland front door."

Tom frowned and turned again to his task. "You really don't give a damn, do you, what other people feel?"

"I do, Tommy," she said charitably. "Why not take him out to Paget's place?"

"For once you're helpful," Tom said, his brow clearing. "I hadn't thought of that. He'll be coming through in about a week."

Carla turned toward the house, dwelling upon Paget's inscrutable withdrawal from the common life of the family. Poor old Paget! The story of Dorie's death had come indirectly to them, a nurse having given it to Adeline Greenleaf, who had told it to David at a chance meeting—or so David had said. Dorie had been dying after the birth of her first child, and people were likely to say almost anything at such times. But certain it was that she had asked them to name her son after Paget Welland, her eyes wide open and not a gleam of sight in them. Soon afterwards she was dead, and the nurse had said that she had looked like a Madonna. Paget had said nothing. He had rented the Kepler place and had gone alone to live there and tend his vines—living, as Dave had said, with a ghost.

She hurried back to the house. Jared would be coming for her to take her out to Redlands. Her eyes closed heavily upon the image of Jared Gale—Jared always there, pulling at the resistant center of her being, demanding acknowledgment. That precious resistance within her was more than a withholding of herself; it was a guarding of all she knew of separate beauty. It was more than a struggle against Jared; it was a struggle against all the engulfing forces that had drawn the others under in their tide.

Jared was already there. He hailed her from the back porch.

"Hurry up, Carla, we'll be late!"

She halted, then sauntered slowly toward him. How delicious it would be to express one's fine contempt for times and places—to be late for everything, to snap one's fingers at circumstance!

They were on their way now, walking through the greenly quiet street that had known their coming and going for years.

"This morning was made for us, Carla," Jared said in a tone of assured contentment.

The inescapable verity of Jared Gale! Did he know that he had grown into her growing being where her ruthless will demanded fulfillment from him? She had known times in the past year or two when only a capricious pity for Jared had saved him from her; his helplessness before her own strong and adventuring will alone had curbed the violence within her. And Jared had never known! If he had guessed her possessiveness, he had guessed it only dimly, and she had found it in her heart almost to despise him for his stupidity. Should she ever loose her will upon him, she herself would be lost, lost in that wilderness of her difference from him.

"What a wonderful thing life is!" Jared exclaimed, squaring his shoulders and walking more briskly. "And what a wonderful world to live it in!"

"The world is as we find it," Carla said, after a pause. "Life is what we make it."

"Life gives us much that is not of our own making, too, Carla. The things I cherish most are those that have been given to me."

"For instance, Jared?"

He cleared his throat importantly. It was a habit she had recently noticed in him. "For instance—a wonderful mother. It's true I've made my own way at college, but the fact that I've been offered a position on the staff next fall was scarcely of my own doing. I have that to be grateful for. By the way, Carla, have you heard anything more about the library position?"

"Nothing new, but I know that it's there for me if I want it."

"You mean you may not want it?"

"I mean—I don't know what I want," Carla replied, her eyes straight before her.

"It would be good experience for you, and you don't want to teach," he suggested.

"I just couldn't teach school," she said.

In a terrible place in memory was the small, dry schoolroom where Sophie sat at her desk and wept, where Sophie moved slowly out of a cruel, small door, forever.

Jared took her arm in a brief pressure. "I know, Carla," he said softly. "I understand. Sometimes I think I know your thoughts better than you know them yourself."

"If you really did, Jared!"

"But I do. Haven't we grown up together—haven't we been like brother and sister for years? Who knows you better than I do, I'd like to know? Why—I can't imagine a day without you somewhere in it!"

Carla laughed lightly. "Jared, I believe you are on the point of proposing to me, right out here in broad daylight!"

"I never really thought of *proposing* to you. I've always counted you among the things—the precious things—that life has given me."

"Oh, there's the car, Jared!" she cried. She ran forward a step or two, waving a signal to the car.

That evening, supper over, Carla took the path that led toward the orchard, then turned instead across the grounds to the shop. David was already there, lighting a wood fire in the iron stove of the back room.

"It's pretty chilly in here, kid," he said. "I think you'll find it warmer outside."

She seated herself on a pile of old papers. "Is that by way of politely dismissing me, Dave?" she asked. "It's no colder here for me than it is for you. Besides, I like this place."

"And what you like you take, eh?" he retorted. "I don't blame you."

She thought of how she had accustomed herself to this new David, who lived his somber life apart from the family, and how the strangeness and revulsion from her knowledge of it had become somehow overlaid and fabulous in the growth of her understanding and acceptance.

Carla laced her fingers over her knees. "I'm going to take the job in the library for the summer, Dave," she said.

He kicked the stove door shut. "Going to settle down, eh? Just another Welland."

"Well, I can go on with my writing there, can't I?"

He turned on her harshly. "Writing? Hell! You can write from now till you're eighty and the whole lot of it won't be worth a damn, if you stick around here!"

"What would you suggest?"

"Get out—get the hell out, before you're mired!"

"Where to, Dave?" She looked at him thoughtfully, and David opened the stove and flung a stick of wood upon the fire with angry haste.

"Where to? Anywhere. Go where people are doing things—thinking things—go anywhere before you smother here."

A late shaft of sunlight falling through the window revealed a broken place in David's shoe. A rush of pain and love for David swept her.

"Why didn't you go, Dave, before it was too late?"

Before he answered, he threw himself into his chair and looked gloomily at the floor. "I was the oldest. I didn't have anybody to set me right."

For the hundredth time in the past year, Carla felt miserable at her own selfishness. What right had she to rise out of the monotony, the narrow confines of this life to an exultant realization of herself somewhere else in the world?

"When I graduate next month I'd like to help somehow," she said.

He looked at her with a wry smile. "Yeah! I stuck around, didn't I? And a hell of a lot I've helped! Sophie stuck around, and what became of her? Ruth is still here, and what are we going to do with her? Old Paget has a lot before him, hasn't he? And Jenny— God Almighty!" His laugh was sardonic. "As for Tom—I had a hand in kicking him out—poor old Tom is just plain gutless. He goes out into the world to get strength to fight the family, and comes home to get strength to fight the world."

He got up abruptly and walked to the window. The sun had gone. "I've got some business to attend to down town, kid," he said, keeping his eyes averted.

Carla rose pensively. "I thought you were warming this place up so you could say here awhile," she protested.

"I'll be back later," he said. "Some day, if I have guts enough, I'm going to put a bed in here for myself."

She knew suddenly where his thoughts had gone. With a melancholy feeling of desertion, she left the shop and went to walk under the trees that knew more than any human creature the secret journeys of her thoughts.

§ 2

Between the house and the tall poplars to the south, the orchard and the garden were steeped in hot, live shadow, a fusion of pink over purple gray. The tops of the poplars were wimpled in a color that was nearly magenta, but over all the lovely glimmer was an unearthly quiet. Carla felt suddenly a burst of impatience at this waiting hush that seemed to have been poised and listening over this place ever since she could remember. The voices of Ruth's children, playing far down in the orchard, came like a tinkle on the air, unreal as the voices of toys. Carla, in an irresistible impulse to smash that spell of silence, burst loudly into song.

"John Hardy stood at the dice room door,
So drunk he couldn't see, Lord, Lord!
His yaller gal threw ten dollars on the board,
Sayin' . . ."

She stopped abruptly, and surveyed with cool eyes the man who stood looking up at her from the ground beside the porch steps.

"Very good," the man said gravely. "Please don't let me stop you. What did his yaller gal say?"

Carla laughed, feeling the quick color in her cheeks. "His yaller gal said, *'Deal John Hardy in the game!'*"

"Fine!" He stood easily, his hat held under one arm, and smiled at her.

"Are you Mr. Kingswood?" Carla asked.

"To the best of my knowledge," he replied. "I saw a young lady asleep on the front porch—Tom's sister Jenny, I suppose. I didn't want to disturb her, so I came around here on the chance of finding somebody awake."

Carla laughed and seated herself on the steps, contriving an air of impudence to hide her overtaking shyness.

"Well—I'm Carlotta—sleeping or waking."

"Yes? I had hoped Carlotta wouldn't be so easy to look at."

A faint flush mounted to his eyes, and Carla settled to her ease again in his momentary confusion. His brows, dark and heavy over deep and wide-set eyes, came together in a perplexed frown, and then the corners of his mouth twitched in a rueful smile.

"How nice that I was able to disappoint you!" she said.

He grinned, and Carla noticed how pleasant and free his features were, lean and irregular and quick to change, his face darkly sunburned except for a light margin close to the dark of his hair.

"I wish that all my disappointments were as agreeable as this one," he remarked. "Now that we are acquainted, may I ask where Tom is?"

She nodded toward the gray building beyond the lilac bushes. "He's still at work in the shop," she replied. "He should be in in a moment—but of course you may go over there if you wish."

"I really don't mind waiting here, if you don't object."

Carla looked searchingly at him sideways. "Tom has been nearly beside himself expecting you this week," she said.

"Yes? It'll be good to see him again."

She got to her feet. "Well, you had better come indoors. Tom will be shocked if he finds me entertaining you on the back porch."

A brief smile flickered in his eyes. "He would be," he observed. "You see, I got to know Tom pretty well. That's really why I'm here."

As she led him through the house, a wonder came over her at the sense of naturalness in his being here, a stranger, alien in every sense to the lives of the Wellands. When she had seated him in the living room, she noted that he looked with keen deliberateness about the room, his eyes quick and friendly.

She could fancy him saying to himself, "So this is Tom Welland's home! It will be interesting to meet the family." It was strange to her that she felt no resentment toward the thought; there was an easy, unsurprised acceptance about this John Kingswood, apprehended as a familiar manner of her own mind.

"I'm awfully grateful for the trouble you took with my verses," she said. "I don't suppose I should ever have tried to get them published, even, if Tom hadn't known you."

"Trouble? I had no trouble. I liked them. I hope you'll let me see more of 'em."

"I'm afraid you will. Are you going to stay over in Thrace for a few days?"

"I hadn't counted on staying at all. I'm on my way up to the lake. Some friends of mine up there are expecting me. I thought I'd crowd in a little visit with Tom to-night, and go on in the morning."

"Tom will keep you as long as he can," Carla said. "He wants to hear all about your play."

"It opened in Chicago last night. That's why I hit for the woods. I just couldn't stand the gaff."

"You mean you ran away from it?"

"Just so. Don't we always run away when a thing means too much to us?"

Carla looked at him challengingly. "I wouldn't," she said.

Ruth and her mother came softly into the house, and Carla called them from the hall.

"Mr. Kingswood is here, mother."

Sarah Welland came into the living room. Carla caught a glimpse of Ruth as she slipped past in the hall on her way upstairs. Carla turned to Kingswood. "This is my mother, Mr. Kingswood," she said.

Kingswood advanced and shook hands warmly. "Tom has often spoken of you," he said. "I promised to come and meet you when I came through."

"I'm glad you did, Mr. Kingswood," Carla's mother said. "Tom will be pleased. Have you told Tom Mr. Kingswood is here, Carla?"

"Carla and I are having a little visit to ourselves," Kingswood put in, smiling.

"Well, they'll be in directly," Sarah Welland told him. "I must hurry with supper. We were down at the sewing circle. I hope you won't mind if I leave you now, Mr. Kingswood?"

Kingswood bowed. "Certainly not, Mrs. Welland."

When her mother had gone, Carla sat down again and motioned Kingswood to a chair. "I'm really playing a trick on Tom," she said. "Poor Tommy had it all set to take you out to Paget's for supper. He has probably told you we're a queer lot. And we *are!*"

He laughed. "And proud of it, eh?"

He was looking at her, bending forward with his hands clasped before him. She returned his gaze, and there was a passing friendly recognition between them. Carla laughed and ran her fingers idly through her hair. "We have a very proud father," she said with faint irony.

There were sounds on the porch then of Dave and Tom and Matt returning. Carla sprang up and went to the door, John Kingswood following her. Tom strode forward to grasp Kingswood's hand, and Carla withdrew and seated herself on the hall chest, to watch with pitying dismay Tom's self-consciousness and confusion as he introduced his friend to Matt and Dave. Dave shook hands briefly and excused himself at once. Then Carla heard her father's resonant, hospitable voice, and saw him draw himself up and stand back in his familiar attitude, the better to appraise the stranger.

"Well, well!" he said. "This is indeed an agreeable surprise! A friend of our Tom's, eh, from the big city! Did I understand Tom to say you were associated with him in the good work of the mission? He has mentioned so many names that I forget—I forget. I'm beginning to get old, I fear. But it seems to me he mentioned your name."

Kingswood smiled slowly. "No," he said. "I was merely a wage slave—forging crank shafts."

"Ah, well," Matt replied, "there is nothing dishonorable in that. Each man to his place. But have the girls looked after you properly, Mr. Kingswood? You will want to wash up before we have supper. Carla, have you—"

Tom broke in. "Paget is expecting us out at his place for supper, father," he said with discomfort. "John is just passing through, and he wanted to meet Paget."

Carla withdrew her eyes from the hurt disappointment in her father's face. His eager brightness faded slowly, and a look of weary age came upon him. "Ah, I am sorry," he said softly. "I am sorry, indeed. I had hoped that we might have had an evening's chat, Mr. Kingswood, but, I guess—we old fellows have to realize our proper place. Youth must be served." He drew himself up erectly then, and smiled as he extended his hand to Tom's friend.

"It is quite possible that we shall meet another time, Mr. Welland," Kingswood said as he shook hands with Matt. Carla saw how gray and penetrating his eyes were, as though he would seize upon something in her father's mind and make it his own. Suddenly, with a tremor of excitement, she knew that John Kingswood was a singular person: he had neither contempt nor fear for Matt Welland.

Her father had left them to go upstairs, and now Kingswood and Tom were moving toward the doorway. Carla rose and Kingswood turned towards her. "I am sorry my visit has been so short," he said. "I may be back this way. I have a feeling there are a lot of things we should find to talk about."

He had gone out then, with Tom, and Carla could hear Jenny's voice in some petulant protest. It did not occur to her to wonder what John Kingswood would think of Jenny. She was aware only of a pervasive vitality that lingered still in the room from his brief presence there.

The lovely magnitude of the evening lay over the Welland place, seeming to lift and expand it to its own brilliant reaches, Carla fancied, as she looked out and away from the porch swing where she swayed idly to and fro, waving a palm fan to the same rhythm. The sun was down, but the watery rose of its setting still dipped into the tops of the trees; the sky margin was a humid lavender. On the lawn, Dave and Jared were playing croquet, their white shirt sleeves rolled up, their collars turned in, and their throats showing duskily red. Jared's hair was damp and clustered richly about his forehead, and now and then he would move his shoulders to free them from the clinging heat of his clothing. Carla withdrew her eyes, her lids falling heavily.

On the porch, in her long wheel-chair, Jenny sat with her slender fingers moving, moving in their constant search over her embroidered spread. Close by her was Matt, and half facing him, the Reverend Mr. Willsie. Carla's mother sat apart with Mrs. Gale, at the other end of the porch, their voices a considerate undertone while Matt talked with the minister.

Mr. Willsie had brought with him a copy of the *Thrace Advocate*, from which he had read an article condemning a play that had fallen under the censor's ban in the city of Boston.

"Thank God for one righteous city in the land," Matt Welland said.

Mr. Willsie cleared his throat thoughtfully. "It seems too bad," he said, stroking his chin, "that the theater has degenerated so pitifully in our time. It was not always so. We have the drama to thank for much of our finest poetry. The plays of Shakespeare . . ."

"I can't agree with you, Brother Willsie," Matt said firmly, shaking his head. "We have no way of judging the influence of Shakespeare upon his day. We know well what happened to the theater after his day, and even the Bard of Avon had his lapses, you will admit."

"Of course, he wrote for another day," Mr. Willsie argued.

"I can't think that other days differed so very much from our own, Brother Willsie. In the sight of God, eternity is but a day. Our times are in His hands, brother. All times are in His hands. Evil to-day is evil to-morrow, as it was evil yesterday. Youth of every age has had the same temptations to withstand. I make no allowances for an evil influence in the lives of the young, no matter what the day or age."

Carla heard the valiantly protesting voice of the gentle old minister, and then her father's voice in reply. Her indifference was pricked to a lively wrath by the fervent earnestness of the two men. She rose lightly, removing herself in body and mind, preserving herself against the ineffectual rage that threatened her. In the house, behind the closed kitchen door, she prepared the lemonade and sandwiches and cake which her mother always served to visitors. Then, leaving the refreshments in readiness, she went upstairs.

Ruth lay on the bed in the front room which she now shared with Carla, her old room having been turned into a nursery. Carla stood for a moment and looked down at her. It had grown almost dark, and the white of Ruth's nightgown made a dim sheath about her. Her arm hung, a faint arc, above her head.

"Are those people still down there gabbing?" Ruth asked, stretching sensuously. "Heavens, what do they find to talk about on a hot night like this? They should have had their lemonade and cake by now."

"I've just fixed it for them," Carla told her.

"Ugh! What clowns!"

"I rather like the minister," Carla remarked.

"Oh—I thought it was our dear Mr. Loftus. Yes—Willsie is all right. Andrew says he plays a good game of tennis, too."

Carla slipped off her clothes and put on a kimono, and went and knelt before the open window, looking out. From the porch below came the murmur of voices. The sky, flushed in the east by the still invisible rising moon, was as mysterious as a hollowed gem. The few stars were hot blurs, insecure and tremulous. Random movements of air tiding up from the garden brought the fragrant shock of peonies and roses, and the deeper, sensational smell of earth. Carla thought of the Welland house, the garden and the old trees, as islanded in the night fluency, but flowing with it on that voluptuous dark sea to some awful drop-away into oblivion. But the vivid chorus of night insects mocked her thought. Whatever magnificent voyage of doom the Wellands embarked upon, these would remain behind, faithful to their own infinitesimal genius. Or were there, possibly, sordid intrigues and furtive romances even among crickets?

On the bed behind Carla, Ruth stirred impatiently.

Not until the visitors had gone home and the family had safely retired, could she rise and dress and go out to meet Andrew, slipping noiselessly down the kitchen stairway, lest she rouse Jenny in the forepart of the house. Ruth would be, to all intents and purposes, trying to dissipate her headache in the open air. And Carla would be left with an explanation of her absence, should it ever be discovered. Upon her return, there would be the performance that had grown so familiar during the past months, of Ruth's throwing her arms about Carla and crying and laughing in incoherent misery and bliss.

The voices emerged loudly now from the porch. Why did people raise their voices in leave-taking? It was as though what they had been discussing a moment before had been full of troublous portent, or even a little scandalous.

On the walk Carla could see Mrs. Gale talking with the minister and Matt Welland. "Yes," she was saying, "it will seem strange to have my little boy turned into a professor this fall. Ah, well, I have much to be thankful for, even if I am getting old."

"Getting old! Pshaw, mother!" Jared was beside her, giving her a playful shake. "Why, she's just a chicken yet, isn't she, Mr. Welland?"

Everybody laughed appreciatively. Carla had a glimpse then of Jared as a professor—urbane, broadly human, a good fellow even though a professor, a favorite with the students. And underneath—she watched him walking away, his back and limbs moving in easy grace. The moon, risen now, flamed over lawn, trees and garden, and Carla imagined that little tongues of somber fire played about Jared's dark head.

"Have they actually gone?" Ruth murmured.

"Yes, they've gone."

Her impatience turned now upon Ruth. "Why on earth don't you marry Andrew?" she demanded. "I wouldn't go sneaking out of the house at all hours—"

"You know very well why I don't marry him," Ruth replied. "I don't because—I can't."

"You can, if you want to. Let father do what he likes after you marry him."

Ruth held up her hand and looked at it, and let it fall limply from the wrist. "Yes—and lose what I have— little as it is," she sighed. "I'd rather live—this way— than not at all."

"You think Andrew would really leave you if father carried out his threat to tell him about you?"

"I don't know. I don't dare put him to the test."

"If he really cares for you," Carla insisted, "he'd understand, especially if he knew all the circumstances."

"And if he refused to understand?"

"Let him go."

Ruth turned her face away in the shadows. "Oh, Carla, I couldn't do that. I want to live. Some day perhaps you'll understand what I mean."

The old impulse to get up and run away struggled within Carla. There was something subtly debasing in even considering Ruth's trouble. From her earliest girlhood Carla's instinct had been to keep herself in the cool heights above the thwarted passions of the family. A downward lapse of sympathy or solicitude for any of them, and she would be confused by love and pain, hopelessly involved, made one of them, drawn into the depths of their frustration. It was out of her determination to keep herself free from her blighting environment that her immeasurable loneliness had grown. People had said of her that she was not quite human. Frieda Gertner had said so, and Jared Gale—accusingly, resentfully. And it was David who had said that she was a leprechaun.

Ruth had risen on one elbow, and in the gloom Carla could see that her eyes were wide with fright. "What if Andy should take it into his head that I killed Clint?" she asked in an anguished voice.

Carla came and lay on the bed, staring widely at the ceiling. A cold dew seemed to be settling down upon her body. "Don't be silly, Ruth," she said quickly.

"I'm not so silly as you seem to think," Ruth retorted. "I wouldn't put it past father to hint that I killed Clint Proles. He probably thinks I did, anyhow."

"Well—are you just going to go on—like this?" Carla asked impatiently.

Ruth was silent for a moment. "Perhaps," she said at last. "I don't know. I think I'm really waiting for father to die."

"Perhaps you wish he was dead—now."

Ruth's body tightened convulsively. "No," she said between clenched teeth. "Only one thing could make me wish that. If I ever found out that he had actually told Andy that I had brought about Clint's death—"

Carla thrust back the irrevocable words that came to

her lips, the words that would release Ruth from her long fear. In a cool recess of her mind, she knew that those words would make her part of the confusion from which she had so long kept herself free. But presently the horror that had taken possession of Ruth's simple mind reached out and overwhelmed Carla's will.

"Ruth," she said, "what would you do if you found out that somebody else had been the cause of Clint's death?"

She had sat upright on the bed, and was looking out of the window as she spoke. The moonlight appeared like a lambent rain over the garden, over all the strangely alive, dark world that she saw there. From within the house came the sound of the family going to their rooms. Outside the house was the live darkness—the darkness waiting for Ruth.

Ruth was very quiet. Presently: "What do you mean by that, Carla?"

Carla felt a little sick. The room throbbed in her senses like a great laboring heart.

"I mean," she said quickly, "I mean that *I* locked the cellar door on Clint Proles."

She sat rigid in the silence, a silence that might go on forever. Ruth might die lying there in that terrible silence.

"So you've waited all this time to tell me?" Ruth asked at last.

"There are things about it you might not want to know—even now," Carla said, a carelessness coming into her voice.

"Things—I might not want to know?"

"Certainly."

Ruth's voice came cold. "What things?"

Ruth waiting, Carla began to talk, quietly, almost with contempt for the tale and for its false importance. Yet, when she had finished, she knew that Ruth was hating her, obscurely, complexly, in ways that Ruth herself could not have told.

"Why don't you get dressed and look as pretty as you can and go and see Andy to-night?" Carla said finally. "Tell him and get it over with. Or would you rather have me tell him?"

Ruth made a curious sound, almost a sob in her throat. "You tell him?"

"Why not? It wouldn't bother me a bit."

"Nothing would bother you," Ruth burst out. "Not—even—murder."

Carla turned and looked down at her. "I think you might explain that," Carla said.

"I mean just what I say. You would stop at nothing," Ruth whispered. "I don't believe Sophie fell."

A rhythmic sensation passed through Carla as though her whole being vibrated instantaneously to some heavy chord struck out of the darkness of the past.

"What in the world are you talking about, Ruth?" she demanded. "Do you mean I pushed her, or what?"

"You fooled her. You got her thinking things. She made up her mind that Bert was waiting for her. You did that."

Carla's lids folded heavily down over her eyes for an instant. "Well, Bert was dead, wasn't he?"

"You didn't know that at the time," Ruth retorted sharply.

"Even so," Carla replied, "the gods were on my side." She rose and went to kneel again before the window. The moon swam, a dead, impervious face in the living tide of the sky.

§3

The summer was loitering through Thrace, the indolent beauty of its days passing over and thrusting negligently into the past the small excited ado of human kind. The town paid its respects to the traditional events of the season, Chautauqua, circus, flower festival, and church social, time drawing each away in its turn, like a slide in a magic lantern, seen and put by.

Carla walked home from her work in the Thrace library on an evening in late August, a mood of change having been upon her all day. In the open space before the orchard Dave's boys were playing catch. She could hear them shouting across the stillness. Dave's boys—the eldest fourteen now—growing tall and uncoördinated. And Dave himself, who had even within her memory been a boy, too, with unmanageable long legs and eyes that dreamed beyond Thrace, was given over now to resignation and a shabby substitute for romance. He had shut the family away from him, had shut Carla away from him, too. He had become unapproachable, just as Jenny with her pitiful china-painting and her ingrowing

283

malice, and her stark and hopeless hunger for love, had grown unapproachable. Carla went into the house, her mother calling to her cheerily from the kitchen. "The children want a picnic supper outside," she said. "I wish you'd come and help me when you've washed up. Ruth's not feeling well."

Carla replied quickly, brightly, hiding her thought of Ruth. For weeks Ruth had been moving about in a sort of trance, seeming to recover life only when her eyes turned upon Carla in an unwholesome and speculative regard. Not yet had Ruth gained to the point of courage which was clear before her. Not yet had she gone to Andrew and ventured her confession.

Carla hurriedly fastened her dress about her, a worn white dress that was sheer and cool. It made her feel extended to a fine litheness, airy and untrammeled.

She found her mother setting the picnic table under a plum tree at the edge of the orchard. Farther down among the trees the children were playing, Ruth's children and Dave's, their voices coming sweet and shrill. The evening was a prism through which one looked with a catch of sadness in the heart and saw summer die again. Carla could look back now and see the shoals of brilliant leaves on the trees of the east garden, flickering like goldfish in their translucent captivity. It was Sophie who had loved and dreaded in her mute way this melancholy time. It was Sophie who had said, "We'll be seeing the falling stars again soon now." But Sophie would never again say, "Money, money, money," to the breathtaking fall of an autumn star, or call to mind her childhood belief that it marked the passing of a soul into eternity.

She helped her mother deck the long table, fetching from the house the prepared salad, the cold meat, the deviled eggs, and the cookies and small cakes Mrs. Welland had baked for the children. Carla folded the flower-bordered paper napkins, without which the children would not consider a picnic complete.

She looked up to see her father guiding Jenny's chair through the flower garden, pausing now and then while Jenny with deft shears cut the wine-red dahlias that grew to her hand.

"I wonder if it won't be too cool for Jenny out here, after all," Mrs. Welland reflected. "She's bound to come, and father won't have her crossed in anything. Ah, well . . . there! The table looks just lovely, Carla." She glanced toward the house. "I wonder if Seena will get back before we've eaten," she said.

Carla flashed a look at her, a look of sudden comprehension, and laughed. "I hope, too, that she doesn't come."

"Carla!" her mother admonished gently. Her slender brown face lighted with a sly humor.

"Well, you'll admit," Carla said, "that the children are heaps more fun without her."

"Live and let live, Lottie," her mother said softly.

"What you really mean, mother, is—die and let die."

"Lottie, Lottie!"

Carla had always known that behind her mother's passive acceptance lay a stoic resignation to the foreordained, and a proud and bright refusal to interfere in the shapings of destiny.

"All right, mother," Carla replied, "but for years I've had a feeling that it would have been far better for all concerned if Dave had never married Seena—or having married her, had left her before it was too late."

Her mother stood looking into the green gold spaces, and Carla could not follow her eyes. They must be looking into a past of inconceivable struggle between love and love, fear and other fears, hope and hopes beyond.

"It is always easy, Carla, to look back upon what has happened, and say what should have been. It's not so easy to know at the time what one should do. There are so many things that enter into it. When I look back upon my own life—"

She paused and Carla looked at her closely.

"Would you have married father if you had known?" Carla asked suddenly.

Her mother was gravely silent for a moment. "Your father is really a good man, Carla," she said at last. "He is his own worst enemy. When I married him I was devoted to him. I am devoted to him still, I think. We learn to overlook things in life, Carla. It was a long time before I discovered that the only person that father ever really loved was his only brother Felix. When they parted, I did what I could to make up for his loss. I have never quite succeeded."

Her eyes moved slowly to where Jenny's chair had come to a stop beneath the red torches of a sumac tree.

"Could any woman have succeeded?" Carla asked.

"I might have succeeded myself, Carla, if I had begun early enough to assert myself. But I didn't have the courage. I hoped that things would somehow come out right after all. I thought my children would have it in them to live their own lives in spite of everything. That was where I failed."

Carla felt all her being moved out in compassion, as though it were she herself who had remained so steadfast through years of anguish to a first devotion, a first resolve, harsh and inexorable in its nature.

"But, mother," she said, "if there had been no Felix—"

"If there had been no Felix, Carla, *I* might have acted differently. Ah, well, it's all very complicated and hard to understand. Come, we'd better get everybody to sit in. There's Seena coming, now."

Matt was wheeling Jenny's chair across the grass. A ripe purple plum dropped with a thick, soft sound, and Carla stooped to pick it up, polished it on her sleeve as the boys did, and buried her teeth in its wet sweetness.

Jenny glanced up at her and said, "Would it be asking too much of you to reach me one?"

"Not at all, your highness," Carla replied, and reaching out an arm, plucked a plum from the tree.

"It *would* have a worm hole," Jenny said, examining it.

Carla quickly snatched a half dozen plums from the tree and tossed them into Jenny's lap. "Choose your own, then," she said lightly.

"Lottie, Lottie!" her father remonstrated. "What in

the world has come over you? Such a temper, such a temper! And with little Jenny, of all people."

Carla sauntered away to the house to call David and Tom, who had come in from the shop.

After supper, Carla seated herself alone in the coolly lit vacancy beneath the poplars. She thought of Tom and his curiously excited restraint during the meal, when he had spoken of seeing Paget on the street that day, and of Jenny's sweetly acid comment upon Paget's avoidance of his own home. She recalled, too, how her father had soothed Jenny. "Paget's work is very demanding these days, my dear," he had said. "He would have come to see us if he had had a moment to spare. Of that I am confident. Our Paget isn't forgetting us, Jenny." David had leaned back in his chair, his eyes full of shameless laughter.

Tom was coming along the lane now with Jared. That afternoon, Jared had come into the library and asked her to walk out with him to Paget's place in the evening. Her mother had baked some things to send out to Paget.

Jared and Tom came and stood above her. "I was just telling Jared," Tom said, "that John Kingswood is going to be out at Paget's place again some time next week. I had a note from him this afternoon. He says he's going to stay for a few days this time. I mentioned it to Paget this afternoon."

"What day is he coming?" Carla asked.

"He didn't say. John wouldn't. He'll just drop in when he's ready."

"Won't he be coming down to the house at all?" Carla asked.

"Not if I can help it," Tom told her.

"Still ashamed of us, eh, Tommy?" Carla jibed.

Tom looked down at her angrily. "That has nothing to do with it!" he flared. "I mentioned his name in the shop to-day in father's hearing and when he asked me what John was doing for a living, I had to tell him. He flew off and told me he would have no such person enter his house, if he knew it. If you know what's good for you, puppy, you'll not mention John's name around the place."

He turned and left them, and Carla watched him go back along the path. There had come a great distance between her and Tom. She watched him as he left them, and it seemed that she could see him far away, a dwindling, retreating figure, growing more and more remote, swallowed up by heedless space, as one might see the diminishing, lonely form of a friend with whom one had lately parted, vanish into the white distance where a lonely road merged with the horizon. She looked at Jared and saw that his brows were knit into a troubled frown.

"We'd better be going, Carla," he said.

She was alone with Jared now, walking the mile to Paget's place, that lay beside a wooded road north and east of Thrace. The sky became deep and green, and stars shook out in the green like bits of a shattered mirror. They walked the mile together, scarcely speaking, Carla permitting all her being to move forward into mystery, refusing to let her mind play upon any consequences of the moment.

Jared spoke, keeping clear still of the swing of feeling between them. "This fellow Kingswood," he said heavily, " is something of a puzzle to me. What is there about him that Tom likes so much?"

"Tom probably finds him stimulating."

"I don't think he's done Tom much good, filling his mind with all sorts of irresponsible ideas."

"Tom's mind is good soil for irresponsible ideas," she observed.

"Well, I think this Kingswood must be pretty thick-skinned to come out here when he knows that you people aren't his kind."

Carla's mind made a sharp recoil. She walked on in silence, Kingswood becoming suddenly more real to her.

"His kind?" she said quickly. "What kind are we, then?"

They had come within the light that fell through Paget's open doorway, leading down a small path through a scramble of gnarled old trees and wild undergrowth. Jared took her hand in a swift, blind pressure.

"People know when they belong together," he said, his voice almost harsh with a sound of fear. Then he let her hand go, and while they walked to Paget's door, she folded her fingers tightly within her other hand, the wild clamor and ringing of her blood seeming to fill all the night about her.

Paget was playing solitaire at his kitchen table when they entered. He rose to bring chairs out for them, then reseated himself again and went on with his game. Carla took the parcels Jared had brought, unwrapped the ginger bread and cake and placed them in Paget's tidy cupboard. She felt a twinge at her heart as she glanced about the kitchen, which was as immaculate as though a woman's hand were here to tend it. She looked at the cards spread out before Paget on the spotless white oil-cloth, and it came to her mind to wonder what curious reassurances he saw before him there.

"Tom tells me his friend Kingswood is going to pay you another visit, Paget," Jared said, and Carla felt an unsteady vibrating within herself at the sound of his voice.

"Yes," Paget replied, gathering up his cards and shuffling them deftly again in his sure hands. "I saw Tom in town this afternoon, and he told me about it. He's a queer sort of bird, Kingswood. I rather like him."

He laid the cards out once more in a carefully sym-metrical pattern, a thoughtful caress in his motions. His look became absent now, and he remained without speaking for so long that Carla felt, even through her own separate and vivid agitation, the sadness of his dis-regard of them, of anyone.

Jared had not looked at Carla, and his few remarks to Paget were tense with uneasiness. Very soon Carla rose, the room having become intolerable to her with its presence of Dorie, escaping and unescapable.

Away from Paget again, they moved without any

pause to determine the way of their going, instead of directly to the road, through the shadowed thicket to the open hillside, and beyond, where the moonlit aisles of Paget's vineyard showed like mysterious rifts in the earth. Here they paused to look out over the downward flow of the world, a silver gray web buoyant on the flow, a web of tears and passion, of the blood of the earth and the blood of man, a web of dreams in a dead heart. Carla's hands rushed to her throat, where a cry had come out of all her insupportable knowledge of living.

Jared's arm brushed her shoulder, and she looked up to see his immaterial shadow built against the illumined sky. But he did not seem within reach of her, he was intangible, slipping away, as everything slipped away. She looked down at the pale luster of her dress, and it seemed to sway rhythmically upon her. Jared's hand was on her naked wrist. Her flesh seemed terribly naked.

The sky rocked above her, beyond Jared's shoulder, and his face that bent to hers in a pale fixity. He had kissed her—and then again it seemed that he was not there—that a wall of moonlight obscured him. He had brought her to the shadow of the nearer vines, where they had seated themselves. Close above them hung the darkly shining burden of the grapes, and the sky beyond of the same voluptuous, unnameable color. The presence of Jared was very near her—an abiding demand within her own body. She drew her arms tightly about his shoulders, urging him down to her, her lips moving close and quick over his mouth and throat, her fingers going swiftly, then, to his hair, and straining its crispness vehemently back from his brow in the strength of her grasp. She felt the sharp indrawing of his breath, and sensed herself as going into his being, knowing the deep strong mysteries of his body. Then his breath had been suddenly expelled on a low exclamation, and he had seized her by the shoulders and thrust her back from him.

"Carlotta Welland!" he whispered. "Have you lost your senses? You're acting like a—like a wanton!"

The moonlight slipped down between them, a high white wall, built to heaven. Carla released herself from his hold, and leaned back with her arms straight and her hot palms pressed against the cool, dewy earth. Her fingers clutched at the grass, the dry blades sharp on her skin.

Jared reached for her hand, and she heard his voice coming toward her, tender and contrite now.

"Carla," he said, "I didn't mean that. Please forgive me. It was my fault. We mustn't be foolish. Sit over close to me and let's talk things over. We've a lot to think about, dear."

She let him take her hand, her eyes moving intently over his face. The thought possessed her suddenly that she was committing to memory the features of one whom she was never to see again. And as she looked, the face of the small boy she had known long ago, wavered dimly over the face of the youth, and the youth became a man, and the man was lost to her. She closed her eyes on tears that came burning up from the very heart of her loss.

He put his arm about her again, and his head close upon her shoulder.

"You've always belonged to me, Carla," he said. "I know it now. We've always belonged to each other. Why shouldn't we be married before the term opens? I won't be paid any too well for the first few years, but mother is a great little manager, and she'll help us get along. We're much better off than most people are when they get married."

Carla's eyes roved over his head, down the grassy slope that bordered the vineyard, and saw how the moonlight had washed sky and earth into a radiant monotone. A great pity filled her for all the melancholy wrongness in living, the waste of the fierce, pure moment that could never be recalled.

A slow rhythm moved through her, the rhythm of her own will set free once more into solitude and isolation, released from Jared. She began to speak, her thoughts coming clearly and going out to him in the full knowledge of their purpose.

"No, Jared," she said, keeping her eyes from him lest he guess her pity of him. "You don't know me as I am. I'm just—that kind of woman—the kind you said. It wasn't your fault. It was my fault. Let's not talk about it."

Jared had grasped her wrists. "Don't say such things!" he said. "It isn't true!"

"Oh, but it is true! I could tell you many things about

myself. I do only what seems natural to me. I can't help it. And I shouldn't be able to do anything else—even for you, Jared."

In his silence he seemed to be going immeasurably far away from her now, but she knew that this was not true; he had never really been close to her. Her mind weighing herself and him deliberately and coolly now, she perceived that in his ultimate value he could never have been more to her than a commonplace physical release from the bondage of the Wellands.

"It's late, Jared," she said, getting suddenly to her feet. "Let's go."

There was very little talk between them on the way home. Carla walked separately in her thoughts, where Jared became again the piteous figure dwelling within the close limits from which her unleashed imagination had tried to lift him.

§ 4

The day that followed was one of quivering, bright heat. Carla came home reluctantly in the late afternoon, to the waiting emptiness she knew would be there. All day she had thought of Jared, with the frail shadow of his mother obscuring and distorting him from boyhood, and a sadness had grown over her for him, and over her ruthless dismissal of him.

With a casual greeting, she passed Jenny, who was seated alone on the porch, languidly sipping iced tea. The thin querulousness of Jenny's voice brought her to a pause.

"Mrs. Peebles just left," Jenny said. "She said she saw you and Jared coming home last night, *quite* late, and she supposed an engagement would be announced one of these days. You'd better be careful, or you'll be getting yourself talked about, even if it is Jared you're playing around with."

Carla permitted her eyes to become blank, and looked in fixed absence at Jenny. "What did you say?" she asked. "My mind was on something else just then."

"No doubt," Jenny remarked. Her voice minced on the air, a tone intolerably dainty. "It would be very interesting to know what it was."

"Three guesses," Carla said, with the same delicate inflection, and went into the house.

Her mother was occupied in the kitchen putting away the tea things she had used to serve Mrs. Peebles. Her face bore a faint, reflective smile, a humor that was at once wistful and wise.

"A glass of iced tea, Carla?" she suggested. "It will cool you off."

"Thanks, mother, it would be lovely."

She watched her mother pour the tea out of the pitcher. She saw the mint leaves floating in it. She heard her mother's voice, mellow now with a grave concern.

"Jared was over this afternoon. He said his mother wasn't at all well to-day. She has taken to bed and the doctor had been in to see her. I was on my way over to her when Mrs. Peebles came, so I think I'll run in on her now, if you'll stay with Jenny. Jenny has been so fretful to-day, and Ruth has no patience with her."

"I'll look after her, mother," Carla said. "Shall I start getting supper?"

"If you're not too tired. I'll be back right away. Call Ruth to help you. You'd better go and get freshened up first, my dear."

Carla followed her mother out of the house and stood on the back porch, watching her straight, slim figure move down the path toward the Gale place. A great, free emotion of pride and tenderness filled her as she stood, and an understanding that was beyond the mean censure of people who would say that Sarah Welland had sacrificed her children to the selfish tyranny of their father's possessiveness. Sarah Welland had been herself, loyal to the first great compulsion of her life.

Indoors again, she heard Ruth coming down from her room by way of the kitchen stairs. Her eyes were narrow with hostility. For some time she moved about the kitchen in the preparation of the evening meal, saying nothing to Carla.

At last, when they were standing together over the kitchen table, each occupied with her task, Ruth spoke.

"You managed to stay out late enough last night, didn't you?" she said.

"Oh, were you planning to go out, Ruthy?" Carla said innocently.

Ruth flushed angrily. "You know very well I was," she replied.

"Well," said Carla serenely, "you can hardly expect me to stay around forever, suiting myself to your plans. What are you going to do when I get out for good?"

Ruth smiled spitefully. "When you get out for good? So that's it, eh? Do you think you'll be any better off when you go to live with Jared Gale and his mother?"

"Don't jump at conclusions, Ruth. I wasn't thinking of Jared—or anyone else in particular. Is there anything wrong with my imagining myself somewhere else than here?"

"I wouldn't count on it, if I were you."

"No? Why not?"

"We never get away."

Carla tossed back her hair and took up the plate of cut bread to carry it into the dining room. She paused in the doorway. "Don't be such a fool, Ruth," she said in a voice that was meant to be placatory. "Why in the world don't you go and tell Andrew all about it? Are you going to be a coward all your life? I'll tell him myself next time I see him. If it hadn't happened, how would you and he have ever got together?"

A look of panic came into Ruth's eyes. "I see. You're going to force me to tell him. God, you're as bad as father?"

"Oh, I'm a lot worse!" Carla taunted. "If it comes to that, I don't think father really would tell him."

Ruth stood stiffly for a moment, then a transfiguring light seemed to come over her. She turned upon Carla. "I wish to heaven you would get out! I can look after my own affairs without your help!"

Carla moved into the dining room, whistling softly to herself. In a dimly defined picture she saw herself away from the Wellands forever, Ruth restoring her assurance and attaining, in final desperation, to the point of courage that still lay beyond her. Then, reality intruding upon her fancy, she heard her brothers coming into the house from their work, and her father's voice in spirited greeting to Jenny. She heard her mother returning from her visit to Mrs. Gale, talking now to Ruth, a tone of troubled uncertainty shading her voice. She saw, as though looking on at a curious continuous drama in which she had no part, the assembling again of the family in their fixed rôles.

§ 5

In the orchard the apple trees stood rich and conscious of their yield, Carla thought, as she strolled through the brilliant morning down from the house to where David and his boys were filling the bushel baskets for marketing. The air tingled sharp and sweet on her senses. She seemed to be contained in one vividly clear enclosure of space with the ripe season of the earth, herself firm and vivid.

David's voice, calling to her as she approached, was brightly distinct in the stillness.

"Have you talked to Tom since yesterday afternoon?"

She moved toward him, picking up a fallen apple from the ground on her way.

"I didn't see him after supper last night," she told him. "He went out to Paget's."

David turned an empty basket over and sat on it. "He went out to see this friend of his—this Kingswood. He arrived at Paget's yesterday afternoon."

Carla's shoulders made a little movement of impatience. "What's all the mystery about?"

"No particular mystery, so far as I'm concerned. Tom just wants to avoid trouble."

"What trouble?"

"Father put his foot down on the idea of having him around at all."

"What if Mr. Kingswood takes a notion to come in?"

Dave smiled. "Tom has probably fixed that up with Kingswood. Why should he want to come in, anyhow?"

"To see me, of course," Carla said. "He likes me."

"Yeah?" David laughed. "I had a hunch! He mentioned you in his letter to Tom."

Carla drew herself up and thrust her hands deep into the pockets of her jacket. "That makes one more reason why Tom wants to keep it a secret," she observed.

"Probably. And he's probably right. When a woman gets her hands into anything—"

"Poor Tommy," Carla said, heedless of Dave's comment.

She turned away, summoning to her mind John Kingswood, a keen, genial sort of man with indolent ways of moving and talking, ways which might well be deceptive, since his eyes, she remembered, had had the power of drawing her own to them, and transmitting the knowledge that in some deep way he and she were kindred. Thinking of him now, she became aware of a tremor of alarm within herself, a fear too delicate upon her consciousness to be really known as fear.

All day, at work in the library, her mind had traveled

two courses, the one eventually yielding toward the other that became bright with new and unknown vistas. Her thought of Jared merged with thought of John Kingswood, became truantly receptive to it, until there was at length nothing of Jared left and her will imperiously demanded meeting with John Kingswood again.

The afternoon had turned gusty with clouds traveling low and films of rain blown deviously in the capricious rain. By early evening, Carla, seated at supper with the family, felt the tug of the wind at the very roots of the old house, and was aware within herself of an abandoned rejoicing in its strength.

Her mood carried her over to a quick resolution. There was her visit to Mrs. Gale to be made first, with the promised books from the library. She dressed securely against the weather—she would go directly to Paget's afterward. Tom, leaving the house at the same time to finish some work at the shop, remarked that there was scarcely any need of her preparing for a walk with Jared, as Jared was not at home. Carla smiled absently and went on her way.

Mrs. Gale's nurse opened the door to her and told her how distressed "the poor young man had been to leave his mother alone even for a minute." Mrs. Gale had not been well, though she was brighter now than she had been. But in heart cases, of course, you never could tell. They may look well one minute—and the next! Carla hurried past her and went to the room where Mrs. Gale awaited her.

Jared's mother lay very frail, very quiescent, beneath

the white spread. Carla seated herself beside her, over-whelmed with pity, and a discomfort of which she was deeply ashamed.

"It was very sweet of you to come, dear," Mrs. Gale said in a dim voice.

"I brought the books mother said you wanted, Mrs. Gale," Carla told her.

"Thank you, dear. Jared may read for me when ne comes home from Redlands. He had to leave for a while to attend a special faculty meeting before the opening of the term."

"They're having a number of additions to the staff this fall," Carla said.

"Five new teachers, I understand," Mrs. Gale said, brightening. "And Jared will be the youngest on the faculty." The note of tremulous pride in her voice struck at Carla's heart.

"And quite the handsomest, too," Carla added.

"I think so, too, naturally," Mrs. Gale said. "Sometimes I wish he were less attractive. Even a professor may be led astray by flattery, my dear."

"I don't think you need have any fear for Jared in that respect, Mrs. Gale," Carla assured her. "He thinks too much of his mother to be easily led astray."

"Jared has been a wonderful son to me," Mrs. Gale went on. "I've tried not to be selfish. Of course, his greatest love will be for the girl he will some day marry. Not that his love for her will ever supplant his love for his mother."

"I'm sure it won't."

Mrs. Gale's smile was very gentle, very full of understanding. "You know Jared so well, dear. There is no one I would more gladly surrender him to than you, Carla."

Carla's cheeks warmed swiftly. Her eyes moved away from the searching regard of the sick woman, her whole being in search of escape from the sudden stifling possessiveness of love which filled the room. Her lips moved in a numb effort at words.

"You will make me conceited, I'm afraid, Mrs. Gale," she said. "But I mustn't stay any longer now. I'm sure you are tired." She rose and touched the narrow hand on the coverlet, and strove to smile. The nurse came to the door then, brisk and quiet.

Out of doors again, Carla faced with a fierce zest the wind that swept thin rain out of a strangely colored sky. Through great torn spaces in the rain clouds the west showed murky yellow, a color sinister and lonely and terrifying. Carla turned toward Paget's place, away from the somber glare of the western sky.

John Kingswood was standing half way down the slope toward the vineyards, the damp wind blowing his flannel shirt flat against his back. His head was bare, and now and then his fingers ran through his hair to keep it off his brow. Far down in the lower valleys the fog lay blue and wet and palpable.

Now, as she watched him, a conscious alertness seemed to come across Kingswood's shoulders. He turned quickly and faced her.

"Hello!" he cried, his smile coming a little tardily. "It's you!"

"Didn't you expect me?" Carla asked.

"Expectation is one thing—realization is quite another," he replied.

He came toward her slowly and took her outstretched hand. For a moment he stood looking down at it, then let it go and placed his hands easily on his hips.

"Didn't Tom come with you?" he asked then.

"Do you think I'd be here if he knew it?" she replied.

He looked at her with one eye half closed, a quizzical grin about his mouth.

"Yes—I believe you would be," he remarked. "I wonder what he could really do about it—if you had made up your mind."

"Lots! He could bring the whole family down on me."

Kingswood laughed outright. "What a family!"

"Let's go and see Paget," she said quickly.

They walked together to the house, Kingswood with his hands in his pockets, proffering her no help over the rough ground.

Paget was sitting before the stove in the kitchen, smoking his pipe, his feet in the oven while his wet shoes dried at the back of the stove.

"Look what came up out of the mist, Paget," John said as he stepped through the doorway.

Paget turned about indifferently, giving Carla a lazy survey.

"Huh! You! Did father remind you to put your rubbers on?" he chuckled.

"No, I'm just over at Mrs. Gale's," she replied.

"Oh, I thought perhaps you were going around the block to get rid of a headache," Paget said solemnly.

They began to laugh, uncontrollably, at this sudden discovery of each other, this sympathetic recognition that had within it an element of the grotesque and the sardonic.

John Kingswood had seated himself near by and was unperturbably smoking a cigarette.

"What's the matter with Tom?" Paget asked finally. "I thought he was coming out."

"He'll be along later," Carla said. "I didn't want to ask him to be my partner in crime."

John laughed and leaned toward her, his face lighting with a swift change of humor. "Open up a little on this family of yours, Carlotta," he said. "I've been thinking of nothing else since I was here last. Tom won't talk—he's cagey. And Paget is too lazy. If I could get you to talk—"

"Go ahead, Carla," Paget urged.

Carla told simply and directly of the Wellands as they were known to each other—leaving in shadow the colors which she alone knew. Kingswood leaned back in his chair, his eyes contemplatively upon her, and Paget regarded her with one eyebrow raised in wry amusement. When she had finished, she made a gesture of dismissal of the subject and asked Kingswood abruptly about his play. He told them of it, a simple and tragic story of a workingman and his defeat in love, and admitted casually that the play had been well received.

"You don't seem to be a bit proud of the fact," Carla remarked.

He regarded her whimsically. "When that sort of a job

is an accomplished thing," he said, "it no longer belongs to you. Raising grapes, now—that's a different matter."

Carla saw him and Paget exchange slow smiles. There seemed to be some curious understanding between them. She felt an abrupt and disturbing startle of intuition. "Are you thinking of going in for grape raising?" she asked.

Kingswood looked at Paget, and Paget said, "John seems to like this place for some reason. He is talking of buying an interest in it."

There was a moment's silence then in which Carla, looking forward in amazement and disquietude, saw John Kingswood interwoven with the pattern of her life.

"You don't mean you will live here?" she demanded.

"Would you be so annoyed at that?" John laughed. "Well—don't be disturbed, Carla. I have been thinking of it merely as a pleasant place to come back to now and then. I like it. I feel I could do some good work here."

Very soon Carla rose to go, her astonishment giving way to a reluctant acceptance of the inevitability of John Kingswood's decision. But beneath her acceptance a resistance to the new and hitherto unmet power in him grew, a resistance to the acknowledgment of some force in him that drew her, that possessed her, as she had once sought to possess. Fear ran through her, bright and dark and confused.

John walked with her over the wood road, Carla having refused his offer to drive her home. The blown light rain was susurrant in the darkening trees, and the wind carried the sweet and melancholy scent of dead leaves under the rain.

The drifting mist had become more dense. John's arm was about Carla's shoulders in a casually protective way. She heard him talking to her—her inner stillness hearing him. There came to her then the irresistible impulse to tell him of herself, of Ruth and Clint Proles, of Sophie, and of Jared Gale. When she had finished telling him, a weariness came over her, a faint lassitude, as though her hard and secret self had gone from her.

"And now," she said, "you know me—as I know myself."

Kingswood laughed lightly. "I do not know you—nor do you know yourself," he said gently. "Any more than I know myself. Some day, if you will permit me, I'll tell you all I can about my own life and the poor business I've made of it. I came back here this time partly to find out something about myself." His voice was full of simplicity, almost of wonder at himself. "When I was here before— I talked with you—and went away, only to find myself thinking about you and wondering what I should do to forget you and get along with my work. Now I know it can't be done that way. Why should I try to forget what I want only to remember?"

He paused and looked down at her, then lifted her face lightly in his hands. "You will be very nice to love," he said. "I'm going to stay here with Paget until you are ready to come away with me—or until I know that I shall have to go away alone and not come back."

His eyes were half obscured above her. She drew back

in fear and anger at the sensation of power that came from him. Then they continued their way along the road leading into town. They walked apart from each other now, without speaking. Where the road merged with a street on the outskirts of Thrace, they looked up and saw Tom approaching, his shoulders hunched forward, his hands thrust deep into his pockets.

Kingswood put out one hand and caught Carla's arm. "Shall I come to take you for a drive some evening soon?" he asked quickly.

"If you wish," Carla replied, her face lifted to the mist. "Though father will make you wish you hadn't."

"I'll come to-morrow evening," he said, and turned to meet Tom, who had halted, amazed, a few paces away.

"What are you doing out here?" he demanded of Carla. His consternation was too much for her. She laughed aloud.

Even Kingswood laughed. "We've been shooting rabbits, Tom," he offered by way of explanation.

But Tom was in a truculent humor. "She knows what a row there'll be at the house if they find out she's been out here."

"Tommy," Carla replied, "will it never dawn upon you that I have never been greatly concerned over what I cannot help?"

"You could have helped coming out here, if—"

"I could have helped coming out—but since I'm here, I see no way of preventing a row, if they choose to make one."

"Look here, Tom," John put in, "you're treating Carla like a child."

"I'm thinking about her," Tom said defensively.

Carla broke impatiently away from them and hurried off down the street. Alone, she shook herself free from the effects of her meeting with Tom. She returned in thought to the walk through the mist, Kingswood's voice moving her with its simple earnestness, its frank fearlessness, its calm assurance. "You will be very nice to love," he had said.

The air scarcely stirred now, and the world seemed becalmed in the white hold of the fog. All thought, all sensation, was becalmed, too, waiting.

§ 6

The night passed, and another day, and again evening came with a sullen wind and rain. The house was deserted, except for Jenny, whom Carla avoided. Her mother and father and Tom had gone to the Gales' an hour ago, upon Tom's learning from Jared that Mrs. Gale had taken a turn for the worse. Ruth had seized the opportunity to slip out after she had put the children to bed, Carla granting a moment's wonder to the question of whether or not she would to-night dare put Andrew's love to the test. Jenny, in her accustomed place in the living room, varied her diversion between the knitting of a woolen scarf and the reading of a magazine which lay on the small table beside her.

Carla moved nervously about the house. She recalled

that when she was a little girl nights such as this one had seemed to her possessed of poor ghosts half drowned in their shrouds by the dark, wind-shattered rain, of frantic witches caught by the hair and screaming in the tossing branches of the poplars, of Norns of vast and bleak antiquity, wailing and sweeping terribly by, overhead in the upper regions of the storm.

Presently, when Ruth returned, her step on the porch set Carla's heart to beating oppressively. Ruth there to attend Jenny, the house became intolerable. She got into her coat, and with her soft hat in her hand, went out to sit on the porch.

There John Kingswood found her.

They were in his automobile now, the rain and the wind lashing about outside. A white spume whipped away from the headlights, and the trees made a tumult that came dimly in to them in their sheltered place. They were on a country road at last, out of town. John stopped the car.

He turned and looked at her, his face lean and cut clearly in the wan light from the instrument board. She held her hand before her, her fingers spread fan-wise against the white glow of the windshield. He reached forward and drew her hand toward him, gathering the slender tips of her fingers together against his lips.

She felt herself drawn to him, herself submerged and a soft darkness moving over her. In that darkness all her being grew rich and pliant, swaying like a frond with some voluptuous life. She drew her hand from his and looked straight before her where the white rain swept against the darkness.

"I want you to talk," she said, guardedly.

"There is so little need for talking, Carla," he replied. "You know what has happened to me. Talking about it would not explain it. There is something there that can never be explained—until chemists have succeeded in explaining life."

"You make it very simple," Carla said.

John laughed, a deep sound that made her close her eyes suddenly. "It is very simple, when you face it," he said. "You and I—what do we matter—except that we both have one brief and precious thing—a passion for living."

He lit a cigarette and sat looking at her reflectively, not speaking. Carla sat quiet and listened to the stormy surge of the night about them, conscious of the violent life within her which had found its instinctive complement in John Kingswood. With odd perversity, her mind went back to Jenny Welland—the Jenny Welland who had gone away on a night of rain and had come home again. Somber curiosity stirred within her. Had Jenny sat like this, perhaps, her poor salesman lover beside her, and listened to his deep entreaties? And had he taken her hand and kissed the tips of her fingers and sent the blood racing through her veins? And had her body ached to go over to him, in a strange and mysterious way? And had she let that moment pass, had she come home, her life ended? What a fool she had been!

Carla felt John Kingswood's arm about her shoulders. She did not move. Jared had called her—a wanton. But it did not mean what Jared had understood it to mean. It meant a relinquishing of that remote self, Carlotta Welland, to John Kingswood. It did not mean possession—it meant being possessed, utterly, irrevocably, in forgetfulness of self. Beyond her physical response to John Kingswood, she knew nothing of him. Perhaps she would never know more. Surrender to him would be a capitulation in passion to the unknown. And yet—

John Kingswood drew her toward him and kissed her once, holding her so for an extended moment.

She pressed away from him, her fingers brushing her eyes. Suddenly, all the fear in her blood—the Welland blood—shrank from him.

"Drive back to town," she said softly.

He turned from her unhurriedly and swung the car back into the road. "You are not really afraid of me, Carla," he said. "You are afraid of losing that hard little identity of yours that you've fought for against your damnable family. Keep it, my dear. It's your own."

Carla made no reply. Her hands were gathered tightly in her lap. She watched the rain spinning against the headlight.

Ruth met Carla in the hall, her eyes bright with penetrating accusation. The house seemed full of subdued voices, a tension over them.

"Mrs. Gale is dead," Ruth told her.

"Dead?"

"Yes. Jared is taking it terribly."

Carla stood looking at her, trying to gather her words

into a meaning. Mrs. Gale dead—Jared alone, broken-hearted. Herself, Carlotta Welland, suddenly blind with tears for Jared, the little boy of long ago. Her hands were shaking, moving helplessly out toward Ruth. Ruth had hold of her now, steadying her, talking softly, relenting toward her.

"Jared asked for you. He's alone over there. He wouldn't have anyone else around. He wanted Tom to ask you to go over."

"I'll go."

She passed through the house, out along the path, and under the rushing sob of the wind through the poplars.

Jared was lying face downward on a couch when she came quietly into the living room of the Gale house. She seated herself beside him and put her arm lightly about his shoulder.

"Jared," she said, "Jared—I am so sorry."

He groped for her hand and held it in a convulsive grip. "It's you, Carla," he muttered.

"Yes."

The rigidness of his shoulders seemed to give way under her arm. "It was kind of you to come, Carla. I didn't deserve it."

"Don't say that, Jared. I couldn't have stayed away."

She clasped her hands before her and stared at them in an effort to keep her tears from falling. Jared turned so that he could look at her; he took her hands and buried his hot face in them.

"Oh, I can't bear it!" he said suddenly, his voice broken with sobs.

She stooped and placed her lips close to his head. "Jared, dear—you must not!" Then, suddenly, she could say no more.

For a long time, then, there was silence between them—a silence broken only by the sobs of Jared. Finally he sat up beside her and took her hands in his.

"Forgive me, Carla," he begged. "It's just—hard to face—all at once."

"I wish I knew how to help," Carla replied.

"You are helping, Carla—far more than you know. You are so sweet and so gentle to-night. You seem very different, somehow."

Her mind formed an answer to him that remained unspoken, echoing hollowly only through her own consciousness: I am your mother to-night, Jared—that is why I seem so different.

But to him she said, "I am not different, Jared. I am as I have always been."

He clasped her hands more firmly in his own. "As you have always been, dear? Carla, Carla—do you know what that means to me now? I have wanted you—as long as I can remember. Now—I need you, dear. God has taken my mother from me—but He has given me you, Carla."

A great trembling seized him and Carla looked across his bowed head, the tears dimming her eyes. But something came clear to her vision then. It seemed that she was standing once more on a sunlit lawn, in a summer when she was only ten years old. It seemed that she saw her sister Ruth, standing in her wedding dress, the long mirror revealing her—and Sophie's face glimmering and strange through the cascade of Ruth's veil as she knelt on the floor and made the veil flow over her hands. It seemed to Carla that it was herself now, standing in the dress, in the long, white silken prison of it. Then, in turn, she saw herself as Sophie, as Jenny, running away from life when it came to her, running home, into oblivion.

She withdrew her hands gently from Jared's grasp and touched his shoulder. "I think you had better try to get some rest, Jared," she said. "Won't you let Tom come and spend the night with you?"

He raised his head and looked at her. "No—it isn't necessary—now," he said.

"Good night, then, Jared. We'll be over in the morning."

She stooped and kissed him lightly, out of her great pity for him.

§ 7

Carla sat on the steps of the front porch, the September evening spread in beauty before her, a pale sky, a pale star coming. The copper beech glowed in its fixity, and on the other side of the lawn the garden was rich with late flowers.

She turned her head slightly at the sound of Ruth's voice behind her.

"Father wants us to come in for a moment," Ruth said.

Carla got up and went into the house. Ruth went before her into the living room, where Matt sat at his desk. He continued his writing for a little while, then looked up

315

at the girls. He smiled and raised his glasses so that they rested on his brows.

"Well, my chickens," he said, "you're wondering, I suppose, what your old father has on his mind now."

He leaned back in his chair, passed his hand over his chin, and frowned.

Carla's eyes glided over Ruth and saw the color drain from her cheeks. While Ruth continued standing, Carla seated herself on the arm of a chair. Jenny sat in her place beside the windows.

"What is it, father?" Ruth asked, her voice a trifle high.

"Ah, well," Matt said. "I am perhaps being a little over-anxious. I can trust you both—I am sure of that—but you are young, you are young! And youth is not always wise." He paused for a moment, then continued. "I have learned that this young man—this Kingswood—who has been at Paget's, intends to remain for a while. He has even prevailed upon Paget to grant him some interest in the Kepler place. A very strange thing for a man of his kind, I should say."

"An affectation, I presume," Jenny put in, from her chair beside the windows. "I can't imagine any sincerity in a city man and an actor—or whatever he is—buying a share in a vineyard near Thrace. No doubt he thinks it's cute, having a little vineyard."

"Or he may just like raising grapes," Carla suggested dryly.

Matt cleared his throat. "Now, girls, please! My boys are men now," he went on. "It seems I can no longer offer them the advice I once gave them—advice, I may say, that has rarely failed them. I regret that I no longer mean anything to them. Paget has gone his way. David is still with me, but my words seem to carry little weight with him. Tom—I find Tom very difficult at times. However—my girls are still my girls—and I am still their father. I trust my word still means something to them. I have always been gentle with you, my dears. I have rarely demanded obedience. I have rarely found it necessary to demand it. You will bear with me, I am sure, if I seem to demand it now. It is because I am older than you and know something of the ways of the world."

He paused and Ruth shifted uneasily. "What is it, father?" she repeated.

"I'm coming to it, Ruthy, my dear. I want it clearly understood that none of you will have anything to do with this man—this Kingswood. I will not have my girls come under any such influence so long as I am alive to prevent it. You must not see him, or speak to him. I should prefer that his name is not mentioned anywhere in this house—or within my hearing. Now, my dears, do we understand each other?"

Ruth replied with a hurried relief that made Carla want to laugh. "Of course, father."

Matt got up from his chair and stood for a moment arranging the papers on his desk. His mood became blithe once more. "And now, girls, let us forget all about it, eh? It's an unpleasant subject. The less thought we give to it, the better for all of us. Eh?"

He smiled at them all and stepped lightly toward Jenny. "Come, my dear. Let me move you out to the porch for a breath of the evening air. Brother Loftus will be here in a moment."

A little later, Carla heard her father's voice in greeting to the Deacon, and heard the scrape of chairs being drawn up close for the evening's discussion. She had gone to the kitchen, where Ruth was preparing a cold fruit drink for the visitor. Carla opened the bread-box, cut two thin slices from a brown loaf, went to the ice-box for a bit of cold meat, and made herself a sandwich.

She seated herself on the kitchen table and began to eat the sandwich.

"I forgot to tell you," Ruth said, "Frieda Gertner called up while you were out in the garden. She wants you to come over to her house to-night."

"Can't," Carla said.

"Why not? Is Jared coming over? He hasn't been here for days."

"Jared isn't coming any more—to see me, at least."

Ruth looked at her for a moment in silence. "No?"

"No. It was difficult—he made it difficult—but I had to tell him that I could never take the place of his mother."

"It wouldn't be so difficult for you to tell him that, I imagine. You have a heart of stone."

Carla regarded her for a while before she replied. "I might have expected you to say that," she said at last. "Whatever my heart is made of, Ruthy dear, it is my own and I propose to have something to say about what becomes of it."

"Well—I can't blame you for that, either," Ruth remarked. "But why can't you go over to Frieda's? She seemed very anxious to see you."

"I'm going out to Paget's," Carla told her.

Ruth's eyes narrowed. Then she laughed, almost giddily. "To Paget's? To see John Kingswood?"

"Who else?"

Ruth stood back with her hands on her hips, gazing at Carla. It was difficult to say whether she was about to laugh or cry.

Carla swallowed a mouthful of her sandwich, then threw back her head and began to sing:

"My soul to my God and my body to the sea,
And the dark blue waves a-rolling over me!"

From the front porch came the sound of her father's voice in heated discussion with Deacon Loftus: "The younger generation is our only hope for the future, Brother Loftus. If we save the youth, we save the world. If we lose our sons and daughters—the world is lost to us, brother!"

Carla paused for an instant to listen to her father's stern prophecy—then continued her song, swinging her legs to the calamitous words and the nimble, jaunty melody.

THE END